CATCH AS CATCH CAN

CATCH AS CATCH CAN

MALCOLM HOLLINGDRAKE

This edition produced in Great Britain in 2021

by Hobeck Books Limited, Unit 14, Sugnall Business Centre, Sugnall, Stafford, Staffordshire, ST21 6NF

www.hobeck.net

A CIP catalogue for this book is available from the British Library.

ISBN 978-1-913-793-27-2 (pbk)

ISBN 978-1-913-793-26-5 (ebook)

Cover design by Jem Butcher

www.jembutcherdesign.co.uk

Printed and bound in Great Britain

❧ Created with Vellum

Dedicated to my wife, Debbie

You make dreams possible

Believe nothing ... trust no one!

My childhood ended around the time of my ninth birthday, shamed into sex, obedience and fear.

Billy Childish, *My Fault*

PROLOGUE

The transparent Perspex disc spun in the air, a flat earth launched skyward by finger and thumb, to become a virtual rotating globe, a levitating optical illusion. The gilt dollar sign, easily read when static, was now a golden blur. To one of the men watching, time stood still as the spinning disc slowed, the sound going from inaudible to a deep, slow bass – almost sibilant – a stretched-out drone comprising one instruction of three words.

'Heads or tails?' The man tossing the disc moved his hand out in readiness to catch its fall. Eyes watched until it reached its apogee. 'After all, this belongs to you.'

For one man this was not only a game of chance. It was, he knew, a matter of life or death. The disc landed on the outstretched, gloved palm and fingers immediately clasped it, hiding it for what seemed an age.

'Heads or tails, my incompetent, traitorous bastard?'

* * *

The guilty are often psychologically beaten before they begin, as more often than not, they have realised, possibly for some time, the true and frightening consequences of their unacceptable actions. There will be little resistance on their behalf, in the hope that mercy will be shown and their professional skills and their usefulness will be realised, and hopefully valued, within the culture of criminal brotherhood, where tolerance and forgiveness might thrive. Benevolence, however, only applies to certain misdemeanours – treachery, in any language, is both insufferable and punishable. The difficulty for anyone controlling this court is knowing how much force to use to gain the truth, as truth is often hidden by the very process of extraction. Pain will bring about an acceptance of guilt, history has taught us that.

Imagine for a moment if you can a razor blade hovering close to your forced open eye.

'Did you take it?' The inquisitor reassuringly asks this simple question.

If you did, do you admit it or deny it? After all, you have another eye. In that position, what would you do? You are naked and tied to a stainless-steel table, just as our man is here. Like you, his shoulders are positioned just over the edge leaving his neck exposed and his head feeling too heavy. Strange hands are now supporting your head, keeping it still, immoveable; in some ways, that is a relief, but in others it is not. They are in full control. Now imagine, like him, that there is a light facing directly into your eyes, bright, yet familiar and if I were to be cynical, almost blinding. All you can see for the moment are silhouettes against the bright contrasting blue. Initially, they are stationary and then the figures move. There is the sound of rap music, loud and thumping. You can feel it vibrate through the cold of the metal table. You are terrified as you know you are guilty. You have no control over your bladder and the wet warmth of your urine seeps beneath you. There is laughter. You know, and more importantly, they know that you are a traitor.

Never in your worst nightmares does this scenario exist. It cannot as it is beyond the dreams of a law-abiding citizen. The nearest we have to this sheer terror is the panic we would experience if facing being attacked and eaten by a wild animal; the thought that there might be a shark beneath you in that dark water whilst you are open water swimming or suddenly seeing a pack of rabid dogs on an unknown, dark and empty street. You feel real fear, fear you would struggle to psych yourself to deal with, if those scenarios were real. That intense fright is a form of torture on its own.

Sadly, for you now, those around you do not feel that way. There is a strange and unusual atmosphere. It is a frisson, an amalgam of your utter fear mixed with their pure enjoyment, a nerve tingling excitement that is always there when human life is harmed, when pain is caused, felt, seen and heard.

The simple question *Did you take it?* might be the penultimate words you hear … and the answer to that question will be your last. To one person in the room, the silly game we have just played is not a game, and we see that the denouement is when a frightened and tormented human life is simply snuffed out. In many cases, it is to the relief of the one who answered that simple question with a one-word answer, *Yes*. At that stage, for them, life had ceased to matter and all pain had gone. This was not Armageddon as such, there is no *good* fighting evil in this war. *Good,* in fact, was never in this equation. For Sadiq and his master, it was just perfect, a thorn in the side had been extracted and he could now move on.

CHAPTER 1

The smooth, brindle coat beneath her neck was reassuring and the rise of Tico's chest comforting. The tranquil setting of the Freshfield sand dunes, protected from the wind that seemed to blow constantly off the Irish Sea, brought quiet to a busy world. Even here she could not subdue the gnawing doubt that had attacked her since making the decision to move. *Promotion, just how important was it?* It was the question that rolled through her mind like a constant, encroaching tide.

April Decent had always been committed and determined to rise swiftly through the ranks. She was focused on developing her police career even if it meant not settling in any place for very long. Moving counties was, she had thought, of little consequence until now. Her two degrees, bolstered by the police policy supporting positive discrimination in order to see more female officers rise to supervisory ranks, contrived to see her in this position of flux.

She knew that she could have remained in Bradford with

Clarkson, her boss, and the team for a number of years, not only being challenged but also contributing significantly. She also realised that DCI Clarkson and DI David Taylor were a formidable team, and one that would remain so for many years to come, after all, Clarkson was a wonderful leader allowing his officers to work both independently and as a unit. Taylor's recent promotion had backed her into a professional cul-de-sac. Even though she had been in the force for a number of years, she had never before felt more secure and needed. Whether that was because she filled a niche left by a trusted female officer or that she offered certain skills, she would never know. What she did realise was that for the first time in a long while, moving on was going to be more difficult than she could ever have imagined.

After speaking with a number of high-ranking officers, she had found out that Clarkson had been the instigator. He had encouraged her to complete the application. She had comfortably achieved the Constable to Inspector fast track promotional process and she knew that she might have to play the role of a DI for at least two years. Her career had taken her from Leeds to Bradford and now here to Merseyside.

She focused now on the white cloud that contrasted with the deep blue of the sky, a formation that would not have looked out of place on a child's painting. It blocked the sun allowing April to gaze directly at it, to investigate its curved peaks and valleys. Razor-sharp rays burst from different areas along the cumulus edge to become bright, accurate triangles that search-lit the sea below. The soft sand felt warm to the touch as she scooped up a handful and let it fall through her fingers, like time passing.

Tico's back leg twitched and April lifted her head and stared reassuringly at the dozing greyhound. She recalled the first time they had met. He was a rescue dog, his racing days had been declared over and it could very well have been the end for him. Little did she know then that they would become so close. She chuckled to herself as she remembered her then police partner, David Taylor, refer to him as a cross between a dog and a donkey. She gently tugged his ear and he yawned in response.

'You're just a soft lump, Tico Decent!' She paused, the anxiety returning. 'Have I done the right thing, Tico? Have I gone from the excitement of Team Clarkson to some place where I might be way out of my depth?'

The dog turned, looked at her, licked her hand, yawned a second time and returned his head back down on the sun-warmed sand. He always seemed so understanding. A sudden flash of coloured light penetrated her peripheral vision as a kite came into view, its tail, a collection of bow-tie ribbons, streaming and dancing in the fresh onshore breeze. Its aerial jig accompanied by laughter, a child's cries of excitement and wonder. Lifting her head for a clearer view she realised she could mope no longer. Standing, she stretched, her eyes focused on the kite's aerial ballet before collecting Tico's ball and throwing it hard against the wind. Having the appearance of a Star Wars *AT-AT Walker*; Tico reluctantly climbed onto his stilt-like legs, stiff and temporarily unsure, before he shook off the sand that had adhered to his coat. Lunging himself into the fresh air from the high dune, he headed after the ball and onto the extent of the beach below with newfound elegant grace that only greyhounds seem to demonstrate.

* * *

The small cottage April had rented since arriving in Mersey-side sat away from the main conurbations. It was an oasis of peace and calm for her. She had viewed apartments in Southport and Liverpool, but none were suitable for Tico and neither did they offer the seclusion she needed. A chance meeting led to her finding this rental property situated on the edge of the pinewoods close to, and part of, Belle View Farm which was owned by Colin and Sue Martin. It had needed a little TLC but she was not afraid of hard graft, and after only a fortnight it was home from home.

Sue Martin had been more than eager to see a friendly face move in, and to have a police officer too was an added bonus. April and Sue had immediately formed a bond; it was clear that they both had a similar understanding of the world. In the first hour of their meeting, they had put most of it to rights.

However, there had been one problem; Tico had not been as warmly welcomed by Sky, the farm's Border Collie, and for the first few weeks a great deal of barking and raised hackles had been evident. Since then, they seemed to be in a period of truce; neither trusted the other and lines had defi-nitely been drawn.

Back at the cottage now, April wrapped her hands around the mug of hot chocolate before moving to the room she used as a studio. She smoothed the paper positioned on the workbench, the design for a stained-glass window she had promised to make for a former colleague from Yorkshire. She was not happy with it so she decided that she would adjust certain lines when time allowed. Moving away, she made a beeline for her desk. She was on early shift the next day and paperwork beckoned.

CHAPTER 2

The dock road was quiet of traffic and that was not always how they liked it. More traffic meant more anonymity but it was what it was and this would be their last run. From what they knew, this would be an easy target. It was assumed from the riding style they had seen and the colour of the scooter, that the female rider would neither struggle nor race away. For one thing she would fear damaging the pink paintwork; from the look of the learner plate, the machine could not have been more than a week old. It should be like taking candy from a baby.

Even though the girl must have had a few lessons, she still seemed uncertain in the way she handled the machine. Looking behind was proving a difficult manoeuvre for her and she needed to master using her mirrors. They had watched her now for two mornings and like clockwork, somewhat wobbly and unsure clock-work, she had cautiously travelled the straight main road before always turning right onto Upper William Street. It was decided that it would be there, as she approached the inappropriately named Love Lane, that they would strike.

Chelle saw the scooter's indicator flash yellow as the rider half-heartedly looked behind, before moving to the centre of the road to turn right. The girl's nervous inexperience was evident as she tried to avoid putting her feet down while waiting to turn. When a gap appeared in the traffic, she uncertainly opened the throttle – too little, the engine stuttered, too much, a surge of speed, then sudden hard braking. Relieved, she headed along Upper William Street, a featureless piece of tarmac hemmed in by windowless brick buildings that ran along both sides of the street. The noise from her bike was amplified on this inhospitable stretch, there were no pavements and the low railway bridge was further ahead. She preferred a quiet road to busy main roads but this one did make her feel edgy. It was so empty.

Swiftly, Chelle pulled alongside. Her pillion raised his boot giving the girl's thigh a tap, not hard, just enough to bring about enough instability for her to wobble and then stop. The pillion leaped from Chelle's bike and grabbed the handlebars facing the now frightened rider. They had misjudged her. A struggle soon developed. She screamed but her helmet muffled and nullified the desperate cry. Chelle, realising things were taking too long, flicked her bike onto its stand whilst keeping the engine running. She removed the ball hammer from her jacket, normally used for smashing bike locks. Swiftly she moved behind the rider who was still intent on wrestling the handlebars from the first assailant. Raising the hammer, she brought it down with all the force she could muster. Initially, she glanced the side of the helmet. The deflecting force guided it to the intended target. She felt it sink into the padded jacket and flesh before striking the rider's collar bone.

The burning pain shot from her disintegrating clavicle as the hammer's ball swiftly smashed the bone. She immediately released one side of the handlebars. Within seconds, she felt the second blow crash into the other shoulder and her other arm went limp too. Chelle did not need to raise the hammer again. She could see the girl slide from the seat and slump to the ground. Her fight was over. Within seconds the two bikes were racing down Love Lane. As a final insult they had taken her bag, forcefully tearing it from her damaged shoulder. She could offer no resistance, only tears. It was fifteen minutes before she was found, by which time her assailants and her belongings had long disappeared. It would take a further ten minutes before the police arrived at the scene and that proved to be too late.

The afternoon's sweep had also been very profitable and as was usual the riders had sung into their helmets: *Like taking candy from a baby.* They drove off at silly speeds between the lines of stationary and moving cars and often bewildered pedestrians, before rendezvousing some time later with the van in order to disappear. The song was a habit they had acquired over the months as their confidence had grown.

Later, as they sat in Sadiq's apartment, the panoramic windows offered an unrestricted view of the distant buildings known as Liverpool's Three Graces, down the Mersey and then to distant hazy refineries almost hidden on the Wirral. This view in all weathers held a different beauty.

'Listen!' Sadiq told them. 'What's good for the south is equally as good for us boys and girls up north. If they can do it, then so can we only we'll use a bit of bloody nous. Even if we're out of the capital it won't matter as we'll move in and out of the local cities and towns. In and out, striking in different places on the same morning. Teams. My teams – efficient, cruel and brave – my band of brothers and sisters.'

He had been right too. Not only did it prove easy stealing the motorbikes, scooters and personal belongings, the team had also found it fun making the snatch. They had grown rapidly in expertise as they experienced the acute adrenaline rush as each target was stalked and attacked. They relished the punters' expressions: that look of disbelief, the moment of paralysis as the phone or bag left their hand, the shouts and then the mad scarper, the weaving through the tiniest of gaps on roads and along the pavements where traffic lights were but blinking eyes to be ignored. The experience brought danger, it was exciting but, most importantly, it was profitable.

People had been growing cautious of two-up scooters when the riders were dressed in dark clothing. The public had seen the news and had become well aware of the capital's modern day dangerous, and on occasion, brutal highwaymen. However, that was the capital not the north west and certainly not here in this city – the Pool as it was affectionately known. Sadiq told the group of seven that the way the southern moped gangs performed was now clichéd. No one understood what he meant when he had first announced this; they had simply nodded in agreement.

Holding a mug of herbal tea, Sadiq stared out of the window. The jasmine aroma lingered as he breathed deeply before turning to face those sitting anxiously around the dark grey table. The team served another purpose. As well as collecting, they delivered, if not on scooters, mopeds and motorbikes, then on pushbikes, preferably electric, silent, efficient and easily acquired – a modern take on the milk float. Sadiq called them his swift pedalling apothecaries, emphasising the word *pedalling*. It amused him. However, to many in the team, whose use of English was poor, the humour was lost.

'The coppers here will soon follow their Met colleagues and bring in what they call *Operation Venice.* To you, that's a direct physical attack on suspected muggers and that, my friends, is you. However, we will adapt quickly, like the chameleon. Now, take all of this in, not just the view. Look around you.' He paused as they scanned the apartment and then each other. 'I was born and brought up in Kirkdale. My mother looked after her family of five whilst my father worked for the council. It was not easy being born equidistant from the two famous football clubs. I hated football.' He paused as if dredging the emotions back to the surface of some deep mire. 'I could never see the point of it and when I was asked by others from the streets as to whether I was a *blue nose* or a *red nose*, Everton or fucking Liverpool, it was often my quick thinking, my wits, and the knowledge of those asking, that determined the particular answer.' He laughed, and the faces staring at him grinned, but there was a degree of uncertainty as to why. 'My judgement was not always accurate, and on many occasions, I came away with a red and bloodied nose. These early lessons, however, have stood me in good stead.'

He turned back to the window. Having all of this was due

in part to his quick thinking, partly to self-discipline and partly to careful planning. 'I've not had it easy, but I made sure I got what I wanted one way or another.'

Those sitting round the table were silent as he stared across the balcony and into the distance, deep in thought. He had found school easy and had quickly demonstrated that he was capable, outshining many of the other students. His use of language, his ability in maths and his attitude and courtesy, soon saw him furthering his education and then working as an accountant. Now, he was, by his own admission, a modern-day Bill Sykes, a controller of the gang of seven, and it was beginning to pay well. What he did not mention was the fact that the apartment was only rented and he did not control any part of that. Sadiq was simply another small link in the chain.

From the very beginning he had helped choose his accomplices with great care and he had prepared them well. Strangely, he had welcomed females into his ranks. However, it was Chelle he trusted the most. He had known her since his early teens when she seemed alone and needy and he liked her. She could ride too. First it was the BMX, then mopeds and scooters, but it was her skills riding a small motocross bike that had convinced him that she had all the necessary credentials.

He moved towards the table. 'Let me remind you. We're different. We're professionals. Make sure you look like normal riders on the bike, that way we blend in. We don't intimidate even though we're using nicked bikes. The key to the success of this is that you'll remember always to be courteous to other road users, let pedestrians cross. We'll allay any fears and then we'll strike. *Come into my parlour said the spider to the fly.'*

Immediately he banged the table top startling many. Chelle let out an involuntary scream, but his instant laughter brought to everyone a sudden sense of relief.

'Remember, careful preparation and accurate execution has paid off for many months as we've roamed Southport, Formby, Bolton and of course, Liverpool. We shall, my friends, soon spread our wings further.'

Fetching money from a drawer he placed a pile of notes in front of everyone. No one touched the money. They were not dissimilar to obedient dogs awaiting the instruction to eat. They only looked.

'Go, we have work to do.'

As a hand stretched for the money, Sadiq noticed a small tattoo on the side of its palm and then the markings on certain fingers. He quickly covered Chelle's hand with his and bent forward so his mouth was close to her ear. Suddenly, she could smell the jasmine on his warm breath.

'Gloves, always gloves. You've identified yourself permanently and that's not a good idea in our line of work. Is this new, Chelle?'

She nodded as her face flushed and her stomach tumbled, realising his displeasure.

'Now, my seven little people, it's off to work we go.'

CHAPTER 3

The gym had an aroma all of its own. It was not one direct smell that bombarded the nostrils but an unusual collection of subtle scents that only a perfumier would be able to separate and categorise. However, after a few moments of being there, one smell seemed to overpower the rest – a malodorous pong that grew to mask all others – and that was stale sweat.

The blue mat, an open sea of canvas, spread across the floor, and in the far corner stood a small crowd of different sized, worn leather figures, like wrapped sadomasochistic humans; some with single stumps, one with legs but two completely legless. Each had a purpose and all had endured a hard life.

After running and flexing, Skeeter rotated her head, first in one direction and then the other. She bent at the waist and gently rolled to the left. It was a fluid and controlled move-ment and she was back on her feet before changing into a tucked position. The momentum now carried her to the right. This repetitive alternative flow allowed her to cross the mat quickly and accurately. As she stood for the last time, she found herself directly in front of a large brown dummy, its arms outstretched as if in welcome. No matter how often she did this, and she had done it for more years than she cared to remember, she still felt the tingle of excitement, an adrenaline rush.

Without a moment's hesitation she reached out, her body slipping neatly between the two outstretched arms. Her nose, now close to the featureless face, drew in the smell of leather. She was excited by it, quickly allowing her own arms to wrap almost lovingly around the figure. It was cool and smooth to the touch, but then this soft almost erotic moment of reflection, this casual caress, immediately changed. An animalistic grunt surged from her taut lips as she pulled the leather figure towards her before sending it upward and backward as she fell and twisted. The figure was hurled brutally over her right shoulder, every move was controlled. Its stiff, unforgiving body arched through the air before making contact with the hard canvas. A slapping sound erupted that brought a smile to her lips. Quickly standing, she performed the same move again and was rewarded by the dummy crashing obediently to the canvas; each time a perfect suplex.

The morning dawned and the weather was very different from the evening before. The drizzle was constant. The seductive smell of toast and coffee was consolation as April spread the marmalade thickly. She always protested she needed the sugar rush. Tico and the radio were April's only companions and she liked it that way. She had no desire to look after others and if she had a man in her life, she would have to hold her stomach in and that was a definite burden she did not want at this stage of her career. Standing, she went over to the mirror, toast in hand. She inhaled, pausing as she heard that yet again the M6 from Standish down to the M56 was slow moving owing to an accident. The Radio Two traffic reporter continued.

... four miles of standing traffic. However, the accident has been removed but one lane is still blocked ...

'You cannot move an accident, only the cars involved!' she muttered as she did most mornings. 'The bloody BBC. It's as easy to say the vehicles have been removed, surely!' No one was listening. She took another mouthful of toast and felt its immediate calming effect. Why she had to be critical over something she had no control over she could never understand. She had always been that way. When she had been fresh to the force, a Turkish colleague had once called her *Mükemmel* owing to her eagerness to achieve perfection. *Mükemmel* being the Turkish word for perfect. She was soon known as just *M* and even her strong protests failed to change that. It had stayed with her through the early years when working in Leeds but it had not followed her when she moved. DI Decent could see the funny side, now thinking her initials might be, DIM.

Within the hour, April was sitting at her desk. She checked the Post-it notes attached to the edge of her computer screen. Some had been left from previous days, *aides-memoire* of outstanding tasks. It would take a while to prioritise them and that was a distraction.

* * *

Heterochromia iridum does not slip easily off the tongue but it certainly made people look twice before either turning away or trying to focus on one of the eyes. People had a tendency to be slightly embarrassed, probably through scrutinising and staring too much.

From behind the computer screen Skeeter watched as DI April Decent passed her desk. She had seen her a couple of times before but that was during the previous week. She watched her turn in her direction and slow her pace. April gave a slight smile and a nod, but as usual, there was also a moment of clear confusion on her face, it was almost embarrassment for the stare that was unnaturally and, even momentarily, too long. It was a regular occurrence that now amused Skeeter more than it angered her. It was easier for people to look away and if that be the case, so be it.

At school it had been a cross Skeeter had to bear and it was there she was first given her nickname, the name she had also carried during her time in the force, Witch. To some in the force and at the wrestling gym, she was generally known as *Wicca*, the derivative of the word witch. It amused Skeeter as they failed to realise Wicca was the masculine term, that of a sorcerer and not a female witch. It was a small consolation for someone called Warlock.

This first meeting was only brief and April had felt herself blush during what she deemed to be overexposed eye contact. To make matters worse she had neither taken the initiative to speak nor to make an approach, a situation she realised later on reflection was totally out of character. It was something she knew she would have to rectify. April was determined to address her rudeness and make sure she was properly introduced, but it would have to be the next day. She had a meeting with her boss, DCI Alex Mason, and she would be out for most of the day.

* * *

John Radcliffe moved along the constantly swerving pathway like a drunken sailor allowing the head of the metal detector to brush over the undulating surface of marine detritus. The early morning fall in the tide had left high and dry a clear but irregular line which stranded along the sand. It was certainly plain from where he was standing that the planet was not in a position to digest plastic. The occasional seabirds called, a cacophony of shrill screams that shattered the peace as they dived towards the tumbling grey waves that bullied and swallowed the beach to his right. The constant breeze, the sea's ally, seemed to move magically. The dry grained upper surface of sand appeared almost serpent-like in fine sheets. For a few seconds, it was a dancing mirage.

Pausing for a moment, he glanced across the beach closest to him. He admired the colour change of the wet sand as it turned to the texture and shade of an elephant's back, reflecting the colour of the lead-grey sky, mirroring the water's deep surface. Lifting his gaze further out to sea, he stared at the Burbo Bank Wind Farm and marvelled at this feat of engineering. It was positioned about seven miles from the mouth of the River Mersey. This is where thirty-two of the planet's biggest wind turbines stood, catching and harnessing the constant breeze, the myriad blades seemingly dancing in total synchronisation in all weathers. They exhibited a beauty all of their own.

He adjusted his earphones and started to sweep an arc over the strandline flotsam and jetsam. A change in pitch in the signal told him that he had found metal. He kicked the seaweed and what appeared to be straw away only to discover a rusting bottle top. He had lost count of the number of bottle tops he had found that morning. Patiently, he started again. Within a hundred yards, however, the next find would change his opinion of metal detecting forever.

Upon her return to the police station, April parked her 4x4 around the back. The building had little to commend it. Aesthetically, it had the architectural merits of concrete boxes placed one above the other. It might simply be referred to as 'functional'. Up until a few years ago, CID officers had been spread around the Merseyside area but more recently, it had been thought politic to bring them all under one roof. The fact that the Southport Police Station and other smaller stations within the Merseyside force did not have the interview rooms necessary for officers to perform their jobs had a great deal to do with the decision. Although still the newcomer, she was growing more comfortable. *Change needs time,* she would often whisper to herself whenever self-doubt crept into her mind.

The briefing had been anything but brief and she was now with two of her team. There had been a serious road rage incident on the East Lancashire Road and it was decided one of her officers, DC Lucy Teraoka, would work with Traffic to investigate. The other immediate concern was the 999 call, taken fifteen minutes earlier. April and DC Bradshaw listened to the recording. Within five minutes they were on their way. Bradshaw had ensured the area of the beach had been securely cordoned off and CSI had been notified.

DC Pete Bradshaw drove. 'The section of beach is not too far from the Altcar ranges.'

He turned to look at April; he could clearly see the puzzled look on her face. She had heard of the Altcar ranges when researching the area of her new posting but could not immediately bring any facts to mind.

'It's a major centre for small arms training for different elements of the forces. There are a number of ranges to accommodate the many different weapons. They have loads of land too for training but they only use live ammo at the site ranges so we'll be safe.' His tone seemed to patronise. 'We'll also check for the red flags though. Our firearms people have been known to use it too.'

April lifted an eyebrow. 'Reassuring,' she whispered before making a note to find out more. She looked across at her new colleague suspiciously, realising that fairly soon she would have to have words. He was too informal and she had a distinct feeling that he was pushing boundaries, a male trait she had frequently experienced in the past.

He turned left off the B5424. 'We have someone with a 4x4 waiting in the carpark at the bottom of this road to take us along the sand until we're close enough to the body. I checked the tide times and we're okay for quite a few hours.'

April lifted a map from her knee. She checked the area quickly orientating the folded sheet to familiarise herself.

She then cross-referenced co-ordinates of the discovery site she had marked.

'Unusual to see a female able to use a map!' Bradshaw's tone was annoyingly sarcastic, and to make matters worse he began to giggle. He glanced sideways before adding further insult to injury. 'You can trust me to get us there. It's got a sat nav this car.' He nodded towards the screen. 'Give a woman a map and we're doomed!'

April did not pause. She felt the anger immediately. 'Stop the car!'

Although April's tone should have left him in no doubt as to the course of action he should take, he ignored her continuing to negotiate the narrowing lane. She slammed the palm of her hand on the dashboard.

'Stop the bloody car now, DC Bradshaw. That's an order!'

He pulled the car to a halt, the tyres sliding momentarily along the puddled track. She could immediately see the annoyance etched on his face.

'How long have I been with this force? Two weeks? Seventeen, eighteen days?'

Bradshaw pulled a face that clearly expressed confusion and uncertainty. He was certainly puzzled. *Must be the wrong time of the month,* he thought before answering. 'Not sure.'

'Not sure?' she slowly repeated, looking directly at her colleague. 'Well let's see if I know something about you. Let's see if I've taken any trouble to discover just a little about the colleagues I'll be working alongside, colleagues I'll be trusting and helping. Your birthday's the thirtieth of January. You've been a detective for exactly fourteen weeks, before that you were in the Skelmersdale area. Your probationary period was somewhat mixed, a curate's egg you could say.'

His facial expression quickly changed and he was about to say something when she raised her hand.

'Not your turn, Constable, as this Inspector hasn't finished. Where was I? Curate's egg. You received a commendation for tackling a man with a knife in your second week there. Throughout that period, you always stressed that your intention was to join Serious Crime. I know that you're a traditionalist, an atheist, that your parents separated when you were eleven and your mother brought you and your two sisters up.' She continued to look directly at him. 'You're a rugby league supporter, Wigan. I know that you have a fiancé and that you live together ...' April allowed the last few words to fade as if there were more she could say.

Bradshaw nodded but was also filled with a growing unease as to why she had looked into his records.

'You'll now be thinking, nosy cow or something even stronger.'

She paused as if to give him a short length of rope by which to hang himself but then owing to her generosity of spirit continued.

'But it's got nothing to do with nosiness or personal curiosity, it's professional preservation. I take an interest in every member of my team, because it's just that, a team, that's our strength and if we're not careful our weakness. It's a lesson I learned early on. "Know them and know their strengths and their weakness", I was advised. I'd then know when they'd be able to help me and when they themselves might be in need of support. I want to know if I can trust your judgement, your integrity. I want to know if you're blessed with a degree of intelligence, common sense but also,

25

significantly, whether you display compassion and professionalism that will allow you to act quickly and safely.'

She paused allowing her words to sink in – wanting the meaning to cross what she saw as a clear, deep professional void she thought just might be too wide.

'Let's get one thing straight, DC Bradshaw. As we shall, I hope, be working together for some time, I want to know if I can trust you to watch my back in difficult times like I'll be watching yours. Now that you understand me a little better, I'll promise, as your superior, to treat you fairly and with the utmost respect. I'll have a laugh and a joke with you and I'll even, on occasion, buy you a beer but I won't tolerate racist or sexist comments to me or any other officers. I, for one, believe there's no room for sarcasm or patronising pricks in my team. I'll expect total professionalism from you and from now on you'll always refer to me as ma'am until I say otherwise. I want you to think before you speak. As someone once said, "It's easier to be a smart arse than to be kind."'

At this, she looked directly at him, not allowing her gaze to drift one millimetre from his, hoping what she had said had gone home. His expression offered little by way of a clue.

'Is that understood?'

Bradshaw paused momentarily and nodded before apologising. April saw him swallow.

'Now drive.'

Within a few minutes he was relieved to see the other police vehicle at the rendezvous point.

CHAPTER 4

April moved towards the cordoned area. The blue-and-white police tape was fluttering frantically, the wording a complete blur and the sheer force making the plastic strip snap and crack on occasion. The officer, on seeing them approach, lifted his hand.

'DI Decent and DC Bradshaw.' Both held out their warrant cards.

'The doctor's been but can only confirm the death. According to his brief chat, the body is that of a badly decomposed male, probably early twenties to thirties, naked apart from a chain that appears to be wrapped around the body. The torso was totally concealed until discovered. Nearly all of the corpse is still trapped within the sand and in six hours the tide's due to cover this area.'

Bradshaw tapped April's arm and pointed. She saw the Land Rover in which they had been conveyed return, following in the previous tracks it had carved in the sand. Three CSI officers moved quickly from the rear towards the tape, carrying cases of various sizes. Within minutes two of the officers were fighting and manhandling a forensic tent against the stiff breeze. The Crime Scene Manager noted the arrival time on the log.

'Where's the man who found the body?' April asked the officer as he was logging in the new arrivals.

Without lifting his head, he swung an arm in the direction of the dunes.

'John Radcliffe. He gave me a quick statement but to be honest he was rather shaken. The doctor checked him over and he's okay otherwise we'd have got him away. We put him behind that makeshift windbreak, the beach patrol guys always carry them to hide what gets washed up or dumped that they don't want the public to see.'

'It happens often?' April questioned as she watched the white-suited figure photograph areas of the beach.

'Usually, sea creatures or dogs are washed up. We had a whale once. Bloody huge it was. Got the nickname, Acker Bilk.'

'Sorry?'

Tucking the board beneath his arm he mimed the playing of an instrument before he started to whistle a tune. Seeing her confusion, he stopped.

'Meant to be a clarinet.' He waggled his fingers in the air. *Stranger on the Shore,* it was a famous tune by Bilk in the sixties. Before your time I guess, and mine, but I'm an old-fashioned guy. Got to number one in the charts.' He shook his head. 'The whale was known locally by the guys who patrol the beach as Acker Bilk.'

He could see from her expression he was getting nowhere. Retrieving his board, he checked the names.

'Bilk? Never mind.'

'Right. As you say, before my time.'

April walked across the sand towards the billowing shelter that had been turned away from the prevailing wind and the sea. She lifted the collar of her coat conscious of the increasing chill. Walking around she ducked down, immediately feeling the benefit of the hooded shelter. Radcliffe was sitting on what appeared to be a blue plastic crate and he was wrapped in a foil blanket, his detecting equipment to his right. April proffered a hand and looked into the man's eyes, judging his first response.

'DI April Decent. You've certainly found more than you bargained for today, Mr Radcliffe! How are you feeling now?'

She was surprised to see a brief smile appear.

'Decent you say?'

'Decent by name and I hope decent by nature.' She smiled.

Radcliffe returned the smile and then the frown returned.

'You can say that again, young lady. Not the treasure I was seeking that's for sure.' His strong Liverpudlian accent seemed as cutting as the wind. 'You're not from here, love, are you? Wiganer or are you from St Helens?' From the look in his eyes he seemed genuinely interested.

'Yorkshire. I'm a long way from home. You were telling me about the body.'

'Right, yes. It was about this far below the sand's surface.' He moved his index finger and thumb apart to represent the depth. 'I saw the object first and then after moving more sand, I noticed the chain and hoped that it might be connected to something else. The signal from the detector was massive. It was then that I saw a hand, bloody strange colour it was too and I noticed what appeared to be plastic. Looking more closely I could see it was a head; it was wrapped in what seemed to be cling film. At first, I thought it was one of them shop window dummies but the smell gave it away … hard to describe but it's still in my nose. Strangely, there was no ear. I had to look twice but … Thank goodness for mobile phones.

'The guys in the 4x4 were here within fifteen minutes. As you can see from today's weather there aren't many swimmers.' He laughed at his attempt at a joke. 'Just a few people up by the beach parked on the sand as usual but they seldom come this far unless they're walking the dogs or on horseback.' He took a breath and pulled the foil blanket around his neck. 'The famous racehorse, Red Rum, was trained near here. Did you know that? Not many do now. Long time ago.'

April paused before speaking. Everyone seemed to have a tale to tell about the beach, what with the musician and now a horse. She tried to appear interested and smiled. 'Really?'

'You know who I'm talking about, don't you, miss? Won the Grand National three times but that was probably before you were born.'

April suddenly felt young and naïve as he talked about horses. She needed to bring him onto a different tack.

'You mentioned an object. Had you found anything up until this point?'

'Mostly bottle tops, can you believe, they're easily carried within the surf and left on the strandline. The best thing was what I found just before I discovered the body.'

He fished into his pocket and retrieved the find. He brought it to his lips, spit on it and rubbed it with what looked like an old rag before passing it to April. April held the round object on the palm of her hand before looking back at Radcliffe.

'It's a medal of some kind. It's heavily tarnished and could be silver but I won't be too sure until it's been cleaned. It's old too as you can see from the edges, but it has some writing, foreign I think, inscribed around the edge.'

April looked carefully at the object and immediately understood the wording to be Latin. She removed her phone and took photographs from different angles, trying to capture as much detail as possible.

'How far from the body was this?'

Radcliffe used his hands like a fisherman describing the length of his catch and after a few guesses he settled on a length to demonstrate the proximity.

'So, would you say it was possibly with the body?'

Radcliffe shrugged his shoulders. 'Who knows? Could be coincidence. On finding that I laughed out loud, as just a piece of metal like that wouldn't have given the strength of signal I received. Thought there might be hundreds! I moved more sand and then swung the detector to the right and bingo. Instead of treasure …' He pulled a face. '… Story of my bloody life, love.'

April quickly took another photograph before she produced a plastic evidence bag from her pocket and dropped in the medal before sealing the top.

'Sorry, evidence. You may get it back in time. Are you sure there was nothing else?'

Radcliffe shook his head. 'No. Just bottle tops. You want them too?'

His disappointment at losing the medal was evident in his

tone. On standing April heard him chuckle. She paused. 'Something else?'

'Your name, love, and that man in the sand brought to mind something my old dad used to say when he'd had one too many.'

'And what was that?'

'"Carry me home and bury me decent." Maybe not as funny out loud. Sorry.'

As she left the shelter of the windbreak, she placed a hand on his shoulder.

'My dad said that too.'

She walked back to the taped area. Members of the public had started to congregate by the police vehicle but none had moved nearer. A pop-up tent was now covering the scene where the body had been located. It swayed in the breeze as the CSI team worked within. After handing the bagged medal to the white-suited figure, she looked up and down the expanse of beach. Bradshaw approached her.

'How's he ended up here of all places?' he asked, rubbing his hands together before thrusting them back into his pockets. Immediately he started to answer his own question. 'I see three possibilities, ma'am. One, he was brought here dead, maybe on a quad bike as they sure didn't carry him. A quad would get you over the dunes and along this beach. Two, he came from there.' He pointed to the sea. 'Dumped overboard from some kind of boat or ship. And then three, he walked here believing he was in the company of friends and he was wrong.'

April smiled and nodded. 'Good, that's good. And if you could only choose one?'

'Considering the chain, for me at this stage in the investigation, he came from Davy Jones' Locker.'

April rested her hand on his shoulder. 'Possibly correct but let's keep an open mind.'

She heard her old boss in her head. It was at this moment that she finally realised the true value of the lessons he had taught her and this knowledge brought a sense of contentment and a smile to her lips. Maybe this position was right for her after all. It reminded her of another of his sayings.

'Remember, dead men can still tell tales. It was a lesson my first boss told me and I've never forgotten it.'

'Suppose you just have to learn how to listen.'

April smiled. 'True.' She turned and scanned the beach as they walked. 'It's certainly a beautiful place, remote and not easily accessed with the dead weight that comes with a body. You may well be right. Interestingly, the treasure hunter discovered a medal. He didn't know how old it was nor in fact what it was but I believe I might know. We'll walk back to the car, Pete, and we can chat as we walk.'

'Ma'am, I've always been known as Brad since I've been in the force and I'd be grateful if you'd call me that.'

April nodded. 'As I was saying, Brad.'

CHAPTER 5

Contemplating the events of the previous day, April looked out of the upper room window of Copy Lane Police Station, the current hub of Liverpool CID.

The view from April's window was neither inspiring nor interesting but it allowed her a few minutes to consider what she had witnessed on the sands the previous day. Suddenly, a paper dart flew over her left shoulder and collided with the window, blunting its nose before falling to her feet. It was quickly followed by an apology.

'Sorry, meant for Brad!'

Looking round April noticed the grinning face and then the eyes peering over the screen of a computer.

'Never could get the bloody things to fly straight. Make a shit pilot, me.'

April did not allow herself to make the same mistake twice and quickly moved across to the far side of the room.

'April Decent. I saw you a few days ago. You're the new DI,' Skeeter said, noticing that April stared directly at her left eye. She smiled moving her hand to her face. 'Makes people forget pleasantries, too focused on one blue and one black. They never know where to look, like you. I might also get the words, *David Bowie ...*'

'*Heterochromia iridum*,' April replied, trying to move her focus.

Skeeter raised her eyebrows. 'No flies on you, April Decent, but then I'd heard that. Mind, you rarely get such a contrast, ice blue against nearly black. Some people, can you believe, think I've got a glass eye! Anyway, pleased to eventually speak. Thought you were avoiding me. DS Skeeter Warlock.' April smiled warmly waiting for the punchline but one did not follow.

'I seem to stop people in their tracks. If it's not my eyes, it's my name. Bane of my bloody life if I'm honest. Always been known as Witch.' She lifted her shoulders in resignation. 'All through school since I was a nipper and then during my time as a beat copper. What I do know is my eyes frighten some crooks shitless, especially foreign ones. The evil eye and all that.' She grinned before standing and holding out her hand.

April was initially taken aback by Skeeter's height and build. She assessed her to be no more than five feet five but she could see that she was extremely fit. She also noticed her hair was tightly plaited and there was damage to her left ear. The swelling was definitely what was unfortunately referred to as a cauliflower ear. It gave her an impish and yet thuggish demeanour.

'I see why the name Witch has played a key part in your life but Warlock and Skeeter?'

Skeeter explained. 'When you live in a city where they once had an Archbishop named Worlock you find people are

35

familiar with it, but Skeeter, that's quite a different kettle of fish. My grandfather's favourite tune was *The End of the World* by Skeeter Davis. Cheerful title and miserable tune but he loved it. The name was different and my mother was too easily influenced. You make the best of what you have I suppose but it wasn't easy when I was a kid. Witch became preferable.'

April smiled. 'Someone tried to nickname me Jester believing they were smart at school but the swift fist and the resulting bloody nose seemed to stop anyone else calling me anything but April. If you want me to take the paper dart to Brad, I'm heading for his desk.'

'From April Fool I guess?'

April nodded before looking again at the retrieved paper dart in her hand.

'Just a silly game we sometimes play,' Skeeter explained, pointing to the snub-nosed dart. 'Good to chat.'

As April moved away Skeeter called after her. 'You're the lucky one, with the failed swimmer I believe?' The sarcasm in her voice rang out clearly. 'I'm chasing down some bastards who think it's clever to steal and snatch using scooters and motorbikes. They're like will-o'-the-wisps these bastards but I'll have them … *Catch as Catch Can*, that's my game and I'm good at it.'

'Story of my life, Skeeter.' She winked, grinned and started to move away.

The phone vibrated on Skeeter's desk. 'Warlock.' She listened raising one eyebrow and turned to look at April. 'On my way.' She put the phone into her pocket. 'Scooter attack. Ormskirk market. Another student's been targeted.'

April paused and looked back.

'It's rich picking there with the university. The kids wander around with their phones, earphones in and their bags facing the roadside. They're oblivious to what's going on. Community Police have been in to lecture and advise and they've put up posters but they'll take no notice. The other week, a girl was dragged along the road for some distance resulting in a serious head injury. According to witnesses, the bag was round her body and so they stopped as cool as you like, the pillion on the scooter casually walked up to her, cut the strap, kicked her in the mouth and they rode off. This one is the second today, one down by the docks, almost identical to one yesterday. Been going on too long. There's a greater depth to all of this if you ask me. Drugs. You mark my word.'

'And nobody intervened as the girl was being dragged?' April sounded incredulous as she moved back and leaned on the desk.

'A person filmed it on their mobile instead of using it to ring 999, tosser, and before you ask, nothing from that. The bike's been found, but it's a charred mess and we know it was stolen. These bikes can get where muck can't and there are enough ginnels and snickets about for them to weave their escape. They plan well and we suspect these attacks are part of an organised gang, probably based here in Liverpool.'

'How many of these attacks have been recorded to date?'

'Across the region we have twenty-two reported but many will have gone unreported. The public is losing faith which is, I'm sad to say, understandable. With the shortage of man power and the rise in the more serious crimes it's hardly surprising that these cases slip through the net. I think we're only seeing the tip of the iceberg.'

'You know what the iceberg did to the unsinkable? It sank it and if we don't get a grip of the smaller crimes we'll be sunk as a force too,' April added in all seriousness.

Skeeter pointed to a map of the north west containing red spots that was on the far wall.

'The spots represent places of attacks but if you broaden the boundary to include the other forces you can double that figure. They're marked in yellow and green. Let's not forget that those fourteen have resulted in two stabbings and the injury I've just mentioned. What we do know, April, is that these people are not riding to and from the towns. They're being transported in the backs of vans before being released; they then meet up again at a set rendezvous point. As I said, it's planned and well-executed. We also believe that it might be the arse end of a drug run, county line in modern parlance. An easy way to meet up with kids, drop off and collect. The sad fact is, we note there's greater activity at the end of the day when schools are out and during holidays. It's easier to order a drug drop today than ordering a kebab and drugs might be safer too.' She winked.

April looked directly at Skeeter's blue eye; she found it easier to focus on the one that looked alive.

'I don't suppose CCTV has helped?' She did not wait for a reply before adding, 'I'll not delay you. Good hunting. And Skeeter, let's see if we can be a little more combative against these mopeds. It's worked in London. Leave it with me and I'll take it higher.'

'Ta!'

* * *

Pete Bradshaw was busy cross-referencing information on his computer screen, his finger following the highlighted information. Post-it notes of various colours were stuck to the wall by the side of his desk giving it a furfuraceous quality. The slight movement of air from the fan hidden within the back of the computer seemed to make the lower portion of Post-its flutter as if alive. An image that did not move was a photograph of a metal statue, waist deep in water, taken at sunset. It was one of the many Anthony Gormley figures set in the sand at Crosby. The sky and part of the beach looked like fire, the rest of the sand resembled quicksilver. April stood for a minute fascinated by his expression of concentration before launching the dart onto his desk. 'Bandits at two o'clock. It's from your admirer.' She flicked her head in the direction of Skeeter's desk.

Initially startled, he quickly placed a smile on his face. 'Strange woman that.' He saw April's expression change and remembered the reprimand he had received when in the car. 'In the nicest possible way. We're all different but I'll say no more. You'll soon see how good she is and I can tell you from rumour and the limited knowledge I have of her, she's frightened of nothing and nobody. Been here forever too. Her motto, I believe it's tattooed somewhere on her anatomy and written in Latin, is, *By any available means or method.* You read into that what you like. I personally wouldn't want to tackle her on a wrestling mat, never mind in a dark alley. She's a bloody good copper and hard as nails.'

He wanted to say that in his opinion she was also a nutter but after his last bollocking he decided to only suggest that she was well-balanced.

'She's working against the moped gangs that have sprung

up since the Met cracked down on the epidemic witnessed in London. It now seems that we have either the gangs moving north into other major cities, the copycats or it's the cancerous tentacles that are simply spreading. Skeeter believes they're part of the county lines. Diversification in all forms!' Pete raised his eyebrows and smiled. 'Anyway, enough of that. You've seen the report?'

April smiled and tapped the desk. 'Neck broken – garrotted – our man in the sand.'

'Pathologist's results are here and from what you've said you've seen them I presume, ma'am?'

April's facial expression did not alter. 'Eastern Med, possibly Syrian but they can't be so specific. No positive ID as yet, I note. He'd been dead some days. All the evidence suggests that he was placed in cold storage for a period and then buried in the sand whilst still frozen. He would have remained there had the storms of a few nights back not pounded the beaches. Yellow multistrand plastic rope was used and interestingly, we initially thought the knot used was a hitch. The more you struggle the tighter the rope could be pulled. It's also easily removed. According to the pathologist, after studying the rope and the marks found on the tender flesh around the throat and neck of the deceased, it's more likely a Lark's Head knot. There was also rope bruising and burning around the ankles.' She deliberately paused to see if he had fully comprehended the finer points of the report. He did not disappoint.

'Suggests he was hogtied?'

'How long is a "cold storage period"?'

'Piece of string comes to mind,' Brad said, his inexperience showing.

'Freezing and salt water can be cruel to a cadaver. They believe up to five days plus. The grave has been water-logged twice daily. The waxy, soapy appearance of the flesh, I'm informed, is a result of the cold water encouraging the formation of adipocere. It's formed from the fat in the body and it partly protects from decomposition. However, sea lice and worms have helped Mother Nature in trying to return the corpse to nature. You're correct with hogtied, Brad. Legs tied bent behind as close to his buttocks as possible with the other end of the rope around the throat. Any flexing of the legs would cause restriction and difficulty in breathing. It appears our man was tormented or tortured for a period of time before he died. Evidence of razor marks to both eyes. Possibly blinded before ...'

Brad shook as if shivering at the thought. 'Can't stand people touching my eyes.'

'Anyway, it's interesting to see there may have been amateur removal of tattoos to the hand, arm and fingers. Total skin removal often into the muscle. They're trying to see if they can get anything from the lower dermis layers but they're not optimistic. Something to do with the standard depth of a tattoo needle. If we have any trace it could be the key to identifying this guy.'

'It's amazing what science can find these days,' mumbled Brad as he shifted some papers in front of him. 'I'd imagine he was transported to the spot he was found either by quad bike or horse, possibly in a large holdall. Nothing on the transparent, Perspex disc found in his hand but you knew about the medal from the outset?'

April's face showed her approval of his attention to

details. 'King's Police Medal. You're aware of the history of those I take it?'

'I'm supposed to be a detective, ma'am. Your photographs were clear so I looked it up soon after we got back from locating the body. The medal was created by a Royal Warrant in 1909, 7th July if you want an exact date, but it wasn't only for the police. It was given to the fire brigade too. It was awarded once a year to no more than one hundred and twenty recipients. Given for ...' he looked across to the wall and let his finger rest on one of the notes '... gallantry, saving life and property, a distinguished record of administration or detective services, success in organising police services and a few other special services. Interestingly it was superseded in 1940 with the King's Police and Fire Service Medal and then The Queen's Police Medal. It's a fake.'

'You're right, but why leave it with or near the body and why leave a fa—'

Brad swiftly interrupted. 'Original medals are worth a lot of money and are few and far between, but the fakes can be found on internet auction sites for a few quid. We're only assuming it was left with the body. According to Radcliffe, it was possibly a metre away and so should we be considering both scenarios?'

April smiled and agreed.

'We're checking missing persons but my guess is he could be an illegal in which case ...' He looked up and raised his eyebrows. 'I also believe he was killed for a misdemeanour, some kind of revenge killing if we accept the things found with him were part of this. Being tortured, stripped, the way he was hogtied also points to that.'

April moved to his side and looked at the photographs

displayed on the computer screen. 'One thing awaits investigation, the possibility of tattoo removal from arms and fingers. Interestingly, toxicology found no traces of any drugs. There are scars that show he was shot twice at some stage in his life, in the right shoulder and in the thigh. I'm assured that these were on different occasions although how they know that is anyone's guess. Entry and exit wounds have healed, but from all accounts, there were clear signs of non-professional medical intervention.'

'From a war zone? Middle East? Child soldier possibly? They start fighting young in order to survive. They're made to fight or die,' Brad remarked as he doodled an image that resembled an AK 47.

'Eastern Mediterranean. Either they've got it wrong or he was a long way from home. I'll see if they can be more specific with injury dates. Maybe he was desperate for a new life. Unskilled? Fearless? Foolish? All my speculation.' April paused. 'I take it we've posted his picture on the police website and social media?'

'Yes. Nothing so far. Mind it was a bloody awful image. Dead men don't smile too well no matter what computer jiggery-pokery is used.'

April did not see the funny side of his comment and her expression conveyed that.

'Ma'am.'

CHAPTER 6

Skeeter brought the car to a halt on Walter Street and read the statement taken from the victim of the bike theft. Looking down the road she could see that this had not been a random snatch, it had been another well-planned and well-executed crime. The victim travelled the route daily. The street was quiet and full of parked vehicles of every description. She continued to read the report on her phone before turning to DC Tony Price, who sat beside her languidly chewing a fingernail on his right hand before opening the window and spitting it onto the pavement.

'Bugging me for ages that bastard.' He inspected the result of the extraction before rubbing his thumb across the roughened edge.

Skeeter scratched the back of her ear. She was now familiar with Tony's personal hygiene and habits.

'If you'd used a knife in this attack what would you do with it, apart from clean the rest of the crap that lurks beneath those nails of yours that is?'

He quickly glanced at his nails; she was right. 'Need to do

some baking, that'd clean them. Scones, I think. The currants would camouflage the crap.' He turned and grinned at her knowing what kind of facial expression would greet him, then answered her question. 'Getting rid of any weapon in Liverpool is easy owing to the bloody great body of water that runs past it and the mud that lurks beneath. Christ we're still dredging up bombs from World War Two so the odd handgun and knife will never be found. People disappear too. Just around the corner on Regent Road, past the hotel, there's the bridge separating the two docks, Stanley Dock and Collingwood Dock. Me? I'd chuck it into the water there. It'd most likely sink into the muddy bottom without trace, that's if it is mud. In the past, the city used the river and sea as a shit hole so what you see isn't actually mud at all, it's probably years and years of accumulated turds mixed with nodders and tampons – a glorified human soup!'

'Thank you for sharing that. Ever thought of swopping your career? Make a bloody inspiring tour guide, chef maybe?' She rooted in her pocket, brought out a tube of mints and popped one in her mouth before returning it. 'So, do we know they went that way?'

'The bike was taken at 07.25 and we had a report of a phone and bag snatch along the pedestrian area by the Liver Building twenty-five minutes after. They probably used the new bike; it wouldn't have been in the system as stolen. We're checking ANPR to see if we can identify it having been in the area.'

At Skeeter's suggestion they quickly swopped seats. 'Right, drive the way you think they drove.'

Tony Price revved the car and accelerated down the narrow road towards the river, pausing at the junction before turning left. Within minutes they crossed the steel and wooden bridge that spanned the dock entrance. Tony slowed to almost walking pace. They both knew immediately that if a knife had been thrown from a moving bike then this was the most likely place. However, there was also the chance that the perpetrator would keep it for the next robbery. There would be no point in organising a search as it would be rejected on the grounds of a waste of specialist support time. A body might be different but a knife?

Skeeter glanced at the huge ruins of the tobacco warehouse.

'Biggest brick structure in the world that when it was constructed, supposedly fireproof and to think it's only now being converted into apartments. It's been such a shame to see it unused for so long. The penthouses will have formidable views.'

'And a massive mortgage – footballers and criminals only, please step this way,' Tony mumbled cynically.

She gazed along the surrounding wall and sections of the docks, glancing at the huge, castellated stone block sentinels that formed the gateposts. Built into the high brick walls they were the entry points to the various docks, many now ruined and deserted and a far distant cry from Liverpool's heyday.

'They always remind me of giant rooks, you know, the chess pieces.'

Tony said nothing but increased his speed. It took them ten minutes to get to the scene where the latest snatches had occurred, but it was as if nothing had happened, normality had swiftly returned. A large city soon heals itself; there is little time to stop and lick its wounds. Skeeter knew that too well from the London terrorist atrocities. Within days, it was as if nothing had happened other than the appearance of more preventative structures, like the closing of a door after the horse has gone. Tony's words broke into her thoughts.

'Mounted and ran along the pavement before swerving between pedestrians and then they were away. Nobody hurt other than having their things stolen.'

'And their confidence shaken, don't forget.'

A high-pitched scream of a moped made both officers turn but their fears were quickly allayed; the rider's fluorescent jacket and the red learner plate attached to the rear number plate made them both smile and relax.

'That's the problem,' Tony continued. 'It's the same with the terrorists using vehicles to mow down innocent people. We're surrounded by cars, buses and wagons and some are parked on the pavements or delivering in pedestrian areas. You can't be on your guard all of the time and that's the key to their success. People don't expect them. Many are wired for sound and oblivious to what's going on. They are never forewarned. They make perfect victims, they're vulnerable and easy.'

CHAPTER 7

The narrow street flanked by terraced houses seemed claustrophobic, their proximity denuding the direct sunlight. Every house, although built at the same time using the same materials, looked different. Some still displayed their original brickwork whilst others were painted in various colours in an attempt to modernise their appearance. In many ways, time had been cruel. They were what they were and however many coats of paint were applied they would never be anything different.

On the pavement, leaning against or stuffed behind a downspout that ran down the heavily graffiti-daubed wall, lay a number of wilted remnants of bouquets of flowers, glass candle holders and two small bedraggled teddy bears. They had been left there two weeks previously to remember a victim of some turf war gang knife crime, their presence now having no effect on those passing by. The murder was simply a moment, a heartbeat in the city's history and it would not be the last. It might not be the last by the end of the day, the observer knew as he read one of the inscriptions.

Allways in our thoughts and we prey each day for you to be with the angles.

xx

The spelling errors somehow made the sentiment even more poignant. He tucked the card into his pocket before standing to look to the far end of the street. As if blocking the exit was the dominating presence of Goodison Park. With all the talk of the new stadium down by the docks, it might not be there much longer. He began to walk along the street. A dog barked, trapped behind one of the many doors; telephone wires hung lazily across the void. A suspended pair of training shoes oscillated their warning in the light breeze. Within a few minutes he would arrive at the shop.

Thin strands of light squeezed through the edges of a second-floor window. Even though they appeared razor sharp, they lost their battle to cut through the blackout material and allow in adequate light. There was a stale smell of urine in the room, mixed with the stronger smell of kebab and garlic. The bed on which Chelle lay gave little comfort. With one wrist secured using an electrician's cable to the metal frame, she had a limited range of movement. If she listened carefully, she could hear music and the occasional passing car. Twice she had heard the distant wail of a police siren and her heart had fluttered, a mixture of excitement and fear but this had quickly been replaced by the bitterness of disappointment. The music was Middle Eastern or African, definitely unusual and only broken by raised human voices. She neither understood nor recognised the language spoken. It was as if she had been transported to some distant place but she knew just where she was, she was within walking distance of her flat; she had come here voluntarily.

It had been about five days since she had been brought to the room. Someone important wanted to see her, a reward they had said. She had come willingly, thinking her bloke might be there. She had not seen him for a while which was not unusual. She would be told he was travelling, on business. Sometimes they had to lie low, but now this. She had been searched and her flat key and phone confiscated. The consolation was that she had received some of her clothes. The days were cruel, often passing slowly and her protests fell on deaf ears. All had been acceptable until they cable tied her wrist to the bed frame. It was then she realised the reward would not materialise.

Chelle could not remember the last time she had wet any bed she had slept on but today she had no choice. Despite calling out, her captors had been deaf to her pleas. She had wept, frightened of what they would think or say. If only she had known it, these simple, silly thoughts should have been the least of her worries.

* * *

The sign over the main shop window proudly announced the takeaway served: *Pizza, Kebab and Fish and Chips*. The white lettering contrasted with the blue background. In this part of the city, it would not be painted red. Damaged and bent *Just Eat* signs were displayed on either side and in the upper window. A green food hygiene sticker placed almost as high showed that they had achieved one out of five stars; surprisingly, not the lowest score.

Just sit on your fat arses and we'll bring the unhealthy stuff to you, he said to himself. *No wonder everyone's getting so fucking fat.*

He pushed open the door knowing what aroma that would greet him, after all it was like a third home. Malik heard the bell and turned. The light layer of sweat covering his bald head reflected the yellowing strip lights that ran the length of the room, giving his skin a jaundiced appearance. In his hand was a long-bladed knife that he had been using to slice the slowly rotating kebab.

'She's still upstairs as instructed. There was no fuss. I don't think she believes she's getting a reward now, as she did at first, if you ask me, she's definitely not sure now.' Malik smirked. 'I could remedy that and give her one and so could the other lads if that's okay? A fucking good send-off you might say.'

He grinned and the three gold capped teeth set behind his lips became suddenly visible. Reaching under the counter he retrieved Chelle's mobile before handing it over.

'Key's with Sadiq.'

'Have you touched her?'

Malik knew from the tone and the look on the face staring back at him just what the answer should be. He shook his head. 'No, boss, not without your permission.'

'Good. Check through this phone for anything that might link. She gets it back after you show her this.' He tossed the card he had removed from the street side floral display onto the counter. 'She owes me five phones, two wallets and who knows what else considering she didn't inform us about that knobhead of a boyfriend of hers. "Trust me", he insisted, "I know what I'm doing. I can double your money, Boss. I've done it before." He laundered the money right enough, made it fucking shrink. He'll not do it again.'

He looked directly at Malik, his eyes cold and lacking any emotion. 'Fortunately, my friend, I know what I'm doing, I know what must be done and it has been executed. Finito!'

Malik quickly looked down, read the card and frowned, the tip of the knife's blade resting on the counter like a vertical guillotine.

'Listen and listen good. You keep it in your trousers and so do the rest but you tell her we know and that the next time she thinks it wise to feather her own nest and not speak out, this card will be addressing her passing. You understand? She's young so she has one more chance and besides, she rides too well.'

Malik smiled at the connotation.

'I've warned you!'

The smile quickly turned to disappointment.

'Just make her aware, frightened. Make sure she says nothing about the boyfriend. Tell her that all walls have ears and that he'll be away a while. Business.'

Malik's smile returned as he looked at the knife. 'That's one more than her fella had.'

Even though the music continued to play in the background, there suddenly appeared to be a silence that dragged on as both men looked at each other.

'What do you have to do?'

'Frighten her, that's all.'

'For the moment that is. Tomorrow you take her to Sadiq. He will decide when she can get back to work.'

CHAPTER 8

April Decent should have been at home but two key pieces of information had come to light making her gut tingle with excitement. Even though she had a list as long as her arm of outstanding domestic duties to perform, she needed to be in work. It was not the urge to impress early in the game that drove her, but her natural professional pride. She had taken Tico for his morning run along the beach, the most important aspect of his early routine, and once that was done, April could manage her day as she pleased. It had seemed to her, and probably the others now working on the case, that little progress had been made, not only in finding the identity of the recently discovered body, but of the items found near it. April had set aside one wall and some temporary display boarding that had seen better days. The casual use of duct tape had helped it stand without endangering those walking close by.

She looked at the photographs of the body taken by the Forensics Team, the images from the post mortem and then those of the items found with him. His description failed to match any missing persons from the UK and Europe. This was becoming more common, there had been such an influx of migrants into Europe over the last few years, there were probably hundreds of people missing or buried, still awaiting discovery, that would never be identified. April thought the man she stared at might be one such case. His usefulness had come to an end; he was disposable. DNA tests for determination of place of origin could be used only as a guide and could not be relied upon. Tests on the remnants of any fingerprints had brought nothing new to the investigation. It was clearly a long shot, a procedure.

'He's a phantom, a blend in. No passport probably and no past. Just someone wanting to make a future,' she muttered to herself.

Lucy Teraoka had been standing quietly studying her new boss. From what she had seen so far, she approved. She said nothing.

The police medal had been returned after forensic assessment. It had been identified as a fake and online auction sites had been checked. From the three legitimately sold, two were to private individuals who had bought them at auction believing them to be original. They had then sold them once it was discovered they were fake, accurately describing their true provenance. Investigations had been concluded and the medals were still in possession of the new buyers, but there had been one piece of good luck. The third medal, tracked to the internet, was sold from a dealer in Thetford to a buyer in Liverpool. Neither a record nor a description of the buyer was known. The item had been posted to a collection point in a shop in the Walton area of the city. This had partly been the reason April had given up her day. The CCTV footage from the shop had been tracked for the date of collection and that should be available within hours. Secondly, the results of the forensic tests made using samples of the dead man's hair were also available.

DC Lucy Teraoka decided she had watched April for long enough and approached the area. 'Morning, Boss. A phantom, you said. Christ, chasing real baddies is hard enough but to chase ghosts … we'll need a witch.' She winked and they both understood the implication.

'Phantom folk, illegals without a past, people who travel here and simply disappear within the system. As you know, some acquire a new identity and the old persona simply ceases to exist unless they, for convenience let's say, need to resurrect it.' April tapped the picture on the board and the whole thing wobbled like some cheap theatre set.

'Right. Have you been in long?'

'Came in too early, considering I should be at home washing and ironing today.' She pulled a face as if to show she was not really concerned.

'I know where I'd rather be. Hate bloody washing, me. I heard the boffins have sent good news?' She sipped from a water bottle. 'Never understand it all … like pure wizardry.'

'We are very Walt Disney today what with phantoms, witches and wizards. Not magic, Lucy, just pure science. We'll catch whoever did this by modern forensics and good old-fashioned police work. That part hasn't changed. It's about being organised with the evidence and making sure it's uplifted into the system.'

April sat, pulled another chair next to hers and motioned for Lucy to sit down.

'Look, here's the science bit. What's fascinating is that we can get up to five years of information about the person from their hair. Well, to be factual, more about what the person has deliberately or inadvertently put in their bloodstream.'

April looked carefully at Lucy and could see confusion in her eyes.

'This is what I understand. New cells form in the hair follicle and they take traces of substances going through the bloodstream. As the hair grows, new cells push out the old ones and they die and harden, like information from your computer being put on a stick or a disc. It's a long-lasting record of what was in the blood when it was forming. The sebum, the coating to each hair, traps information about drugs and minerals ingested by the person.'

'So, hair keeps a record of what passes through the body and not just DNA?'

'Right.'

'So, what do we know?'

April smiled and rubbed her hands. 'We know our man enjoyed both alcohol and drugs, predominantly weed and cocaine but that is generally more recent. We can also make a strong guess that he'd been living in a major city for more than three years, more than likely Liverpool. Further comparative tests will confirm that. What I hope is that our man here proves to be the chap who collected the fake police medal from a Hermes collection point two weeks ago. We're about to go and look over some CCTV tapes for the date in question.'

* * *

April parked the car on the small, litter-strewn carpark. A row of steel bollards protected the cash machine to the right of the shop's entrance. It was clear they had suffered a number of parking incidents; however, all were relatively perpendicular to the ground and fulfilling their function.

'We could have collected it and viewed it at the station but I wanted to see it here first.'

April entered followed quickly by Lucy. Two people were behind the counter, one serving a customer. They waited until he left.

'Hi, police, you're expecting us. Mr Hill?'

The older of the two came from round the back of the counter and looked at the warrant card she proffered.

'Didn't expect you until lunchtime but everything is ready.'

They followed as he punched four numbers into the door lock before entering a large store area.

'Originally the police suggested the parcel was collected by a man. That's what took the time. Knew the date and time it was collected but, turned out to be a young woman, although sometimes these days it's hard to tell the difference. So many customers it's impossible to remember unless they or the item they're collecting are unusual.'

He went to the screen and pressed the play button. The image was standard shop CCTV footage, black and white and grainy. The camera was obviously positioned behind the counter facing the customer side with the shop door just to the left. Lucy could see the top of someone's head, probably Hill, as the figure was seen to move cigarettes into a cabinet to the side. It was quickly confirmed.

'That's me, goodness it shows my bald patch too well.'

Both officers could hear a certain melancholy in his voice but it quickly vanished.

'See, here, she's just come in, blue hoody top.'

Instinctively both officers leaned forward and followed the girl's actions.

The angle of the camera did not give the best full facial image but April felt sure it could be enhanced.

'Please go through the collection procedure,' she requested without turning her face from the screen.

'You come in either with a printed sheet showing the order number and a barcode or you can show it on a mobile. See, she's shown me her phone screen. I now scan it which tells the courier service that the correct person has collected the package.'

'Did it have a name and address on it?'

'Can you pause it?' Lucy requested as she leaned closer to the screen.

'Look at the tattoo on the side of her palm running from her wrist.'

April and Hill followed her gesture and moved closer.

'I remember now you've mentioned that. If I recall it was a lizard or gecko, only small but without a long tail. And something else. She had small, random tattoos on the fingers of her left hand, here. Never seen that before. Just above the nail. Not every finger either.' He pointed to the area on his own hand.

'Do you remember what they were?' April quickly asked.

The look on Hill's face told her all she needed to know.

Hill shook his head. 'Here we are. Yes, the collector was a K. Jones and this collection point, no title given. Providing the information they have matches with what I have, then there's no need for a personal address. I guess it's to do with data protection, security. Bloody hell, with the change in the law everyone needs permission from everyone else to keep any sort of data these days. This might be a load of rubbish but you can see the reason. I was told that if you bought an expensive watch online and you have it delivered to your home address then the seller knows your address. What's to stop them coming in a week and robbing you?'

April nodded. 'It seems to make sense.'

'We're shortly going to have secure lockers fitted outside so we don't have to be open. You can send and receive using your debit card and mobile phone, print labels, the whole shooting match. It's a twenty-four-hour service.'

'Sounds like *InPost*,' Lucy responded immediately.

'That's it. Quick and easy and it means we don't have to keep stuff here. Protected by three CCTV cameras it is too, so it's really secure. You'd get better images than these as one of the cameras will be looking directly at the face of the person collecting and delivering.'

'Unless you're wearing a helmet or a burqa,' April mumbled to herself but ensuring Lucy heard. 'So, Mr Hill, the courier will have received a mobile number and other details of the person receiving the goods when this was booked by the seller?'

'As I've said, they'll receive the person's mobile contact number and possibly an address but this shop was the collection point. Adding other information is unnecessary. The system works with few complaints considering the number of transactions. The person sent the package and it was received successfully. End of!'

'Have you seen this person since?

'No, on just that occasion. You're lucky the system still had it saved.'

April handed him a memory stick and he downloaded the relevant section. Hill was just about to speak when April raised a finger. 'Data protection ... you'll get a receipt.'

Once in the car, Lucy contacted Control giving the details they had learned from Hill and requested the courier release the mobile numbers involved and the seller's details.

CHAPTER 9

Chelle rubbed the tattoo on the side of her hand. She repeated Sadiq's words at the back of her mind: *You've identified yourself permanently.* All she knew was that she had bonded with Abid and having matching tattoos seemed romantic. The fact that they did not match was never considered an issue. Her eyes went to her wrist, she could still feel the chafed skin made red and sore from the electrician's tie. It had been hard trying to sleep attached to the bed but it was the memory of the man's hand that startled her awake as it had grasped either side of her face. His grip had been hard and deliberate, causing her involuntary muffled scream to be forced through her dry lips. The strong stench of onions clearly lingered on his fingers positioned deliberately too close to her flared nostrils. She recalled how she had struggled to breathe and his words.

'Listen, bitch. Fucking thank your lucky stars you're getting a second chance, not everyone does in our game but you know that, don't you, Chelle.'

Chelle remembered the coldness in his eyes and the fine flecks of spittle that had hit her face.

'You'll now behave and forget the past as that's gone and buried. All you need to worry about is what's ahead as we have a busy time coming. Just do as you're told, ride well and you'll keep seeing the sun set.'

It was the knife in his other hand that dominated her full attention. It moved close to her eye.

'One more chance to see the sunsets! Don't end up a shell on the beach, Chelle.' He emphasised the syllables of each word and then laughed at his own joke.

The blade moved quickly away and sliced through the plastic tie, releasing her wrist from the bed. He stood away. It was the moment hearing the word sunset that would remain with her.

* * *

Checking her watch, she realised there was no time for reflection, what was done was done. Slipping on the glove she twisted the throttle on the bike and moved away into the traffic. Within minutes the second bike followed. They would take routes different from the meet and there they would wait a few hundred yards apart. It was all in the planning and all about patience. When the target arrived, they would be ready; surprise would be their weapon.

They heard it before they saw it, the shrill open exhaust of the bike before it slowed, probably due to traffic. It was late. Chelle flicked down the mirror-like visor and started the bike in readiness. She knew the other bike containing the two riders would also be prepared.

The late afternoon sun sat low and a mist hung grey, a heavy mantle along the dark water of the Mersey, bringing with it a chill. The narrow streets in this area were claustrophobic, wrapped by the tall buildings that edged the dockside. It brought an early darkness, occasionally slashed only by blades of yellow-orange light that stabbed their eyes as it hit the riders' peripheral vision. They followed the Honda Activa along the A565 before it turned left onto Howe Street. This was the moment. Both bikes followed and Chelle quickly pulled alongside the Honda rider. Initially, he had not seen the bike move to his right-hand side but he quickly registered it as it eased him into the kerbside. He moved his left hand off the bars and gestured before calling out a warning. Returning his hand, he pulled up, now gesticulating with both hands. Chelle blocked his path and turned to face her victim, her identity protected by the reflective visor.

Quasim jumped from the pillion seat of the second bike and drew a large knife, jabbing it at the Honda rider's arm whilst shouting, 'Run, or I'll kill you!'

The Honda rider initially twisted away. His eyes were drawn to the blade as the two bikes seemed to surround him, like two angry wasps, their engines' screams adding to his confused state. The noise amplified as it echoed from within the close brick walls. Seeing the man still holding the bike, Quasim thrust the blade down hard aiming for the rider's thigh that was close to him. The tip quickly penetrated the jeans he was wearing and sank up to the knife's hilt.

There was a moment as if time stood still. Quasim watched the rider's face in the open-faced helmet. It was not a look of fear that he was faced with, but one of uncertainty and disbelief, but then as the pain registered, his expression changed. Quickly extracting the blade, Quasim was careful not to twist it and cause too much internal damage. He could still see the intensity of pain and horror in the man's eyes reinforced by the accompanying scream. Without hesitation, Quasim grabbed the handlebar of the scooter and with the knife hand punched at the rider who instantaneously backed away and fell from the bike. It was done. Quasim slid onto the scooter, opened the throttle and followed the other two bikes before turning onto Regent Road. Within a minute the knife was thrown from the moving bike into a fenced yard containing tightly stacked blue shipping containers. It would remain there. Whilst the Honda was still fresh, they would destroy one of the older bikes before planning the next grab.

The rider lay on the semi-cobbled road and watched the ground beneath his right leg turn deep red.

Working with the youngsters at the wrestling club was the highlight of Skeeter Warlock's week. Training the Tough Tots, as the group was known, filled her with pride as she remembered her early days, many of which had ended in tears. Today, however, was different, it was more structured and far more safety conscious. Two tots were in the centre of the mats on all fours and two, also on all fours, were tasked to get past them. There was much excitement, laughter and encouragement as those sitting around the edge encouraged and shouted. Skeeter knelt on the mat's edge and the smile across her face signalled her delight at the progress they were making.

'Wicca!' Roy yelled from the far end of the room, trying to be heard above the noise of the excited screams.

She turned briefly to see what he wanted before looking back at the kids.

Roy was moving towards her. 'Your phone's been dancing inside your locker and annoying the hell out of me for the last ten minutes. It's on and off, persistent, whoever they might be. Probably work calling their favourite police woman.' He winked and tapped her shoulder. 'Go, I'll watch the nippers.'

The early evening air felt chill after the warmth of the gym. Some youths were playing football on a distant, floodlit field, their shouts drifting towards her. She checked the phone to see she had five missed calls and an answerphone message.

'It's Lucy. We have another report of bike theft, broad daylight. Knife attack and a bad one.'

Skeeter could hear the anger in Lucy's voice; there was no way of concealing that degree of professional concern. She checked the time of the message before returning the call.

* * *

April and Pete Bradshaw were standing discussing the latest findings on the police medal when Skeeter entered. They turned to see the forlorn figure move to her desk.

Brad watched her before moving over. 'More attacks?'

She let her eyes rise to meet his whilst shaking her head. 'Bloody broad daylight, the bastards. Broad daylight and then they stab a guy in the arm and thigh because he put up a struggle. It won't be long before these shits kill someone, knife attacks, hammer attacks … If I could get my hands on them.'

'How's the fella?'

'In hospital, knife missed his artery by this much.' She held her thumb and finger apart to show the distance.

Brad whistled. 'Lucky bugger … if you can call it luck. I guess he survived.'

Skeeter responded. 'There's long-term psychological damage that's sometimes difficult to treat. All for a fucking scooter.'

'Bastards,' Brad mumbled under his breath.

'The scooter?' April queried.

'Vanished. There were two other bikes involved, one single, one two up.'

'Back of a Transit more like,' April added.

Skeeter nodded her agreement. 'It'll be stripped, painted black and back on the streets used as a modern-day Black Bess.'

April moved towards her, clearly sensitive to her distress. 'Funny how we have this romantic notion regarding the highwaymen of old. Stand and deliver, until you put them in a modern-day setting and then they become the bloody scum of the earth. We could do with setting up our own riders, make them look old or vulnerable but then they'll find there's nothing old or feeble about them when they give chase and stop them. They did that in the capital and rammed the buggers off the bikes. Believe me they soon started to think. I've had a word with DCI Mason. He thinks there's a chance of following the same tactic.'

Although April was only stating what she knew, she could

see the idea of taking the fight to them had registered with Skeeter. Fortunately, she quickly changed the subject. 'What about you?'

'Bit of a head's up on the medal that was found near "Sandy Shore" here.'

April's tone lightened and it reflected immediately on the general mood as April pointed to the boards.

'Our name for the guy dug up on the beach – Alexander Shore.' She allowed Skeeter's chuckle to die away. 'It was sent from a collector after it was purchased online and collected by a woman from a local store. We have her on CCTV but the images are not too clear. The technical people have managed to get some improved stills on the tattoo she had on her hand.'

Skeeter walked over to April and looked at the images on the wall. 'What exactly is it?'

April answered immediately. 'It's some kind of gecko or lizard. The shopkeeper also remembers seeing some random markings tattooed here on her fingers. They're not visible on any of the shots we have. We received a later call from Hill, the shopkeeper, to say the finger tattoos might be fancy foreign letters or numbers but he couldn't be sure. We've also received two mobile numbers and the sender's address from the courier of the medal. Number of the purchaser turns out to be a stolen phone and yes, debit card used was also stolen. We have local police interviewing. When you look at the position of the tattoos, they match the area where evidence of skin removal was performed on the corpse. According to the forensics' report they are suggesting there was hasty tattoo removal.'

'Did we not already know that? The fact they might have

been there and removed could be coincidence,' Skeeter announced with no real conviction.

April tapped the side of her nose. 'That's the million-dollar question. Now, if they were done together ...'

'Local tattoo shops will hold consent forms of anyone receiving a tattoo, they need to keep them for six years, providing she had it done locally that is.'

'Providing it wasn't done in a backstreet shop abroad on a drunken Friday night,' Brad responded quickly, putting in his two penn'orth.

Both women looked at him and it was Skeeter who answered for them both.

'The pot's always half empty for this man isn't it, Brad?' She grabbed his cheek.

He knocked away her hand. 'Just bringing all options to the investigation.'

'Had experience, have we?' Skeeter moved closer, her body language matching her mood.

There was a pause and both saw Brad's face flush. Neither took their eyes off him as he rolled up the sleeve on his right arm before turning the inner part towards them. The tattoo contrasted with the soft pink of the tender flesh. Both women looked at each other, back at Brad and then at the tattoo.

'Kyrenia, Turkish Cyprus, eight or so summers ago after a day's drinking ...' He started to sing. '*Regrets, I've had a fe ...* Me and the mates thought it would be a good idea to have our nicknames tattooed on our inner arm in Turkish. *Brad,* I asked for which they told me translated to this ... *Ekmek.* Being pissed I believed them and was happy.'

April smiled as if she knew what was to come but Skeeter concentrated on Brad's face.

'Either I didn't explain the word clearly enough or his English was worse than I remember but *Ekmek* when translated means *bread*.'

Neither Skeeter nor April knew whether to laugh or gasp but Brad simply rolled down his sleeve.

'I don't tend to tell many people that story. It's part of my embarrassing history – wild child. The worst thing was when I started in this job, I had a flat above a Turkish takeaway and in summer I had to wear long sleeves. I was fed up of having to explain why I had *bread* tattooed on my bloody arm.'

That lightened the moment as both put a reassuring arm on his shoulder. 'Your secret's safe with us, barm cake and you can spell that whichever way you like!' Skeeter chuckled.

The light-hearted banter was just what Skeeter needed and she smiled at her colleagues. Turning, she studied the photographs attached by coloured magnets to the whiteboard.

'You could get an artist to interpret the tattoo design and forward it to all tattoo shops in Liverpool to begin with, then post it on missing persons on the Merseyside police website. Someone will have seen something.'

CHAPTER 10

It was while working in the local Sunday school in her teens that April had become fascinated with the art of coloured and leaded glass. She would relax after the classes, staring at the church windows, intrigued by the artisans' careful positioning of the colours to bring out the best in the images depicted. She had vowed one day to learn the ancient craft. A six-month night school class had seen her work with copper foil and then quickly progress to the serious art of leading. At the height of her enthusiasm, her then partner had remarked she would have leaded the windows in the car if he had allowed it. She often chuckled at the thought. However, now owing to work commitments, she only used her skills as a form of relaxation; a way of closing the hangar door and leaving work behind, as her father would say.

April stretched a flaccid piece of 'H' section lead came until it was stiff enough to hold horizontally before laying it on the cartoon diagram of the window design on which she was currently working. She allowed it to follow the carefully cut coloured glass before pinning the outside edge of the lead with a horseshoe nail. She forced a fid into the lead channel to ensure it was a snug fit to the glass. She tapped another nail into the board. Cutting the lead to neatly edge the glass, she butted it to another lead section. Moving away, her hands now supporting her back, her smile showed she was pleased with the abstract, patterned window that was taking shape before her. A row of nails held the flat collage together until it was soldered.

Her police mobile illuminated and danced across the workbench. She leaned forward and caught it as it collided with the old tobacco tin that held the nails.

'Ma'am, it's Brad. We have a hit on the missing person website although I realise she's not necessarily missing.'

April listened, trying to place to whom he was alluding.

'The tattooed girl … We've had a call to say that someone hasn't seen a Michelle Pearson for nearly a week. She rents an upper floor flat on Rosslyn Street, Walton, from the couple who live below. According to the report she was co-habiting with a foreign bloke for a while but he hasn't been seen for ages, like. They thought he'd cleared off. They used to row a good deal, they say. Now she's gone too. Strangely they don't owe any rent. Says they always paid in advance – cash – and have always been good tenants, apart from the disagreements and slamming of doors on occasion that is.'

'So why did they call in? Because they were missing?' She moved one of the nails with her thumb and it tightened on the lead.

'She keeps a scooter-like moped in the yard at the back and although she's not been seen, the bike went missing last night. There's more. When they checked on the Merseyside Missing Persons' website, they identified our Sandy Shore chap, the guy on the beach, as the bloke who stayed there and they also think that he had a similar tattoo to the one described. Could be a total time waster but …'

The pause before starting to answer was lengthened as April assimilated the information. It was unusual to reap such a bonus, two for the price of one and she immediately hung on Brad's last few words … *time wasters*.

'So where are we with that? Has someone visited to check it out?'

'No, I thought you might like to visit and check it personally after all, ma'am, nothing ventured.'

'Arrange it and have me picked up in fifteen minutes.'

Brad's car was already outside the apartment when April arrived. After sending her driver away she climbed into the passenger seat beside Brad. He smiled.

'This one.'

April's glance followed his finger to her left. The house was immaculate. There was no garden and the front door opened directly onto the street. Positioned within the bay window she saw an Aspidistra in a brightly coloured pot.

'Upstairs flat, you said? There's only one entrance?' On closer inspection she could see there were two doorbells.

'There's a back ginnel between this and the next row, but it's been fitted with a security gate, an initiative by the council a few years back after having trouble with youths. These hidden rear passages once made great escape routes for youths when being chased by the police as well as being secluded corners for God knows what activities … just let

your imagination run wild and you'll have thought of some.'
He raised his eyebrows.

'You mentioned that a scooter has been taken even
though it was secured by having locked gates at either end.
How come?'

'Someone had a key or the combination?'

April read the report quickly detailing the call.

'Come on. We'll not learn anything sitting here.'

As they left the car, the front door was already opening.
Eileen Toland was older than April had anticipated and more
than a little overweight. She filled the door space with barely
room to spare.

'DI Decent and this is DC Bradshaw. You called 101
regarding a missing person's enquiry?'

Eileen immediately started to speak, her rich and
treacly Scouse accent was a clue to her origin. April
stopped her.

'It might be better to chat inside if that's okay?'

Toland looked up and down the street but could see
nobody.

'Yes, do come in. Please wipe your feet.'

The lounge was neat and orderly. A large flat screen television dominated the space. Once seated, Eileen repeated
what she had started to explain at the door.

'Do you remember the last day you saw her, Mrs Toland?'

Toland pulled a face to suggest she was thinking hard
about the question, and then looked across at her husband
who sat looking blankly.

'Er, it must have been a week last …' She paused again. '…
Wednesday, yes, Wednesday evening, about six. I know this
because I'd had my hair done, and Michelle said she liked it. I

bumped into her in the corridor there. She lives upstairs and we'd often chat. That's right isn't it, Francis?'

Brad looked at Toland's hair and mentally tried to describe the colour, it was the hue of a two-day old bruise, a cross between grey and blue.

'So, today's Tuesday. Nearly a week, you believe? Is it usual for her to be absent for such a length of time? Could she have gone on holiday?'

'I have rules, Ms … Decent, did you say?'

April nodded.

'If the flat's going to be left for any length of time, we tell each other, like. It's so we can keep an ear out. You never know these days, especially round here. It's not what it used to be. A lot of foreigners have moved into the street over the last few years. You just have to look at the bloody colours of some of the houses. Sorry for the language but blue, I ask you, and I know they don't support the team at the end so that's not the reason. To make matters worse some haven't a word of English.' She wrapped her arms under her ample bosom and swayed gently. 'Don't get me wrong, Liverpool's always been a melting pot for all and sundry, being a port like but … well … I'll say no more or you'll consider me one of those racists and I can assure you that couldn't be further from the truth.'

April thought of the number of expats who have gone to live abroad and had never taken the trouble to learn one word of the language but she did not comment.

'Could your husband have heard from her and forgotten to mention it?'

Both turned to look at Francis whose face flushed. There was an embarrassing pause.

'Forgot to say, love. I got a call a few days ago. She said she'd had to go visit her mother who'd had an accident, from what she told me it was serious. Said she'd had to dash off. She told me she'd given the key to a friend who was going to collect some of her stuff for her. You were out at bingo and I must have fallen asleep as I don't remember either of them calling.'

April turned to look at Brad and they both quickly reached the same conclusion.

Brad slipped his hand in his pocket and withdrew an enhanced definition photograph of the girl taken from the shop's CCTV showing what was determined to be the hand tattoo.

'Did Michelle have a tattoo on her hand?' He passed it to Mrs Toland. 'I'm aware this isn't very clear but you can get a rough idea. I believe this is why you telephoned the missing persons' helpline.' He handed it to her.

'I thought I recognised it, like, when I was scanning the people on the missing person site. Der's more people missing than you think.' She pronounced *th* as a *d* and elongated the word. 'I was really surprised. I know it's a city full of docks and a bloody big river but all that lot can't have all fallen in and got washed away can they? With her going missing and this silly sod not mentioning anything I thought I'd check.' She let her foot crash against Francis's leg as she shook her head. 'Glad I did. Is she alright?'

Brad glanced at April and back at Toland but neither spoke. Brad pointed to the photograph eager to get an answer.

'Anything?'

'She had tattoos der and der.' She pointed to the photograph. 'It was some kind of lizard.'

She looked at April hoping for some encouragement but none came.

'She also had what appeared to be lines or marks on her fingers, not where you normally see them but right down by her nails. Her boyfriend had them too, looked the same.' She anticipated April's next question and quickly added. 'Can't remember which though, as they were only small, but dead fancy.'

'Do you have a key to the flat?'

Toland's offended expression spoke volumes and her answer was short and to the point. 'It's my house. Of course I've got a key.'

'Have you been in her flat since she disappeared?' April asked.

'I beg your pardon, I wouldn't ... Francis, have you?'

He shook his head.

If she told him to die on the spot, he would oblige, Brad thought, then he said, 'Forensics will tell us all we need to know. Amazing what they discover these days.'

Brad's nonchalance caught her off guard and for a moment her eyes darted between the two officers sitting opposite as she fidgeted on the chair.

'Well ... professionally, like. I am the landlady.' She bristled as she spoke. 'Just to check she wasn't dead, like, or that she'd left things on and I went up once to pop her post in. Mostly leaflets. There was no real mail.'

She blushed briefly but was saved further embarrassment when April asked about the missing partner.

'Never liked him, shifty type, you know the ones? Those who undress you with their eyes.'

Brad glanced at April trying to keep the smirk off his face.

'Bit of a geek. Computers, like. He had a couple of those laptops on the go. Didn't see him as often as her, a few times a week maybe, but I recognised the photograph on the police website even though it was grainy and blurred. Hubby said it reminded him of a corpse he'd once seen floating in the canal. Put him off his tea and it was his favourite if I remember right. Dreadful photograph.'

Brad immediately looked at April again.

'Do you have internet in the flats?'

'Yes, they requested it, in all rental properties now, they said. All homes have it. We don't in our flat do we Francis? In our opinion it's just full of pornography; that's what I understand anyway. That's probably what he was watching. Who knows?'

After questioning her further about her husband's comments, they took the key and went upstairs. April pulled on some plastic overshoes and gloves.

'You wait here. Just need a quick look. What about that marital relationship?'

'Rules him with a rod of iron the poor, bloody sod.'

Brad leaned against the wall and looked at the photograph of the girl and smiled before fanning himself with it. He listened to hear if Mrs Toland was still in the lounge or whether she had moved into another room. After thirty minutes the room was sealed and they left.

Within the hour, CSI were attending. Brad was uncertain as to whether Mr and Mrs Toland found their visit embarrassing or exciting but he sensed there was a feeling of self-importance by the way she spoke. He also found it difficult to believe they had kept themselves boxed in the flat below after the couple's disappearance.

As the CSI moved up the stairs, she bustled into the hallway. Checking their feet, she watched as they climbed the stairs carrying equipment whilst issuing stern, almost aggressive warnings to them that any damages would have to be paid for. She hovered either at the bottom of the stairs trying to see what was taking place, or stood by the lounge window watching the neighbours' curiosity get the better of them. Once the flat had been checked the officers worked the rear yard. It was now just a case of waiting.

'Mrs Toland?' The lead CSI removed his mask and let it dangle at his throat. He smiled but then his expression swiftly changed.

'Thank you for your time. The room has now been sealed. I don't know if we'll need to return so I'd appreciate your co-operation and leave it as is. No entry.' The smile briefly returned but the warning was clear.

CHAPTER 11

April faced the five members of the team. The forensic search of the flat had identified that the corpse found on the beach had been there and, considering the DNA traces, had occupied the place for some time. The man had also been identified as of eastern Mediterranean origin. The team had also announced a new discovery. April addressed the team.

'We've put concealed CCTV in the flat and also facing the rear yard. It's monitored round the clock just in case she returns or our landlady gets nosy. We've checked the files from the fingerprint and DNA analysis and although they've drawn a blank on our Sandy Shaw, we now know more about Michelle Pearson.'

April tapped her computer and a projected image of a young white female hit the screen on the far wall.

'Let me introduce you to Kelly Jones, nineteen. We know from experience that many kids who are either on the streets or involved in crime, whatever the degree, have had issues in their past, not all, but the majority. Kelly was no exception.'

April tapped again and the image changed to a chart showing the girl's chronological history.

'Kelly was born illegitimately to a convicted criminal and drug user. Father still unknown. The mother received a five-year term for aggravated robbery, removed the eye of a shop assistant who wouldn't let her take freely from her shop. She also had previous relating to ABH, self-harm and prostitution. To put it into perspective, the mother was then twenty-two. For those quick off the mark, the DNA found in the flat was linked to that of the mother who, according to records, was removed from Styal prison for the birth. Kelly was then kept in Manchester Neo-Natal Intensive Care for five weeks. The child was born dependent on the drugs taken by her mother and immediately after birth exhibited severe signs of going cold turkey. Mother was found to have been addicted to OxyContin, cocaine and methadone. The child was treated over that period with neo-natal morphine solution and a lot of TLC. If anyone doesn't know the symptoms that are manifested in children like this, you should check it out. It's all here.' April lifted a booklet for them all to see.

'What a shit start to life,' Brad chipped in. 'And I thought I'd had it tough.'

'Her life gets better – for a while, at least. Moved to foster mother and made good progress in all areas. It's safe to say Kelly bloomed in the months she was there. However, there was clear evidence of mental instability. Adopted at just over twelve months old, she continued to make progress until the age of six. Started showing signs of mental illness, anger, aggression towards the two other children in the house but that again, after support was put in, stabilized. School was fine but she was more creative than academic. Reports tell us she was precise in her presentation but she was also reported as being rather sly, untrustworthy and unpredictable. As her behaviour and school work began to decline, she was given specialist educational and emotional support and then she was moved to an EBD special school placement. At twelve she disappeared from school and home. Numerous appeals but she wasn't found until now.'

There was a pause and silence apart from the slight hum of the laptop fan.

April looked at each member of the team. 'All we have to do now is find her before …' She let the sentence hang in the air.

Lucy was quick to break the silence. 'Knowing what we now know, we can presume children like this disappear initially and they find the streets both lonely and frightening, not what they imagined. So, they would look and find someone who will help them; this often can mean older males. They give them a safe place to stay, treat them like an adult, show affection and love, maybe buy gifts and then when they've established a degree of trust, abuse them, share them, frighten them. This would also most probably mean ply them with alcohol and maybe establish a dependency on drugs in order to gain and maintain control. Free prostitutes, to put it bluntly. It's always a vicious circle. Our Kelly may well fit this bill.'

'Indeed, Lucy, indeed. Now, let's think back to the flat. You've seen the photographs. It doesn't resemble a shit hole. It's neat and orderly. Now that tells me it's been cleaned. You tend to get a feel for these things, and I'm pleased to say I'm not the only one to comment, CSI agreed. Seeing that there was a complete dearth of personal effects, no photographs, jewellery, and more importantly, none of his clothing, confirms to me that we can assume the room was searched and selected items removed. Considering the length of time Michelle, whom we shall now refer to as Kelly Jones to save confusion, had occupied the place too, you'd think she would have had some token, a memento, maybe? It's interesting to note that there was no underwear, personal hygiene products or jeans left. She's either done a runner or ...' April paused to allow discussion from the group and she did not have to wait long.

Lucy responded first. 'It might have been purely for convenience. My experience tells me with recruitment of gang membership you come off the streets, you're desperate and will happily live where you're put. Look at the number of illegal migrants who have entered the country in lorries over the years. They're rarely found. They vanish into attics, cellars and lofts in shops, restaurants and we've even discovered them in warehouses and garages. Not suitable for an animal let alone a human being. If you think about it, it's easy to imagine. To me, she's now running scared.'

'If only we knew the real number of these folk coming here, Lucy. It's easy for the puppet masters as they know there are no records or references. Easy come and easy go,' April replied sceptically.

Brad was nodding thoughtfully and added, 'Besides, if the room were cleaned, whether that be by the girl or persons unknown, it's been done thoroughly. We're talking professional criminals and the fact that traces of Class 'A' drugs were present puts this death into better perspective. It adds credence to our belief that the death and disappearance are gang related. In my opinion, ma'am, someone has done something they shouldn't have and paid the price.' He tapped his pencil on the table as if adding a full stop. 'That's my take on it.'

'Right, it's work time. The medal, why? The transparent disc. What? We need answers. Brad, check with Skeeter and see how she's getting on. There's a link here. I feel it deep down and so does she. Lucy, I've had a tip off from a contact at Greater Manchester, someone I met when working in another force. We've co-operated in the past and there's the possibility they might let us link with an informer who's proved effective before.'

'Very MI6, ma'am.' Lucy started humming the Bond tune and giggled.

April said nothing but continued to study Lucy before raising an eyebrow. Lucy laughed again. 'Very Roger Moore if I may say so.'

'It's a case of meeting and collecting. You don't say much to them and they don't say much to you. It's a hidden transaction. Don't worry, you'll be prepped.'

'When you say *you*? You mean me?' Lucy's facial expression was one of shock. 'Me?'

'It's right up your street.'

'Right.' Lucy raised her eyebrows. *And which street might that be*, she thought as a tingle of nerves filled her stomach.

* * *

April walked Tico along the beach. The spring days were beginning to stretch out and their closing was often reflected in stunning sunsets. Tonight was no exception. She stood admiring the distant horizon, now showing deep slashes of red and orange. The sea, a deeper palette of similar leached colours, seemed almost static the further her eyes travelled into the distance. Clouds had grown, thin at first but now more threatening cumulus were dragged into the picture. Sleet had been predicted but rain was definitely forecast. The drone of an aircraft could be heard, carried on the breeze which seemed more cruel, cutting and chill, than it had been earlier. April turned up her collar. She knew it would not be long before the wind would change and blow from the land. She watched the fine-grained sand move in clusters, whipping along the surface, a light whispering accompanying the movement. She breathed deeply. Her thoughts turned to the buried man and she shivered. Tico moved to her side as if he sensed her sudden disquiet.

'You are special.' She ran her hand along his arched back. 'Come on, Tico, home.' Tico turned and started to run; his motion was pure grace. She looked forward to settling down, working on the stained-glass window whilst listening to some music and then wine – yes, definitely wine.

The cottage was warm. Tico made an immediate dash for his bed in front of the Aga. April made her way into the area she called her studio. The horseshoe nails stood in rows trapping the glass within the lead. She would clean the lead joints, tallow them, tallow being the best flux, and solder them closed. She retrieved a small bronze brush and a stick of tallow – it looked like a candle without the wick. Rubbing the dulled lead joint, she brought a shine. She covered the surface in tallow; a strange aroma came from it, for her, a pleasant smell. After cleaning five or six joints the soldering gun was hot. Testing the heat against the solder; it melted easily. She could now seal the joints. Within the hour the first side was complete.

* * *

The queuing traffic moved slowly, more stop than creep. The progression in the early evening dark seemed like a penance. The term *rush hour* was a total contradiction to what was a twice daily, frustrating experience. Drivers' patience and concentration were tested whilst travelling at a pace that would not have been unfamiliar in 1890, therefore making a mockery of the term. The stop start motion on a stuffy double-decker bus was nauseating but the last thing Lucy wanted was to get off and walk. She had felt the need to do it before when travelling on public transport as she began to feel the early signs of motion sickness grow. As a child she could never travel far. The yawns, the beads of sweat to her forehead and the clammy warmth she immediately recognised. Walking would be certainly quicker but the inclement weather was against that.

She swept the misted glass window with her hand, bringing together a collection of water droplets that swelled and burst before rolling down the window like snails' trails. She allowed her gaze to follow the leading droplet until it collided with the rubber window surround. Lifting her gaze, she stared out of the window wishing the traffic would move.

The approach to this junction was always the same. Why the few buildings were left as if on an island, surrounded and awash with a complex road system, she would never know. It seemed irrational, and to her, obvious that a bottleneck had been created; three roads into one was a recipe for chaos. To make matters worse, in heavy rain, the narrow river that was artificially fed beneath the roads would often flood the whole area. That would not be the case today but tonight there was a rugby match at the nearby stadium adding to the normal congestion.

The street lights, fresh and glowing orange, seemed to wash smudged colour on the wet surfaces. She stared at nothing in particular and time seemed to stand still before the bus lurched to a sudden stop throwing everyone forward. A few passengers grumbled, a child began to cry a few seats behind Lucy, adding to the misery. Lucy's senses suddenly seemed under attack now that her hearing was bombarded. It was at that moment she leaned closer to the glass, trying to allow her warm and sweaty skin to feed from the cool, wet surface. The bus had pulled up abruptly just before the archway of a railway bridge. The train crossing above brought a rumble and a slight vibration. More droplets moved ever faster down the glass. At this point along the road there was no pavement and the bus hugged the stone wall that gave way to a row of stout, Victorian iron railings. Littered amongst the uncut grass along their base was a collection of life's detritus; ejected over time from waiting and passing cars. Lucy looked down, amazed at the variety of objects. She tried to identify each one in turn but the length of time they had been trapped there had denuded both labelling and colour.

Failing to stifle a yawn, she raised her eyes to scan a much greater area, illuminated in the street light, when her attention was drawn away from the railings and through them onto the steep railway banking. Mounted on a stout stick trapped amongst a tangle of brambles and buddleia was what appeared to be a head. Startled, she moved her face back a little to find a cleaner area of window from which to get a better view. The object leaned to the left as if nodding in the same direction the bus was travelling. The hair, golden and bedraggled, hung lifeless apart from the occasional flick by the drizzly wind.

The bus began to move forward and Lucy inched closer to the glass until her nose was almost touching it, her breath misting the lower area. She wiped the window again as she focused on the object. Her heart rate rose, partly out of uncertainty but more through excitement and a morbid curiosity. It brought to mind the graphic photographs of the stranger on the shore, the pallor, the eyeless sockets. It was then she chuckled. She realised that it was in fact the discarded head of a doll or a shop mannequin. Smiling, she wiped the window for the third time whilst keeping her eyes on the object until it was no longer visible. The bus crept under the bridge and as if in concert, the object disappeared from view and the child stopped crying. *I wonder how long it's been there?* she thought and the photographs on the Incident Room boards swam into her mind.

Stepping from the bus a stop early brought an immediate relief as Lucy felt the slap of the cold air collide with her perspiring face. She popped up her umbrella and the wind made her slightly unsteady. Pausing, she took a moment to study the veil of drizzle as it moved in waves across the road like ribbons of fine organza, collecting the colours of the lights that blazed in the background. She took three gulps of cool air. She was beginning to feel human again, helped by the almost theatrical trick of nature. It was magical, and she took a few moments to admire the beauty. Red and orange from the cars' lights joined forces with the illuminated shop signs and the myriad of brightly coloured lights set within the pavements. They ran parallel with the roadside, before the same sheets of rain patterned the wet road surface turning black tarmac into liquid silver. Alchemy. She felt the momentary tug of the breeze again on her umbrella, like an encouraging hand pushing her forward. She smiled and started to walk.

There was always something magical about the town centre at night, no matter what the weather, and tonight was special. If only people took the time to look, but then many of them were wet, cold and wanted nothing more than home. It was true that the dark masked the time-ravaged, blighted, densely packed streets but there was also such beauty. Lucy's mind returned to the vision of the head on the stick and it brought the nerves she had felt when April proposed her doing this job flooding back.

'You've seen it all tonight, girl,' she said out loud. How different that area of the town seemed to this, the centre. Checking her watch, she realised she was early. Turning left she watched her bus disappear down the side road, relieved no longer to be on it. Quickly crossing behind, she walked through the small piece of parkland. She could see the Cenotaph nestled by the side of the parish church. Lights were on in the Old Court building, now an evening concert venue. She took a moment to reflect. How many people over the many, many years had gone in through those doors innocent to later return guilty? *All part of my job*, came to mind. The thought of a coffee had an immediate effect on her pace. She quickened her step. There was now only the sound of the traffic moving somewhere out of sight.

Passing through the park gate she noticed two people huddled on the lower steps of the Cenotaph to her right. Neither looked in her direction but one belched loudly. One threw a bottle against the low railings on top of the church wall which shattered like tiny jewels on the wet flagstones. Lucy paused, her anger growing. Removing her mobile she checked her contacts. How she would have liked to deal with these two herself, right now when the immediate consequence of their action could be clearly remonstrated. Unfortunately, she had neither the time nor the footwear. Dealing with delinquents was always about planning. On the wet flagstones, her shoes would be more of a hindrance than a help. Neither man, looking at their present state, was *compos mentis*. She would leave it to others and besides, this was not the time. She made a call.

The four arched wooden mullions of the façade to Caffè Nero were familiar. Pausing, she tried to glance through the steamed-up window, made artificially opaque by the contrasting temperatures. She could see little but sensed it would be busy. Turning, she put her back to the door and eagerly pushed whilst at the same time shaking the umbrella. Inside the warmth and the aroma were welcoming. Lucy found a table and dropped her coat and brolly, as per her instructions then ordered a latte before slipping to the toilet.

She glanced in the mirror and sighed. The weather had been unkind. Producing a lipstick from her bag she carefully applied the brush to her lower lip before moving both together. The rich gloss red was now perfect. Running her hands expertly through her hair she was done. Her coffee was waiting.

* * *

Colin Patterson's journey had been much easier. He had set the alarm in the shop, closed the door, pulled down the shutters to the window and then the door. The alarm's shrill cry was still clearly audible. It would soon go silent, when the alarm was set. He popped the laptop bag strap over his shoulder, turned up his collar and headed along the narrow lane. He heard a clock strike six somewhere in the distance. Hugging the edge of the pedestrian precinct, he avoided the majority of the puddles and the drifting rain. One doorway was full of bags and what might be considered a heavily blanketed body. A small polystyrene cup sat to the left. Rummaging in his pocket, Colin collected some change and dropped in the offering. The vagrant raised an arm in thanks from beneath the protective covering but nothing was said.

'My daily act of kindness,' he whispered to himself. 'It could be me in there ... it could be me. One always has a duty to perform.' He adjusted his collar against the wet wind and moved more quickly before entering the rear yard to the church. Sudden angry shouts and abuse echoed just around the corner. Turning to pass the Cenotaph, he saw the many weatherworn poppy wreaths, now scattered around the base. He watched four police officers manhandle two men in the direction of a police van.

The protestations were both loud and abusive with many of the sentences slurred. 'You can all fuck off! It's my fucking town and I can fucking do and fucking say what I want. Just fuck off! Are you fucking listening? You're hurting my fucking arm!'

A sudden spindrift of sleet flushed the confines between the buildings without warning, whipped up from the direction of the railway and the park. It seemed to cleanse the foul air. Magically the protestations died away. Colin pressed on through the narrow passageway. Seeing the café, he made a dash for the door. He was not alone as three others followed him in. He looked cautiously at each.

Lucy had watched the four enter but focused on the one man. Appearing to look through her bag, she observed him as he collected his coffee and settled into a corner seat. Unlike many of those in the room, he immediately brought out a paperback and allowed his fingers to locate the folded page.

It had been the signal Lucy had been anticipating. She produced a phone from her bag, waited a moment before standing and crossing towards Colin.

'I'm sorry but I just wondered if you had a phone charger? My phone has just died and I need to send an urgent message.' She turned the phone to him as if proving the point. 'Left the charger at home this morning. Rushing as usual. Sorry.'

Colin moved his hand to his laptop bag and brought out a small, emergency charger. 'Never without it. You just never know when someone will need one.' There was neither sarcasm nor sincerity in his voice as he handed her the device. 'I'm sure one of the connections will be compatible.'

He studied her carefully. Taking the charger, she plugged in her phone.

'You need to press the small button to the side. When the

lights show it's charging. There's no rush as I'm here ...' he looked at the clock on the wall over the counter, '... for another fifteen minutes.' He quickly glanced across at the windows but the condensation obliterated any possibility of seeing outside.

Lucy smiled. 'Not a good evening to be out.' Raising her eyebrows, she followed his instruction and watched four blue LED lights illuminate the front of the battery charger. She returned to sit down. He picked up his book and then his coffee.

Ten minutes later, Lucy popped the charger back on his table. 'That was so kind of you. Thank you.' She smiled widely.

Colin looked at the charger and then at Lucy. 'A pleasure. They're so cheap these days I don't go anywhere without one. Most supermarkets stock them. Got this from Lidl. Cost next to nothing.'

Lucy smiled again, turned to her table, collected her things and left. All she had to do now was suffer a return journey on the bus.

CHAPTER 12

E verything seemed so grey. The walk along the beach with Tico had been brief as neither had any enthusiasm for the wind nor the rain. Within minutes of their return, Tico was curled up in front of the Aga. Entering the studio, April checked her work from the night before – she was pleased. First, she needed to change.

April wrapped her hands around the coffee mug. The half-an-hour walk was over, and now, dressed for work, she could take a moment to reflect. Once she would have considered taking time out in reflection a waste of precious time, but a wise superintendent somewhere in the past had waxed lyrical about allowing thoughts to percolate, to filter. Just like a good coffee, they cannot be rushed.

The pine trees to the south of the cottage bent inland from the years of supplication to the demands of the sea winds. Clouds, low and brooding, continued to head her way bringing the sheets of misty drizzly rain that had dampened their earlier walk. She thought about each of her new colleagues, categorising their individual strengths and weaknesses. Had someone been watching they would have seen her facial expression change with each considered thought. Had she done the correct thing by asking Lucy to go in place of herself? Her position was growing in responsibility and therefore delegation was an essential key to that role but it was one of the hardest to come to terms with. She remembered Lucy's face when she had asked her and it brought a smile.

Drinking the remains of her coffee she went and checked on Tico who looked up from his bed, giving a slight wag of his tail. It was clear that he was settled. Fed, watered and walked, he needed nothing else. Seeing Sue Martin, she waved.

Sue called as she moved to the barn. 'I'll check on Tico later in the day. Have a good one and take care!'

'Thank you. You too.' April waved as she jumped into the 4x4. How lucky she had been to find this place.

* * *

April sat at her desk and checked the Post-it notes attached to the edge of her computer screen. Some she had left from previous days, *aides-memoire* to remind her of outstanding tasks. She took the phone from a basket, letting her fingers run over the surface once it was removed from the plastic, protective sheath. It was the one Lucy had charged in the café. She was eager to know its contents but she would have to wait until the tech guy she had requested arrived. Lucy tapped on the door and popped her head round. She held a mug of coffee.

'Morning. You have it I see. You wouldn't know from looking at him. Seemed such a nice chap.'

'They're not all dressed in cloaks, Lucy. He'll be paid. You're aware there's a system in place for this kind of thing. It's above board, as I said when I asked you. It'll not be much but hopefully it will be significant. How was Wigan on a wet night?'

Lucy frowned. 'Wet and dark. I live nearby and the town centre behaviour hasn't changed since I worked there.'

April sat back and tapped her fingers on the desk. 'Did you live near the centre?'

'Those were early days. King Street on a Friday and Saturday night was educational. Town centre's not what it was. Like most big towns, there's a dearth of shops and as they close you see fewer people other than the homeless. The town was a good grounding for me. Stayed five years and then moved to Merseyside. Promotion into plain clothes. Love it even though my new boss gives me challenges.' Their brief burst of laughter was interrupted by a second tap on the door. The tech guy popped his head round and smiled.

Sadiq stared at the view. It seemed to stretch for mile after mile, blackness illuminated by a wealth of urban colours. An aircraft flew down the Mersey, the noise distinct and the lights the only visible feature. Planes occasionally disappeared within the low cloud only to reappear further along in the dark. Even now he could make out the Wirral but there was a blur, a watery mix of predawn and drizzle.

His feet resting on the coffee table, the man on the sofa

interlocked his fingers before gently flexing them back-wards. The resulting slow pattern of clicks from each of the knuckles brought a slight shiver to Sadiq's spine. The sound was not too dissimilar to that of a snapping neck.

'The shipment comes in on Thursday, providing nothing gets in the way at this late stage. You know what can happen on these cruises, what with food poisoning and the like.'

Sadiq's expression said it all; he was helpless. 'I've no control, bro. What will be, will be.'

The pause was palpable.

'You know the procedure, it's all set up.' The other man tossed a large brown envelope onto the coffee table between his feet. 'The cruise liner docks on time according to the schedule. Remember too that this is a new couple so they'll be skittish. Let's hope they remember what Abid told them. He was good at some things! They seemed confident when it was first organised, but the closer they get to home, the more the nerves will be kicking in. I'm sure they'll be doubting their sanity, desperate people do. If they're successful then they'll do it again. We haven't put all our eggs into this one basket. Stay well back just in case they bottle it. They have a key to the car parked in the same carpark as their car. It will be positioned next to theirs and they'll drop our goods into the boot. I only want it collecting after forty-eight hours. I'll have it watched and then you can send in one of your boys. And Sadiq ...'

Sadiq turned briefly to glance at the river and then back.

'Make sure the fucking driver is over twenty-one, no bloody kids. Is that understood? And put that in a super-market carrier bag.'

'Bro. Fully. It'll be Doc.' He moved across and collected

the envelope. 'Supermarket bag, sure thing. This goes into the safe until then.'

'Did you do a thorough job? The body was clean, Sadiq? I have your personal assurance, do I?' The tone of voice conveyed the point subtly but it clearly still registered as a definite threat.

'I checked myself, bro. The tattoo removal, he was shaved, finger pads, teeth removed as instructed. Considering what we did to the poor bastard, I'm amazed the coppers managed such a good job with the photograph they posted. Amazing what computers can do nowadays. Reincarnation you could say.' He laughed, but it swiftly faded as he was laughing alone.

'It's no joke,' his companion stressed. 'They can bring the dead to life, you're right. Now, the flat?'

'It was cleaned whilst we held Chelle. All his stuff and some things she'd kept were collected. I've taken pictures.'

Sadiq grabbed a remote and a large flat screen television lowered from the ceiling to fill most of one wall. He then ran through a slideshow of a number of photographs showing the flat before and after.

'Inevitably, bro, there will be prints and DNA as we can't get rid of that other than by torching the place.' He paused letting the thought sink in. 'We waited till she was out and let Toland know that Chelle was visiting her mother. We informed her she'd had an accident, Chelle would be away for a while and that someone would be calling for her things. Seemed to go well.'

'So where is she now?'

'She was brought here as you requested. We'd collected some of her things from the flat. She wasn't clean after fucking Malik had held her ...' He did not finish. 'Not clean in that sense, abused like ... I don't think so anyway.' Doubt was clear in his voice.

'If I find out Malik or any of his boys didn't keep it in their trousers they'll not be worrying about trousers or girls as they'll have to sit to piss.'

'No, no, nothing like that I don't believe. I know that he does that to the slags he collects for pleasure and the girls he kindly shares around. The pass round girls, as he calls them. He does as he's told and if you've told him *no* then that would be final. He'd just forgotten she might need to piss and ignored her for too long. She was bloody furious. Anyway, she had a bath and then a shower. She was in ages. I ordered food and she watched a film. I warned her not to expect to see Abid again as he'd been moved. He wouldn't be returning to the flat and to expect someone new to the group. That's all I said. I could see from her eyes she knew it was bullshit but then she knew what he'd done. There was no maths needed. Two and two make four. The puzzle for me and I think for you, bro, is how come the coppers found the flat so quickly?'

'So, answer the fucking question, Sadiq. Where is she now if not back at her place. Here?'

'No, no, bro. I've put her in a safe house alongside a friend and his wife. As the name suggests it's secure and she's working again.'

'Let's hope so.' He stood and walked to the door. 'Did you know they also found a medal and some kind of plastic disc? It's mentioned alongside the photo. Maybe that's how they tracked down the flat and if they've got to the flat then they know about Chelle. If he was clean then how come those things were found?'

'Saw it on the police site but when we put him in the ground, he was clean. Could have come in on one of the tides or been in the sand when we buried him. It was dark so who knows? They weren't with him when he was taken as he was as clean as the day he was born.' Sadiq frowned. 'Honestly, bro.'

'Believe nothing … trust no one! Do you hear? I want a list of who was at the burial site.'

It was the first mistake Sadiq had made and they both knew it. Trust was never his strong point.

The printer next to April's computer spewed out a single sheet of A4. She snatched it eagerly and read it before passing it to Lucy.

'I don't believe in fairy tales, for Christ's sake. Snow White!' Lucy chuckled, looking directly at April. 'Snow White and what, the seven dwarves? This must be a wind up.' She began to read on. 'Snow White is believed to be the name of the gang working to the north of Liverpool. Bike and phone thefts, drug and arms running, general street violence and goodness knows what else.' She turned to April. 'We pay for this?'

There were four names listed and a series of incidents linked to each name.

Lucy read the names out loud, 'Bit of a mixed bunch. Asif Rehman, Don Benson, Beverley Gittings, Mansoor Kamman. Your guy's even given us their nicknames. Bully, Blusher,

Scar and Doc. Not exactly original from the sound of it, and neither are they likely to be living with Snow White, apart from Doc, that is.'

She tossed the paper onto the desk, the action deliberate, clearly demonstrating her lack of belief in the intelligence.

April took note but remained silent whilst she added one of the names into the computer and waited. Within minutes it rewarded her with a case file for Don Benson.

'Here we go. Born in St Helens before moving to Liverpool. Institutionalised, in and out since he was fourteen. Petty stuff before moving onto the drugs scene and then ABH. Can you believe only a fine given for that and no community order?' They both looked at the mug shot. 'Taken nine years ago. Puts him in his late teens. Height, five foot six.'

Lucy chuckled. 'Now that might meet the criteria for one of Snow White's boys.'

'Don't let Skeeter hear you! Don't you see the relevance of the title? What's white, expensive, consumed by middle-class professionals and delivered to their door by little people, usually kids, the final tip of the county lines?'

'Bloody hell! I'm slow for a copper, sorry. Is there a current address?' She noted April's expression. 'Thought not.'

To DC Pete Bradshaw, the morning had come late to what seemed today to be an inhospitable stretch of the River Mersey. The sky appeared to sag with the weight of the leaden overcast. The city behind still had a noise, a rumble, an awakening, that greeted the broad river. The tide was low, running deep, cold and an opaque grey colour that mirrored the sky. It ran out towards the estuary, the ever-open mouth, and then into the Irish Sea. Brad could taste the salty air borne on the breeze as his tongue ran across his lips. The distinct smell of ozone filled his nostrils. He leaned on the railing watching a gull skim the corrugated water's surface before climbing high, and yet, to his amazement he was still startled by its shrill and sudden cry. Fascinated by its agility, and what seemed to him to be carefree flight, he admired its acrobatic, aerial morning ritual.

'Bloody seagulls,' he whispered, envying their freedom. He turned, walking to the bronze statue he knew so well and looked at it thoughtfully. It was of Captain F J Walker, Johnny, a man Brad had come to admire: the most famous submarine hunter of the Second World War. His strategy in catching prey reminded him of the people who were roaming the city on motorbikes attacking the unsuspecting. They seemed disciplined, well-trained and determined – a pack. Walker advocated a creeping attack and that was just what the bike gang performed. He and the rest of the team needed to apply a similar tactic to stop them, but would they? That depended on his new boss. Probably not. The distant call of a police siren moving quickly down The Strand brought him back to his senses. He checked the time on the Liver Building clock and moved away. He would be late.

* * *

The meeting with Sadiq was all Chelle had needed to convince her she should run. Knowing what had happened to Abid had, for the first time in years, brought in her a deep sadness. Abid had been kind to her. He had told her he loved her and he was gentle. He had shared a secret and then the tattoos. His idea. His were completed first and strangely he had not taken her to the same artist, but to a friend. She had found that odd but was happy not to ask the reason. She looked at her hand and with a finger traced the shape of the gecko. Salty reminders of his laughter filled her eyes and ran down her cheeks before she wiped them with the back of her hand. She studied the fingers of her left hand. The marks were just above the nails, the numbers he had asked the artist to tattoo. *We're a team. They can never split us up and this is our bond, our security key. It's a recipe when we put them together.* He would slide his fingers between hers and whisper each number in turn.

She had asked more than once what they meant but he had never revealed their significance. He just raised his finger to her lips. *Our secret – only we know. They spell an important word if you know where to look. Tell no one, at least not yet. Tell only when you are really frightened.*

She had noted the marks on the small piece of material taken from his clothing, she never wanted to forget the way that he read them to her, the whisper, the energy as if he were exorcising some demon.

She had gone to the new flat, done as she was instructed – as she always did. That was how life was now. The nagging, gnawing fear filled most of her thoughts taking the edge off her capacity to work efficiently. The Southport flat was on a street running parallel to and just behind the sea front, if you could ever call it that. The sea was always a stranger there too. It was situated on the third floor of what might once have been classed as a holiday boarding house; lace curtains, landlady and dinner gong were distant memories. It was neither tidy nor clean. Positioned near Lord Street, the area was filled with carparks and a number of bars. One disconcerting feature that greeted her on arrival was a large, grey painted face adorning the gable end of one of the houses. West Street seemed cold, wet and to her wild. The consolation, if there could be one, was that it was away from their main hunting ground and was easily accessed by road, bus and rail. Escape routes need, on occasion, to be plentiful. There were people there who assured her that they would care for her but she knew they were more like supervisors.

The next couple of jobs had been easy, *candy from babies,* she sang to herself in one of her rare, lighter moments. She had taken the train, always conscious of the cameras as she had been advised, and met the van in different locations. For a while it made her believe that she might be able to weather this storm of uncertainty. The gnawing was gradually receding. She had faced adversity so often in her young life and survived and she could do it again.

It was always the thought of Abid that seemed to haunt her, bringing with it the amalgam of fear and doubt. It was his genuine kindness, his reassurance and his dreams that had made her love him. If she had been honest, he was the first person she thought about above herself. She had hoped that it might be real love, an emotion she had chased for as long as she could remember. She doubted Sadiq's words that he had gone away on business. Abid was, she believed, in their eyes a nonentity. He was just like her, desperate, frightened for much of the time and alone.

The day before he disappeared, she had seen it in his eyes, not fear but regret, a deep sadness as if he knew he had made a fatal mistake, thrown it all away. It was never expressed in words, only in the way he touched her. He knew it might be for the last time and she had sensed it, an emotion that ran so deep it made her tingle. She had held on to him through their tears. The following day he was gone. She now treasured the piece of his clothing in the bag and occasionally she would inhale and he would be there, his smell. It gave her courage. He had told her to keep it. It would be a good luck charm, an amulet.

If they could make him disappear then they could do the same to her and any of the others with the simple act of clicking their fingers.

Two days later when the first opportunity presented itself, she packed a few things and left. She did not take the train but a bus heading away from the coast – she was alone again.

CHAPTER 13

The contacts with the tattoo parlours had proved fruitful. The trawl had dredged a connection linked to a small shop on County Road. The owner of *Jester's Ink* had responded with the information that they had carried out a design of a gecko on the side of a man's palm over a month ago.

Brad turned down Lind Street, the nearest side road but parking proved difficult, permit parking only was allowed. However, on finding a space he parked. The registration would show it was a police vehicle should a traffic warden happen to pass. Within minutes he was standing outside *Jesters*. The window appeared partly frosted in which the words *Professional Tattooing* were written and the date the shop had opened, 2010. The door followed a similar theme. It looked, as the name suggested, professional and not at all what he had expected. His mind had conjured some grotty shop with a hand painted sign but this … He pushed open the door.

Entering, he was even more impressed. The area was clean and orderly, there was a deep aroma, more a light scent, feminine. On the counter was a large computer screen. Huge framed photographs of shiny tattooed bodies were carefully mounted along the walls, gallery straight. He looked at the first. The image depicted a semi-naked female, the tattoos covering a large percentage of her upper torso were pure artistry.

What appeared to be a glass patio door slid to the side, the same frosted covering, giving privacy to the studio beyond, but this time patterned with ornate swirls.

'Hello.' A petite young woman greeted him, sliding the door closed before approaching, all white teeth and smiles. She moved behind the counter before perching on a bar stool raising her high enough to look Brad straight in the eye.

'How can we help?'

'DC Bradshaw. You responded to a request for information regarding these tattoos; the gecko and the marks on one hand.' He pointed to the side of his palm.

'You have ID I take it, DC Bradshaw? I have an appointment due in fifteen minutes. The ID is for data protection and all that. I want to stay in business a few more years.' It was said in all seriousness.

'Sorry, yes. I wouldn't expect less. It's all very professional. Shouldn't take too long.'

Fishing into his pocket he handed his warrant card across the counter. He looked at the intricate coloured tattoos she had over both hands, the images trailing off onto her fingers. The designs were a collection of interlocking Koi carp, oriental in both style and colour. They seemingly swam up each arm, their delicately scaled bodies wrapping, disappearing and returning. They were true works of art that left not one square centimetre of flesh exposed. Brad was fascinated by the tattooist's skill.

'You didn't do those yourself, did you? They're fabulous.' He realised as soon as he had spoken how stupid the question was. 'Sorry, stupid question.'

'No, my partner. Thank you. It's about the gecko? I remember it. A simple yet pretty design. He knew just what he wanted and then some fancy numbering on his fingers; Arabic numbering and script. Unusual place for solitary art. We see a lot there if the design is an extension.' She held out her own hand. 'See, here, the design runs to just above the nail. The skin is very thin there and can cause problems and discomfort.'

'He?'

'Yes, male. Not what you were expecting?'

Brad smiled. 'In a way, the information's important, possibly more so.'

She slid off the stool and searched beneath the counter before bringing out a file. 'It's here.' She passed over the gecko's template.

'Is this to scale?'

She nodded. 'Positioned as you demonstrated here. Wanted a two-colour outline, black with a red inner line. He mentioned that the colours represented the colours of a flag. Each to their own. You learn that in this game. You can see it clearly here.' She pointed to the sheet.

'Do we have a name?'

'All part of the professional business. However, he was over twenty, I'm sure, but we do collect contact details just in case we need to notify clients of problems. Standard procedure.' Turning to the computer she added the reference code from the file. 'Here we go. Adnan Dushi. Might be Russian, may be Arabic but he didn't strike me as such from his complexion. Had one of those accents.'

'Did you ask where he came from?' Brad asked.

She nodded. 'He said Walton!' She laughed out loud. 'I nearly fell off the chair. Took all of my control to keep a straight face. You learn not to get too involved, ask too many questions, after all they're coming for a tattoo not counselling or open-heart surgery. Besides, with blokes, there's always a fine line. You just don't get too familiar or tattoo where they might not want a tattoo. You learn these things in training. That way you keep safe. Normally my partner's in but he wasn't that day.'

'An address? You mentioned contact details.'

'Rosslyn Street. Number twelve. There's a mobile too.'

Brad made notes. 'Was he alone when he came in?'

'Think he had a girl with him but I can't be sure.'

'CCTV?' Brad looked at the smoked glass hemisphere attached to the far corner of the ceiling.

'We do but as you know it's looped and kept for only six days. This business is highly regulated but there's no requirement to have cameras, in fact, having them in can be bad for business. As long as we have the consent form and we're happy with the presentation of ID that's enough. After all, I trusted your ID.'

She had a point. He said, 'The symbols on his finger. You said they were Arabic numbers?'

'I said possibly, yes, apart from the last one which was a series of what looked like Arabic script. He said it meant "love".' She looked through the file. 'I thought I'd kept those too but obviously not. They'll be somewhere. They were here, here and here with the "love" on this finger.' She demonstrated on Brad's hand.

'You didn't work on a girl, similar things?'

'No, sorry.' Seeing her client appear at the door she immediately turned.

A customer came in. 'Hi, sorry if I'm a little late. Another one of those mopeds just attacked a woman down the way. Some guy managed to help her. Bloody nuisance. Coppers too busy sitting on their arses, I guess.'

The tattooist covered her mouth with her hand to hide her smile. 'I'm sorry, my next appointment.' Sliding from the stool she collected the file before putting it back under the counter.

'Thank you. Most useful. If you find the missing designs please give me a call.' Handing her his card he turned and left the shop.

'No problem.'

The traffic was busy and a police car, all sirens and lights flashing drove past at some speed. The address that Brad had been given was that of Chelle Pearson – Kelly Jones.

* * *

Over the chill of the wind, Kelly Jones moved along the footpath that linked Up Holland with Orrell. It was away from the road, well-trodden. To keep out of the mud she walked as closely to the barbed wire fence as possible. She had spent some time on the footpath by the golf course watching the golfers putt and drive. Their lives seemed so normal, so stress free; it hardly seemed fair. Now in limbo she wondered if she had done the right thing having left the only family she had known, if it could be classed as such. Leaning on a wooden fence she watched a white golf ball roll along the green leaving but a slight trail. It immediately reminded her of herself.

For most of her life she had been that ball, a life in limbo and then struck and retrieved, cleaned and put away before being summoned and abused again. The worst fear was again realised the moment she saw the ball disappear into the hole. It brought a chill and the thought of her man. She had seen the news of the discovery of the body on the beach. She had seen the police photograph and she knew. He too, like some small, white golf ball, had disappeared off course to be lost in the bunker, eventually disappearing in the sand. She had seen on the same news the image of the medal and the Perspex disc. Digging into her pocket she retrieved a similar disc, but hers was clean. On one side in shiny gilt was the dollar sign. *We'll soon have the real thing, I promise, and this is for you, a token of your trust in this venture together. Those that are with me have one too.* He had spoken with such excitement before placing them both into his eyes, trapping them with his brows like two monocles. *I will see to that.* His accent was strong. They had both laughed. They had fallen into his hands. She had tried to mimic his actions but had failed. The memory was warm in total contrast to the now chill wind. She began to cry and walked on. His luck, his gamble had failed and the consequences had been severe.

* * *

What Kelly did know was that she had to stay away from her old haunts. Sadiq's promise of a reward was three hundred pounds, but at his luxury flat he had intruded into her bed that night, as if it were his right to use her when needed, just like Malik. There was never benevolence nor love with them. She had to earn every single penny and she despised them for that. Strangely, that was not what hurt the most. It was Sadiq's deceit. The call to the landlady, the lies about the disappearance of the one person she trusted, dare she believe, loved. He only ever revealed what he wanted her to know. His words had sounded hollow even though they appeared to be delivered with sincerity. She mimicked him, *Chelle, you're a good girl. We need you. You ride so well. I love you and your body. This sex is our secret, promise?* She then recalled his anger at the tattoos. He did what he was good at. He reeled her in, pretended to love her and then bang! Life was always like that.

Shaking her head, she watched a magpie rise from the field. 'Morning, Mr Magpie,' she instinctively said as her eyes followed its flight away into the woods. She had found a warm, dry place. It once had been a tunnel running from the former Nobel works at Gathurst towards the station. It was hidden and off the beaten track. She never felt safe in shop doorways or parks, too many cameras and far too many people who were ready to take advantage. It would have to do until she could find a hostel, a secure and proper place to live but not just yet. Here, in the countryside, were people who minded their own business, walked dogs, took photographs, ran and cycled. She had time to think and she would be safe for the moment at least.

She pulled up the hood of her parka and threw the bag over her shoulder. Just like the bird, she headed for the woods.

CHAPTER 14

S keeter held onto her opponent with a vice-like grip. The effort performed by the two women was clear from the sweat on their faces and that deposited on the blue mat. She was determined to turn her opponent, to pin both her shoulders to the canvas but despite all her skill, the woman was not for turning. The bout had been harder than she had anticipated and this contestant was no push over. This was the type of challenge she loved at the pit. Over the years many a world-class wrestler had progressed through the ranks.

Lancashire wrestling, *Catch as Catch Can*, had been in her blood from childhood. It was in that of her brother and father. Protesting initially, as she could not be left at home, she had been taken along too, doll in hand. Soon after seeing others her age, the doll was forgotten. The original gym was world-renowned and so too were the early exponents. It was the Japanese on visiting the Wigan gym who gave it the name, *The Snake Pit*. They said upon attempting to throw a

Wigan wrestler, *that he would land on his front and attack you like a snake.* The name stuck.

There would be no break or breather for either Skeeter or her opponent, no bell, no water and no quarter. The rules were straightforward too. No punching, slapping or biting, no kicking or choking were allowed. The wrestler just fought using learned techniques, strength, stamina, skill and cunning. Skeeter had that by the bucket load. There was no talking and no noise from either opponent for fear of disqualification. There was sheer poetry, balance and dignity taking place on the mat, if combat could be classed in such a way. It was a mind game, physical chess as each woman tried to make the other create an opportunity or an error.

It was Skeeter's sudden change of hold that allowed her to break an arm grip and slip down to take her opponent's leg. Within the blink of an eye, she had moved her own leg and applied *face scissors.* A moment later she saw the other woman tap out. She had won. Both relaxed and Skeeter allowed her back to rest on the canvas. Her chest heaved and it was only then she felt the sheer strain and the sweat run into her eyes. This was the best feeling in the world. She replayed the winning move, her eyes closed and a huge smile on her face.

Once outside the gym the cool evening air served as a tonic. She was ready to run home, shower and retire for the night, knowing her body would ache in the morning. She was used to that.

* * *

Brad checked the latest evidence on the case and went over to the Incident Room wall. He added the information from the tattooist and ensured the details were uploaded. It was important he be up to speed for the briefing. He had been late for the previous meeting and although nothing had been said, he could tell from April's attitude that he was sailing close to the wind ... again.

He allowed his finger to hover over the information on the board detailing the Perspex disc. It was found, it was believed, by the detectorist, to have been in or near the corpse's hand. Now, however, he could not be sure. He read the specific forensic report on each of the items.

From the evidence we have, similar discs were used in the advertisement for crypto currencies a number of years ago. They were printed with gilt dollar signs to one face. Tests on the surface detect the gilt ink used was of low grade and would fade after time from light or moisture. They were stuck to the advertising using Gluefast. Traces have been located. Ironically, the exposure to either sweat or sea water has removed the gilt but not the sticky Gluefast suggesting one side of the disc was trapped against a surface, possibly human flesh.

Brad was impressed by what Forensics could actually discover. Three officers entered the room, all carrying a notepad and a mug. Checking his watch, he had three minutes. He quickly went to his desk and retrieved his notes.

The briefing was designed to be informative but informal. There was no need for paper as April had loaded her laptop and would project what she wanted them to note.

'Morning. Thanks, and I know we're earlier than usual but we've been lucky to receive intelligence that might prove key to this investigation.'

She first went through the forensic results on the recovered disc before turning to the key points gleaned. Turning to the screen at the far side of the room, she let her hand slip to the touchpad on the computer and they watched the CCTV footage play. It was brief, grainy and seemed to present nothing.

'Stan, please.' She looked across to where Stan was sitting on one of the tables. Boardman had been with the force for more years than he cared to remember.

'Anyone identify the station?' his voice light and with a lilt.

'Southport!' a number of voices chimed in concert.

Stan chuckled. 'Correct. Collect your winning cigars on the way out. To be serious. Look at the person wearing the green Parka coat. The hood is up and it's trimmed with fur. There's also a peaked cap worn beneath. At no stage can we see the facial features.' He paused the video. 'Remember that.'

The next piece of CCTV footage shown was taken within the carriage.

'Now look. The same person has removed a glove to retrieve a ticket.'

The image was paused and enlarged. Initially no one spoke and then the muttering started.

'Although not clear, I'm assured that it's a tattoo of a gecko. Tattoos too on the fingers in the place identified on Kelly Jones and, we presume, that of the body found on the beach. Sadly, as yet, those missing tattoos cannot be identi-fied but I believe Brad has an update.'

He looked across at him and raised a finger as if needing a moment longer.

'Needles only travel to a depth of one sixteenth of an inch and should not penetrate the third skin layer. When you remove the flesh, you remove the tattoo, that's if it's done by a professional tattooist. We'll soon know if they went deeper and if traces can be found. I digress, sorry.' He looked at April.

'Thanks, no. Do continue.'

'I'd just like Brad to come in here and share his findings from the parlour, where similar tattoos were carried out on a man who gave Chelle's address as his. We also have his name. Adnan Dushi. The five people with that name in the UK do not live in this part of the country and neither do any have tattoos matching these. They've all been checked so we're assuming it's a fake name. One is, in fact, a guest of her Majesty as I speak. Drugs. Funny that. He'll be interviewed.'

Brad ran through the information he had. 'If the tattoos match, we now know they may well be Arabic numbers apart from the last tattoo on the little finger. That too may be in Arabic but the script is for the word 'love'. They were on the right hand. I believe the girl's are on her left. There may well be a significance with what is tattooed there but until we have a clear indication we'll not know. The tattooist couldn't locate the diagrams of what she'd tattooed on the fingers but assured me she'd look again.'

'Thanks, Brad,' Stan continued. 'That information's gone to Forensics to help guide their skin search. The person, as you see, also had their back to the working camera. The one camera positioned forward of the carriage was buggered so we can't be assured of the person's sex. Let's presume female. The hood and the cap remained in place throughout the journey. However, we have a rough idea of height and weight. She left the train at Blundellsands and Crosby Station. On checking the local CCTV footage in and around the station we have assumed she travelled down Blundell-sands Road. Immediately out of the station you have a choice of roads.'

April brought up a street view image.

'Some are cul-de-sacs but that means nothing as she might have been meeting someone either in a car or at one of the houses. At present, the best guess is that she was picked up on one of these side roads. We've requested any dash cam footage of this time and day from Joe Public. Hopefully someone collecting or dropping off might be able to assist but I'm not holding my breath.'

'Stan, is that the only time she was caught travelling from Southport?' Brad asked as he leaned forward trying to get a clearer view.

'That's what we believe at present. We have civilian support checking the days before and the journeys to date. Had the guard not inspected the ticket this wouldn't have come to light. The pedestrian area CCTV in Southport showed the same person crossing Lord Street earlier and then walking along Chapel Street. It appears the person never stopped, just went straight to the station.'

April smiled and nodded her thanks to Stan. 'As soon as we have anything else, you'll hear,' she reassured the collective. 'That's the strongest link we have to Kelly at present. She may well have fled the flat, or simply been moved on depending on her importance. The motorbike taken from the yard at her flat suggests that there's a strong link between the death of her flat mate and the serious motorbike offences we're witnessing. Serious enough crimes to necessitate the murder. From today, we can't be sure, but we are linking the two investigations.'

Brad frowned but he could see the logic.

'And Brad. I want an artist's drawing of that tattoo, the gecko, and I want it in every facility for the homeless starting in Southport. Then here before spreading out to surrounding areas including neighbouring towns within easy travelling from here. There can't be that many. I then want it in charity shops and on the police website.' She watched to ensure she received acquiescence.

'Do people still hitch-hike?' Brad questioned. 'If they do, she could have gone anywhere.'

'We do what we can do.' April stared until Brad frowned.

'You're the boss.'

April nodded and left.

CHAPTER 15

Skeeter and Tony Price walked down Goodison Road.
The façade of the football ground was clothed in what
is best described as a huge, blue, semi-transparent tarpaulin.
It was bedecked with the images of the players from the past.
It was impressive. The breeze, channelled along the road,
brought only a slight movement as the clever design allowed
the air to pass through. In contrast, some of the terraced
homes seemed dwarfed by the stadium's stature but it was
the contrast in colour that struck Tony Price.

'Bright red! Directly facing the Everton ground but then
you look at the plaque showing the door number and it
clearly identifies their allegiance. On match days this place is
alive: the scarves, the banter, the rivalry and then there's the
noise from the trapped crowd when the game is on. The
voices joined as one in common belief and brotherhood. It's
bloody moving. You can stand here now and almost hear the
cheers and songs. For years that noise, that harmony, will
have reverberated down these very streets and into these

very homes. People have lived for this club. In a strange way it's beautiful.'

Skeeter leaned on the wall of one of the terraced homes and stared at him. This rough and uncouth copper waxing lyrical about something he knew nothing about was also strangely beautiful. It was as if he had found his feminine side. 'Bloody hell, Tony, please stop! You'll have me hearing fucking violins and my tears will be washing down these streets. You don't even like bloody football, you tart!'

He grinned. 'Covered too many games as a young copper. Had you going, though! Can't bloody stand it. Wish I earned as much for doing so little. Look, they even put up bloody statues to them.' He pointed up the road towards St Luke's church. Positioned in front was a new statue.

'If you'd done your research when we were at Walton Station, you'd have seen there's a new and fully monitored camera looking directly at it. It's a perfect target for some opposing fans. *The Holy Trinity* it's called as it shows three players from Everton's winning side from 1969 to 1970. Found it a little odd to have that title when it's positioned outside a church. When they shift to the new stadium, if it's ever built, they'll no doubt take that with them. Suppose football in this city is a religion so it possibly is relevant. But it's the CCTV cameras I'm interested in. Michelle Pearson, or Kelly Jones as was, had a flat down there.' She pointed but saw Tony was still reading the wording on the football ground's façade. 'Are you bloody listening?'

He nodded. 'Down there. Kelly Pearson's ... sorry Jones's. Flat. The boss believes they're part of the motorbike gang, Snow White and the ...' He did not finish his sentence.

Looking down on Skeeter his imagination was ahead of the conversation.

'We're calling in all the shops, pubs, takeaways and talking to anyone we bump into. The footage from the cameras that surround this place is being run with facial recognition software and before you say it DI Decent has cleared it. I take it you've heard the Met has made their first arrest using the system and if that moves to a conviction, I can see it being a wonderful weapon. We don't shout about it as every human rights activist will rise up and be supported from the shadows by every bloody criminal. They'll be up in arms about the erosion of their liberty. It's going to be a long day.'

By one in the afternoon, they had drawn a blank. The photograph of the dead man brought more comments but no direct response. A bent Just Eat sign caught Tony's attention. 'Bloody starving. I believe you Woollybacks, you Wiganers, call it *clempt*? All this fresh air. Fancy a kebab?'

Skeeter looked at the shop front and then the food hygiene rating. 'Nope, but we have to go in. You can do and eat just what you want. I've seen you eat your fingernails so a dose of Salmonella would stand no chance against you. Come on.'

Skeeter held up her warrant card. Malik leaned over the counter to read it. 'Police?'

He noticed her eyes but said nothing, immediately turning to look at Tony as if he were the more important. Skeeter tapped the counter with her finger before sliding the photograph across to him.

'This chap used to live close by. Have you seen him before Mr—?'

'Malik, plain and simple Malik.'

Malik brought the photograph towards his face and studied it. 'The guy found on the beach? Heard about it. If he looked like that, he'd be better off in Anfield Cemetery, love, not ordering food from me. My kebabs are good but don't work miracles. We haven't seen Chelle Pearson either. He handed back the photograph.'

'Chelle?' Tony quickly responded.

'The chatter around here has never stopped. Her landlady is better than the television news. Now, I'm busy, is there anything else?'

Skeeter looked around the empty shop. 'Cleaning and food hygiene prep I take it. Looking at the sign on your window you're a past master at that.'

The door at the far end of the room opened releasing a strong aroma of food accompanied by eastern music. A man appeared.

'You OK, Malik?'

Malik nodded. 'The police. I'm helping with their enquiries. You know me, Flam, always ready to help the community.' He grinned widely and Skeeter noticed the gold teeth.

'I think we're done. I'll take a döner kebab,' Tony added. He brought some change from his pocket. 'Skeeter?'

She shook her head and watched Flam close the door. 'Flam? Unusual name.'

'Short for Flamur. Albanian and before you ask, he's legal, legit. Now, is there anything else you want to know?' He did not hide the sarcasm in his tone. Malik looked at her and then back at Tony. Collecting the long-bladed knife he sliced the pitta bread and put it to warm, turned and went over to the vertical meat spit. He began to slice, collecting the meat on a small metal scoop. As his back was facing the counter, he allowed a dribble of saliva to fall onto the meat before covering it with another slice. Returning he filled the bread, adding onion and parsley. 'On the house.' Malik smiled. 'Full of Eastern promise. Enjoy!'

Tony dropped money onto the counter. 'Official rules.' They left.

Skeeter turned to look at Malik, her expression quizzical.

'Hope your eye gets better soon, Skeeter.' Malik grinned, the glint of gold adding insult to injury.

Tony heard her grunt and he instinctively grabbed her shoulder.

'Not now. We have unfinished business.' He felt her body relax and they moved away.

It took barely ten minutes from their leaving the shop to Sadiq's mobile ringing. Malik knew Sadiq would have been informed of the police's visit.

* * *

Tony watched Skeeter move quickly to her desk. The anger was no longer on the surface but he sensed her deep resentment. She was like a terrier and Malik and company had kicked her. He moved through to the kitchen to make a brew. Brad was there leaning against the sink.

'Had a good day so far, Tony? Saw Skeeter from the window here when you pulled up. Looked like she was chewing a wasp.'

'Someone's upset her and she has this nag, the copper's nag she keeps going on about. Kebab shop near Goodison.

You'll read all about it on the board. Shit hole really but made a tasty kebab. Funny they had an unusual way of monitoring the place and I think that might have stimulated her nag but it's probably just hunger. Plain and simple Malik really got to her.' He laughed and threw a teabag into some hot water.

Brad just looked. '*Quelle finesse*, mate, *quelle finesse*. Malik. Remind me not to mention it when I see her.' He leaned over, touched Tony's arm and smiled. 'Let's not aggravate the witch.' He winked and left.

Lucy had researched the three remaining names on the list and was now beginning to feel foolish for doubting April Decent. It had made her appreciate the growing respect she felt for her new boss. Each name had a criminal past, each was in some way linked to drugs. One in particular fascinated her – Beverley Gittings. She read the file. *The jurisdiction of this fair land of ours has been extremely lenient,* she thought as the number of offences was revealed. Prostitution, drink and drug related crime. Here was another girl who had faced all the hardships from birth. Parents were both drug addicts, she was supported through school but had little to show for her time there. Father died of a drug overdose. The mother was imprisoned for breaking all four legs of Beverley's pet dog as punishment for her coming home empty-handed when she was fourteen. The more she read the more she had a degree of sympathy for the girl. She was still only nineteen, the same age as Kelly. She thought of her own upbringing and tried to put each of their lives into some sort of perspective. It proved impossible. She could hardly comprehend the thought of buying drugs for her mother let alone selling her body to help her feed a habit. The girl was pretty too.

Another name listed followed a similar pattern. No fixed address, whereabouts unknown. Two were not even registered, probably illegal. All had managed to become part of the disappeared. She had to start a search somewhere and the place to start looking would be the last known address of the Gittings' family, if it could be classed as such.

* * *

Parking on Webster Street, Toxteth, was difficult at the best of times but she had picked the day the bin lorry was collecting. After some time, she parked in the first available spot and walked checking the numbers until she located the house. Aluminium screens covered the windows and doors to two properties in the row of terraced houses. She sighed. The Gittings had lived in the first. There were twelve to fifteen houses occupied. It was now a case of knocking and making enquiries.

* * *

Skeeter sat behind the computer screen. There was something about plain and simple Malik that was neither plain nor simple.

'Did he get to you?' Tony Price watched the response from across the room. 'Feel insulted? You want revenge?'

He folded the paper into a dart and threw it. It headed in

a descending curve as it crossed the room and struck the back of her computer screen.

'Bull's-eye! Saw you and Brad do this and it always raised a smile.'

She collected it from where it had fallen between her feet and opened it. There was a large round smiley face. She giggled. 'Thanks.'

'You can't use your power as an officer of the law to get one over him. I'd be fucking annoyed too but you've nothing to go on. He answered all the questions you asked and he served a tasty döner.'

'Tony, you might not believe this but it wasn't Mr fucking Malik that caused the hairs on my neck to rise but the guy who came from the back, all aggressive like. You saw him?'

'I did. Big lad? The Albanian?' He did not wait for a reply. 'Put it in perspective. Can you imagine the trouble they could get on match days? Hell's bells you need guys like that to ensure the staff's safety and the premises, no matter how many coppers are on the street. I don't need to tell you how quickly trouble starts as we've both witnessed it and been involved. That's probably why he positioned the mini camera on the shelf facing the counter.'

From the expression on Skeeter's face, he knew that she had been unaware of its presence.

'It wasn't your everyday CCTV either, it was the clock. Has a spy camera that links to a phone or computer using the internet. My attention was drawn to it because it was so clean. Everything else was covered in a layer of fatty grime but the clock's face, particularly one area of the glass, was immaculate. Now whether your guy is always keeping a watching brief from the back of the place or from upstairs who knows? There could be an owner somewhere else who needs to keep a tally?'

'These bloody spy things are frightening and they're sold to the public. In the wrong hands, the hands of a pervert, they are a real danger. Are you sure it was a camera?'

'Looked that way to me. I have one very similar. That's why we have laws about their unregistered use.'

Walking across he took out his phone. 'There, that's my lounge in real time. If anyone disturbs the sensor it will notify me and I can see what's happening. Records too on an SD card.'

'Thanks, Tony, you've been a true support. I'm going to check the background of the place and then I can rest easy. Humour me.'

Skeeter requested as much information on the address as possible: business use, licence holder, employees and their National Insurance numbers, occupancy within the building. She was determined to leave no stone unturned. That would be the start and depending on the results, would determine any future action.

* * *

On the fifth attempt Lucy had struck lucky. The house was five doors down from the boarded property previously occupied by the Gittings' family. Mrs Netherfield was in her mid-seventies. The house was immaculate. She opened the door on a security chain. Lucy smiled and showed her ID.

'Police. Sorry to disturb you. It's a routine call. I'm trying to track a Beverley Gittings.'

Netherfield pulled a face on hearing the name. The door closed and then swung open. 'You'd better come in, love.'

After brief introductions, Netherfield went into the kitchen and put the kettle on. Lucy knew that she would be there for a while.

'They weren't too bad when they first arrived. I believe they'd started life in a caravan and then managed to buy here. Never seemed to have two pennies to rub together, mind. Then the kids came along. I have to be honest and say when they were young the parents tried hard and the kids were always smart. Always spoke. The father was a keen fisherman, not sea stuff, more the canal. Big lad too.'

There was a pause as she seemed to drift off into the past and Lucy watched as her cup tilted. She reached out and steadied her arm. 'Ta, love. I was back then. I do it a lot these days. Being alone it does funny things to you. Old age is not to be recommended. Stay young, love. Funny, I could just picture them.'

'Two children?' Lucy asked as she sipped her tea. Even though she had requested no sugar it tasted very sweet. She said nothing.

'Beverley and Sean, he was the older. The trouble seemed to appear when the father lost so much weight in a short space of time. I remember that really well, the shock of it. I hadn't seen him for a while as I'd gone to stay with my sister in Chester for a week or so. She has such a lovely place – proper posh and not like here. Anyway, when I got back, I'd gone to the shop at the end there and as I went in, he was coming out. I walked past him. It was only because he spoke. Goodness, he'd changed so much. Gambling and drugs people said. He was dead within the month. I thought it was cancer but then I know nothing. Sean went off and the family then started to downward spiral. I've seen it a couple of times. Booze and betting usually, after the husband or man in the house loses his job. Family breaks up and the next minute there's a To Let or a For Sale sign. More often than not if it's rented, they do a flit.'

'So, Mrs Netherfield, what about the mother?'

'Biscuit?'

Lucy shook her head.

'Thought you'd know. Locked up. Broke the dog's legs. Drink and drugs. You'd see them come to the house on push-bikes, those little scooters and mopeds. Sometimes men would come to the house. In for a while and then out. Knocking shop people said.'

'How old was Beverley?'

'Fourteen, maybe fifteen. Suddenly started to wear makeup. Mother put her on the game if you ask me. Some-times I'd see a car pull up and she'd be picked up. Should have been at school.'

'When did you last see her?'

She put her cup and saucer on the coffee table. 'I know exactly when I saw her last, it was after her mother was taken away and the house cleared. She was with a gang, mainly lads, hoods up, you know the type. It was maybe three weeks ago. I was coming back from having my hair done, it was going dark and a gang of about eight were blocking the path. There was a lot of swearing, strong stuff. I could see there might be trouble so I tucked my bag into my coat. I was frightened I can tell you that. Suddenly someone spoke and the gang parted like the Red Sea. It was then I saw who had spoken, it was Beverley. She simply nodded. Last time I saw her. Maybe she's not all bad.'

'Thank you.'

'It's sad when you see them lose their way. She still had a heart, the lass. I'll always be grateful. If you see her please give her my regards and say thank you.'

Lucy detected the sincerity in her eyes. She nodded. 'I'll do that, Mrs Netherfield. Let's hope there's still time to get her straight.'

As Lucy turned to leave, she paused. 'One last thing. Did Beverley have any visible scars?'

'I once saw her arms. Here and around here.' She pointed to her inner forearm. 'Always had a lot of cuts around there as if she'd pulled her arms through brambles.'

Lucy only smiled and left.

CHAPTER 16

The deep red Peugeot 207 sat idling, lights off. It had been stolen earlier in the evening and would, with luck, still not be reported missing. The cemetery, a dark oasis in the centre of the city, sat in marked contrast to its surroundings. A black hole set amongst the city's lights, it was positioned to the right of the main road. The gravestones along the edge were illuminated and shadowed but further in, the dark swallowed the rest. Lights along the far side marked the boundary of the black hole. All three youths vaped anxiously. The time leading up to confrontations was never easy and those that said they were not scared were liars or fools. Clouds streamed from the partly opened window matching the grey curl of exhaust that quickly dispersed. The youthful chatter was a combination of nervous banality and foolish jokes.

Hoover sat in the back, more nervous than the rest. He had fidgeted a great deal since the car had come to rest adding little to the chatter. He had fondled the long-bladed knife with gloved hands, the object wrapped within a transparent, plastic bag. No fingers and no DNA he had been instructed. Its matt black blade was curved and serrated along the top edge. The lower edge was finely honed. He swallowed deeply. Removing the plastic, he tossed it from the window before slipping the blade up the sleeve of his jacket.

'Fucking quiet in the back, Hoover, my old mucker. It's fucking easy. Just make sure it goes in hard and comes out with a twist, like you do your women.' Laughter seemed to fill the small space. Hoover smiled.

It was time to make a move. The location they had chosen was to the far end of the cemetery. The small passageway between two Victorian semi-detached houses led to the top gate. It was narrow, a cul-de-sac and unsuitable for a car, a pedestrian entry to the graveyard. It was also dark. It would serve their purpose.

Within two minutes they had parked within yards of the T-junction. It was an area of the city accommodating many students and therefore a rich and lucrative area for Beverley to ply her trade. The three would now have another nervous wait but if the information was correct it would only be a matter of time before their intended target appeared. Just how many would be in the group was an uncertainty. If there were too many they would stay in the car and when safe, leave.

Two youths, walking hurriedly, crossed the end of the road directly in front of the car. The passenger was the first to spot them and nudged the driver with his elbow.

'Fuck, they're earlier than I thought and there's only a couple of them. She's one of them. Bonus lads. Game fucking on.'

All three scrambled from the car, pulling up their neck tubes to conceal their faces. Each tube was patterned with a different design. Hoover's resembled the face of a laughing clown, another a skull, the third that of Guy Fawkes. All three were disconcerting and lifelike. They screamed as they started to move down the road. The couple paused, looking in the direction of the noise. They then made their first mistake. They started to run instinctively down the narrow passage.

'Are you ready, Hoover? You're going for the girl. We'll take the bloke!' the driver yelled as they took up the chase.

Hoover had already stripped off the sheath from the knife, stuffing it into his pocket. They sprinted towards the junction and then crossed the road to face the passageway. The joking and bravado were left in the car. After the initial shouts, nobody spoke. The sound of their crashing feet echoed between the houses. It was a sharp and frightening warning to those being pursued.

Beverley Gittings turned to see the black figures running and quickly gaining on them. 'Oh fuck!' was all she could say as she turned for the small opening in the gated entrance. She tossed the bag containing the separate quantities of drugs over a wall. At this stage she was unsure as to who was giving chase.

Before them was an ornate cemetery gate. To both sides was an arched opening set in the face of each stone tower. Within that rested a wrought iron rotating gate not too dissimilar to a turnstile. She had been this way so often and yet during this moment of panic she knew it was a wrong move. It suddenly seemed unchartered. She let out a scream, pointing to the left as she went right.

'They lock them at night. Go over, Quas!' she yelled to her partner. With a leap he lodged his foot in one of the ornate openings in the stone arcaded screen that joined the twin towers. He grabbed the top of the wall and was up, one leg straddling either side. He watched their approach. Beverley tried to join him but failed. The three were now only yards away.

'For fuck's sake, Bev, move! They're close!' Quasim's voice was high-pitched and conveyed his fear. He knew there was little chance he could help. He quickly looked again and counted at least three assailants.

Those vital seconds of hesitation were all that it took. Beverley had foolishly created her own place of ambush. It could not have been more perfect for the pursuers. Within ten seconds Hoover had rapidly covered the distance and identified his quarry.

Beverley had one option and that was to try the stile, they might have forgotten to chain it shut but dusk had fallen an hour ago. She moved into the cell, fumbling with the first iron lobe of the turnstile. It was cold to the touch and stubborn to her frantic shove. She realised they had slipped on the chain and her heart sank. Suddenly it moved, but only part of the way and a moment's relief was quickly dashed as the snap of the chain cracked loudly bringing with it a chilling fear. Every time in the past it had turned so easily. Her senses were heightened by sheer panic, as the adrenaline raced round her body. She knew what was happening. She had done the same to others, but this was wrong, this was her own patch for fuck's sake. She tried again. It was turning and she was moving with it. Soon she would be through but the chain snapped tight again. In her peripheral vision she could see her partner was disappearing into the darkness of the graveyard. His two pursuers, also over the wall, had left him to run. They focused their attention on the trapped girl and Hoover.

'Do it for fuck's sake!'

Beverley could go neither way. Her body seemed to relax momentarily, partly in fear. The clown moved so close to her she could hear his breathing, see his eyes.

'Beverley?' He spoke quietly.

'Yes ... No ... please, please.' She held up her hand. 'Don't do this!'

He was hesitating, she could sense that and it brought a moment's hope.

'It's not worth it. Please!'

It was then she saw his arm thrust forward. She turned away to avoid it. A second later she felt the first desperate blow. It had caused the blade to penetrate her outstretched hand. She neither felt it enter nor retract. Curling herself into the enclosed space she turned her back to her attacker, trying to make herself as small as possible. The second blow struck. Initially it seemed as though he had thumped her hard just below her right shoulder. She gasped as her breath temporarily vanished. Winded, she tried to gasp in air.

'No!' was all she could utter in defence.

The third blow swiftly followed and caused the critical damage. It was an underarm blow. This time it hit lower and with it came the severe pain as her kidney was sliced. She turned in desperation, only to see the laughing clown. She could see the sweat on his forehead before the comical face tilted backwards, as if in slow motion, to gain leverage.

Beverley Gittings did not feel the blade twist as it was

extracted. All feeling had suddenly evaporated. She heard voices, initially loud but they swiftly dulled. Those to her left sounded excited. On lifting her head, the clown mask had gone from her field of vision. Confused and in pain she tried to focus on the distant street light at the end of the passageway but that slowly blurred into darkness. The fear now intensified but the pain eased as the world became calm and black. For a moment she felt at total peace. Strangely, she smiled as she sank to the ground within the confined stone sarcophagus-like space.

Hoover felt a mixture of fear and excitement. He had done it. They had assured him that he could and that it would be easy, once he was close to his victim. *To avenge the death of one of theirs ... an eye for an eye,* he whispered the exact words they had told him and he could now see the logic. However, his belief in his ability to do it and the actual act of pushing a knife deep into another body, into a living human being, had proved easier than he had anticipated. To him she was not human, she was a thing, a sack, inanimate.

Maybe it was the drugs, the high he was on. He had looked into her eyes; he had seen her fear and her uncertainty. It was the final moments when he witnessed her sadness that seemed to linger; that was the image that was burned into his memory. That is what led him to lose discipline and panic. He threw the knife to his left into what looked to be an overgrown garden, an action he immediately regretted whilst leaping to take hold of the top of the wall. Shuffling over, he dropped into the cemetery, his feet hitting and sliding on the sloping surface. Collecting himself he began to run.

'Come on, Hoover. Fucking now!' The two at the other

side of the gate had gestured frantically whilst calling in lowered voices. He joined them before all three were swallowed into the darkness.

They had planned to stay together until reaching the cemetery wall next to the supermarket carpark. There they would split, avoiding the CCTV cameras at all costs. They would wait and take the wall in turn, listen for any signs of the emergency services warning them she had been discovered, before moving. They believed it would be some time before the crumpled body was found.

'Get rid of the knife as we discussed and dump all your clothing ... burn it or river them, whatever is best, but get shut!' the lad sitting next to him instructed, his voice calm and precise. 'It's now a case of walking out of here without making stupid mistakes.' He did not wait for a response. 'You've got it, the knife, yes?'

Hoover said nothing, he nodded knowing that he had made a huge error. Looking at the blood on his gloved hands he felt an immediate remorse and began to wipe them frantically on the grass.

'You did good. Pity you couldn't take her fucking scalp! To think I shagged her once. Fucking cost me a couple of packets of the good stuff, but that was before she went to the dark side.' He chuckled. 'Didn't prick her like you though, bro. She didn't scream like that when I screwed her.' He laughed again and grabbed his crotch.

Hoover turned his head and vomited into the grass, resulting in even more laughter from the other two.

* * *

As in most cases, if a body is left in an isolated spot it is usually found in the early morning, often by a dog or the person walking a dog. Beverley Gittings proved to be no exception. It was just coming light when Ben, an old black Labrador, paused by the cemetery gate and barked once. The gates should be unlocked and normally he would squeeze through the turnstile and relieve himself on the first tree to the right. It was a ritual. Today, he did not move. He stood his ground.

'Come on, Ben, I have to get to work.' Sarah Mott paused and looked in the direction of the right-hand portal. There was somebody there. She first noticed some dumped cushions just below the wall but then her eyes alighted on something crumpled in the right gate. Bending, she attached the lead to Ben's collar before moving closer. The body was slumped as if propped up by the central post of the stile. Sarah did not need to go any further, she could see the mass of congealed blood that had puddled the step on which the body rested. Removing her phone, she turned away before dialling 999. Ben, now desperate, simply cocked his leg and urinated on the dead girl.

Within five minutes the lights from the van lit the road running through the centre of the cemetery on the far side of the gate. Thankfully, she would no longer be alone. The security officer was eventually coming to unlock the gate.

CHAPTER 17

I t was still early as Lucy and Brad parked as close as possible to the crime scene. The blue lights within the grille and on the dashboard of their car left nobody wondering as to their role. The paramedic's vehicle was further up Arundel Road and within the taped boundary. Both officers produced their ID, ducked beneath the tape and were directed to the end of the passageway. Sitting on a chair to the right was a middle-aged woman attended to by the paramedic. To her right lay a Labrador.

A warm light had now crept into most of the passageway as the early sun tracked along Lancaster Avenue, and with it, neighbours had started to congregate. Brad immediately focused on the crumpled figure contorted within the right cell of the gate. Some discarded cushions from what could have been a settee were dumped and rested against and near the centre between the two towers. A secondary line of tape crossed the passageway and Brad could make out Crime Scene personnel on the far side within the cemetery itself. Speaking to an officer who was leaning against a privet hedge, he pointed to the woman.

'Sarah Mott, she found the body this morning. The chap who opens the gates, one of the City Watch lads, was late owing to an incident elsewhere. He stayed until we arrived. Have his details.' He offered the electronic pad.

Brad took note and then allowed his eyes to fall on a camera dangling vertically from the gable end of the right-hand building that formed part of the passageway.

'Take it that's knackered?'

The officer turned and smiled. 'According to the students living there it's always been like that. People who use this passageway at night are obviously shy.'

'Do we have any details?'

'Nothing. Paramedic did a check but she was obviously dead. Awaiting the doctor and then CSI can do their stuff here. They're checking the other side. Hopefully we'll know more once she's been moved. Apparently, they call the gates cells, the bit where the turnstile is. According to my colleague at the other side there's a stone plaque built into the wall and considering the gate was built in 1885 it's quite prophetic. One of the names on it is a G Stabb.'

Brad frowned. 'Right.'

Within forty minutes the police doctor, another CSI van and the press, like bees to honey, had arrived.

Lucy had taken Sarah Mott's statement and she had been cleared by the paramedic. There was little point in her stay-ing. She was assured that she would receive a call from police liaison to ensure she was supported. Finding a corpse, particularly someone so young and in such dreadful circum-stances, could have long-lasting psychological effects. There was nothing more they could do once door-to-door enquiries of the immediate area had been organised.

Brad glanced at the parked vehicles both along Arundel Road and Lancaster Avenue before turning to the officer.

'Just as a matter of interest, walk a couple of hundred yards along both sides of this road up there and the immediate ones linking. The killer got here somehow. It's a wild card but on the off-chance they did, check to see if any car is unlocked. Use gloves too, please. I'll check this way.'

Both men set off in opposite directions. Within fifteen minutes the officer called after Brad.

'We have one!'

Brad returned and saw him standing next to the Peugeot 207.

* * *

The Dawn Lady, a medium-sized cruise liner returning from the Caribbean, entered the Mersey. For the first time in a few days, the weather heralded sunshine and a break from the showers. To those on the river's banks watching the maritime ballet, the vessel appeared toy-like as it manoeuvred mid-point in the Mersey. A fine mist hugged the river's surface like a thin skin. From on board, passengers witnessed the nautical link and the architectural splendour of the maritime city with some relief. The news of a sudden outbreak of food poisoning on two cruise liners had brought a degree of disquiet amongst not only the passengers but also the crew, bringing uncertainty for the majority of the holidaymakers. So close to home and yet … For two passengers in particular, it would not be the news they wanted to hear.

For Arthur and Lynn Brinkman it was the end to their twenty-one-day holiday but they had spent the last week in a state of anxiety. They had a deadline to meet and cargo to deliver. The final twenty-four hours of the journey had been particularly stressful for them and for those awaiting delivery. Leaning on the balcony of their cabin they watched New Brighton pass to the starboard side. The lighthouse, a solitary white finger, rose out of the water signalling they were finally home. It had taken them longer than anticipated to navigate from the river entrance. The pilot had come aboard over thirty minutes previously and progress had been slow, but as Arthur had pointed out, it was safe and not the easiest of things to park.

The liner pirouetted mid-river watched over by three tugs. Once the turn had been completed the ship began the slow sideways push towards its berth. The Brinkman looked across at the riverside buildings. Gulls screamed and dived at the churning water so far below, created by the ship's powerful thrusters. The water seemed to boil into a beige froth that lingered in wriggling lines on the river's surface. The birds were desperate to scavenge any flotsam that surfaced.

'The pleasure ceases and the work begins here,' Arthur mumbled with a degree of resignation in his voice.

Lynn moved inside and collected the crutches. 'The thespian in me is rekindled once I have the correct props.' She smiled before modifying her facial expression.

Although falling down the stairs had been planned, she had not bargained for the injury to be so severe. The doctor had strapped the ankle and given her pain killers. X-rays had shown it not to be broken. She had also bumped her face and her left eye was bruised.

'To say we weren't going to draw attention to ourselves we've done the exact opposite. In the minds of some, I, your husband, might now be a suspected wife beater when we leave *The Dawn Lady* after an idyllic cruise. That'll bring unwanted attention' They both laughed. 'Let's just hope we receive the sympathy vote as anticipated.'

Their cases had been taken during the night leaving only their one piece of hand luggage. It was now a matter of waiting, staying normal and trusting to first time luck.

* * *

The reports Skeeter had received were direct and to the point: three staff, their names, their National Insurance details and their addresses. The business was licensed to Malik, as Tony had presumed, for the food trade. The licence did not include any living accommodation. There was also no mention or link to a Flamur, the angry bastard from the back of the shop. Skeeter smiled. 'You've given me the perfect opportunity to ask more questions, you arsehole of a man.'

Within five minutes she had sent a request to Liverpool Council Environmental Health for a full inspection of the premises on the grounds she believed it was being used for illicit accommodation of possible illegals. It should take twelve hours to process. She also requested she be present during the visit.

* * *

Lucy scanned the front cover of the latest newspaper. The report of an aircraft carrier, shortly to dock on the Mersey, seemed to fill the local pages. Aircraft were to be positioned on the sea front and this would attract large crowds. It could be a security nightmare, what with the latest spell of terrorist activity and the motor cycle attacks. Tossing the paper to one side she scanned the report on her screen. She was shocked to read the initial findings from the morning's crime scene, realising that the teenager was, in fact, Beverley Gittings. The severity of the wounds and the position in which the girl was found, trapped and cornered, deeply affected Lucy. She could not envisage just what the girl's final minutes of terror would have been like. Pausing, she tried to visualise those last moments but other than a flush of nausea she had little concept. Nobody should die like that, no matter what they did or had done.

CCTV footage had been received from businesses surrounding the cemetery and a positive lead was being investigated. The Peugeot was traced to an address in Mond Road, Widnes. The owner was unaware of its disappearance as he was on holiday in Benidorm. The vehicle had been recovered and was with Forensics.

'Gang war, patch war, turf war. Call it what you will there's little respect for property or people,' Brad grumbled as he tapped the table with a drumstick.

Lucy frowned, eager to show him the video. She pulled a face and looked at the object he held up.

'It was on the boss's desk, a pair in fact. Saw her tapping away yesterday. She can beat out a rhythm.'

'I'd put it back just where you found it. Women get particular about their personal items being handled by strange men. Then pop back here. The relevant footage from the Asda carpark CCTV has been forwarded.'

He was back within minutes.

'She'll know they've been touched; women always do. I'll say nothing just blame the cleaner! Only this once, though.'

Brad flushed but did not reply before settling to watch the large screen.

'There!' Lucy paused the footage and pointed to the screen. 'Behind that tree. One coming over the wall and then going out of shot.'

She checked the notes then restarted the video footage and they both focused on that area. A second and then a third figure could just be seen illuminated by the carpark lights.

'Can it be improved?' Brad asked.

'Not according to this report but be patient.' She explained that the next section of footage was from the junction of the A562 and Wellington Avenue.

'That's here!' Brad pushed across an electronic tablet showing Google maps.

'You can see from the time that's probably one of the three. The time difference is accurate. It was presumed that they then went directly to Bagot Street as we have footage of them on the corner. Look at the body language. He's moved to the left as if keeping out of sight from the main road. He's clearly unaware of this specific camera.' She checked the notes.

As there was no sound recording the next movement caused Brad to sit back from the screen. The motorcycle suddenly moved quickly into the shot. He watched as the person climbed onto the pillion and the bike vanished off screen.

'Planned, even down to the pickup. Close inspection shows the bike doesn't have a registration plate.' Lucy removed the memory stick.

'Pillion didn't have a helmet,' Brad announced, the sound of frustration clearly audible. 'Not enough coppers on the beat and they know it. These bikes can get where shit can't. It'll either have been burned, in bits somewhere or playing at being a Mersey submarine right now.'

'I guess the other two were collected from different rendezvous points but nothing on camera so far.' Lucy shrugged her shoulders.

CHAPTER 18

Arthur Brinkman checked the memo that had been left in their cabin and then the coloured debarkation tag already attached to the one piece of hand luggage. According to the colour they were due to leave the vessel at eleven thirty and the deck was clearly marked on the plan. They had watched the cruise director's briefing on the television in their room and although this was the first conclusion to a cruise holiday, they had disembarked before during the trip.

'We're in the hands of …' he paused as the word God suddenly seemed inappropriate.

'Neptune, my dear. He might watch over his fellow seafarers but somehow, I doubt it. We're now well and truly on our own. Any regrets?'

'At my age?' He shook his head. 'It's like tossing a coin, love. We either win or lose.' Although the words sounded negative there was a positivity in his tone as he started to whistle.

* * *

Skeeter could barely contain her excitement as she sat in the car looking at the kebab shop. She nursed her mobile and kept checking the time. She was early, very early. She would be meeting with Jane Fairhurst from Liverpool Council's Environmental Health who had agreed to the visit. She was herself eager to review the establishment after the poor result in the Food Hygiene Rating Scheme.

Skeeter's phone rang. She answered and listened as she saw the white Ford pull up further along the road. Jane was early. Leaving the car, Skeeter stopped by the vehicle.

'Are you alone?' Skeeter asked expecting to see at least two people.

'Always, one of the reasons I might be moving away from this role. It can happen especially when the owners don't like my findings, that they attempt to, let's say, bribe their way out of a situation.'

'Money?'

Jane laughed. 'Usually flattery. "Why's a lovely young lady like you trawling round places like this?" The best is when they try to offer you food to take home. They don't realise you've just condemned the place so why you'd want to eat their cooking is beyond all comprehension.'

Skeeter remembered that Malik had offered Tony his kebab *on the house*. She had already decided they were suspect before the offer but that had put the cherry on the cake of guilt.

'This will be a reappraisal and not a full inspection,' Jane mentioned as she straightened her ID that hung from a lanyard. 'I have photographs from the previous visit recorded by a colleague and we'll do some comparatives, take samples and check the paperwork. The fact that you're with me will either inflame or calm the situation. We'll see.' Jane smiled and quickly checked through her bag retrieving a body cam, a small square camera that she attached to her lapel. 'Helps to maintain a degree of respect.'

They approached the door. The smell was the same. It was clearly neither fresh nor hygienic. Malik turned and immediately focused his attention on Skeeter. His expression did not change other than a narrowing of his eyes. Jane had already proffered her ID. 'Liverpool Council Environmental Health, Mr Buruk.' She smiled before letting the tag fall. 'It's a follow-up to see if you've improved certain areas that were highlighted in my colleague's previous inspection.'

'It's not due yet.' His attitude was defensive and he pointed at Skeeter. 'She's police, not health ...'

Jane immediately interjected. 'Shall we get on? I'm going to look everywhere on this occasion. Up, down and out the back if I may. Let's start upstairs and see if we can get you higher up the chart. Remember, this body cam will be monitored live throughout our visit.' With little alternative he turned the closed sign on the door and dropped the latch.

* * *

The passport checks had gone without a hitch. To Arthur's great relief there had not been a sniffer dog present. He carried only the single case he had with him, a porter had taken all their other luggage. Lynn sat in the wheelchair, the crutches to the side. They had agreed to be the last of their cohort to leave the ship to save delaying fellow travellers. Once clear, the porter wheeled Lynn to a seat just inside the Cruise Centre and took away the chair before returning once again with two large cases. He brought a third whilst Arthur went for the car. It had been left for the duration of the holiday in a multistorey carpark attached to the hotel they had used on the night before their departure. It was part of the cruise package. The luggage he carried stayed firmly in his grasp. He bent and kissed Lynn before walking off through the terminal carpark, dragging the case. She took a paperback from her bag and started to read. Not one word registered. Her nerves were at the forefront, but it gave her a barrier of normality behind which to hide. Arthur quickly passed a number of coaches waiting in the cruise terminal carpark and a slow stream of travellers who were dropping cases and boarding.

Sadiq pulled the cap peak a little lower over his face. It was instinctive rather than for any real purpose as he watched Arthur pass between the two closed barriers of the terminal carpark. He looked at the one case he was carrying. Knowing the contents, and that now they were so close, was the hardest part. It was the final hurdle, yet it could still all go terribly wrong. Other members of the team were on watch nearer the carpark. After Brinkman entered, he would be left alone; there were too many security cameras in the facility. After fifteen minutes, Brinkman's car was waiting for the barrier of the cruise terminal to open. Sadiq was still watching, his nerves tight. There was no way of knowing if the transaction had taken place until the car they had left for the deposit was collected forty-eight hours later.

Lynn hobbled to the waiting car, the crutches alien and cumbersome. Arthur held the door open. Neither spoke but she immediately saw the supermarket bag on the back seat. Her heart fluttered nervously; her hands sweaty. She was using all her will to keep calm and under control. She settled in the seat as Arthur loaded the cases into the boot before returning to the driver's seat. He was just about to drive off when he saw someone in uniform run from the cruise centre waving for them to stop.

Both flushed, their nerves on edge. Had they been detected? A rush of fear caused Arthur to stall the car. It was Lynn who saw the book first. The man was holding it high in his waving hand and relief flooded her whole being.

'I left my bloody book!'

With a shaking hand, she lowered the car's window.

'You left this on the bench. Thought I'd missed you. Safe journey home.' Pushing the book through the window he turned and jogged back, lifting his arm this time in a friendly wave.

Arthur rubbed his eyes and looked at Lynn. 'Bloody hell. I'm too old for this shit!' He put the car in neutral, turned the key and started to move towards the barrier.

Sadiq stood with the phone to his ear. 'Delivery dropped, bro.'

'You know about Malik? Soon he'll no longer be with us. Careless, Sadiq, careless.'

'I know, I saw and I heard about him with the girl, the shit.'

There was a long pause. 'Right! What about her?'

'Still looking, bro.'

'Don't cock this up. We need to find the bitch; things are too important right now.'

'What about Scar?'

'I'm on to it. We have an idea, someone by the name of Hoover, probably new in the area. I've put the word out with a reward. You need to find Chelle and you need to keep things running. Cut the attacks but maintain the drops. With new stock coming we can afford to make new markets, spread the tentacles a little further without treading on toes. We'll see what that brings.'

'Right.' Sadiq's answer was concise but there was nothing more to add. There was too much going on, too much seemed to be now out of his control. The only consolation, he was five minutes from his apartment and he needed a drink.

* * *

Skeeter photographed the upstairs room containing the double bed. She ignored Malik's protestations that no one had lived there. She allowed her eyes to scan the full scene. The large sheet of dark plastic over the window was an effective blackout. Light pierced the edges in fine white daggers but the majority of the room was dark and closed off from the outside world. The lone, unshaded bulb offered the only brightness. As Malik and Jane moved into another room she knelt to look under the bed. Ignoring the dust and the two grubby cardboard boxes, she studied the object near the bedhead legs: a piece of an electrician's tie. Putting on a glove she collected it before turning the glove inside out to trap the plastic within. She stuffed it into her pocket. In Skeeter's world a bed and a tie had only one connotation and her gut tingled.

The rest of the visit was as expected. Little had been done to raise the hygiene level but it was not bad enough for Jane to close it down. It met certain standards.

Skeeter had seen enough to convince her there was more to the place than purely a food vending establishment. She moved behind the counter and looked at the clock on the wall. Tony had been right. In contrast to the rest of the place, the glass was amazingly clean.

'Please lift your clock down, Malik. That's right isn't it? You said the last time that you were *plain and simply Malik?*'

Malik tilted his head in indifference. 'Why?'

Skeeter looked at Jane, and then back at Malik. 'You're not posting information to say you have video recording equipment in the shop and if I'm not mistaken that's such a device.'

Jane moved closer.

'Is Flam – that's his name, yes? Your backroom boy. Is he monitoring our visit or is someone else?'

'Security, that's all. You lot surround us with bloody cameras. Even on the statue down the road they've put one. She's even wearing one and you then question me?'

'She notified you, Malik, she told you at the start. It's recorded. Have you notified the Information Commissioner's Office and paid the fee that allows the use of CCTV on your premises?' She leaned closer to him raising herself onto her toes. 'Look into my eyes, because if not, you're breaking the law and it therefore is …' she paused allowing the seriousness of her words to sink in, '… a criminal offence.' She wanted to follow it with the word *arsehole* but thought better of it with the camera running on Jane's jacket.

The post mortem report was clear. April checked the images on screen, shaking her head as she started to read the pathologist's report. The wound to the hand told April everything she needed to know. It was a common injury seen on victims of knife crime. We would all raise our hands in self-defence. It seemed such a waste of a young life but was a scenario that had been on the increase over the last few years. Her finger followed the script on screen, pausing at key places.

Suffering from early-stage Gonorrhoea. Evidence of fairly rough sex – slight vaginal tearing but no other extragenital injury. Petechiae on the neck and high inner thigh. Finger nail assessment shows no damage so it is highly unlikely the victim was raped. Evidence of long-term self-harm. Significant scarring to both arms, some in the shape of crosses and others clearly are marked with what looks like 666.

April looked at the detailed images and could only concur with their findings. This was a troubled girl. *Scar,* her alleged nickname was now understandable. Reading through the toxicology results it was clear she was a regular user. High alcohol register was also noted. April cross-checked with the girl's GP records which were few. Moving into the Incident Room she found the name Gittings on the board. Picking up a red marker she drew a line from the name before printing one word: MURDERED.

Skeeter returned to the office area, throwing her car keys onto the desk. They skidded before colliding with a small trophy that served as a paperweight. The empty water bottle followed but found the bin. April returned from the Incident Room.

'Problem shared is a problem halved.' There was little intonation in her words, her tone was neutral. 'We know why Gittings carries the name Scar.'

Skeeter ignored her; the frustration evident in her expression. 'There's a bloody link, I know it, I feel it. He's a bastard and he's hiding something.'

April moved across to perch on a desk close by and folded her arms.

Skeeter rummaged in her pocket and withdrew the screwed-up glove.

'I think our girl, Kelly, has been in the upstairs room. I also think she was held against her will. Part of an electrician's tie was under the bed, perfect for keeping someone attached to it. Doesn't have to be a bed, it could be a radiator or anything for that matter but it was under the bloody bed. I can assure you the place has not seen an electrician for some time. Bloody shit hole.' She looked across at April. 'It's going to Forensics but I doubt there'll be anything on it. I want a warrant.'

'I hear you. I've received the pathology result for Gittings and something interesting from Forensics. It was found in her coat lining.'

April held up a plastic evidence bag. Inside was a transparent disc. 'Not dissimilar to the one found on the beach. The gilt dollar sign is clear.'

'A pass? They show it to access a place or some goods?' Skeeter speculated.

'Strange but unsure.'

'Pathology?'

'Suggesting gang stuff, drugs and alcohol, maybe prostitution but that can only be conjecture. An STI, yes, but love bites to the neck and thigh might contradict that, as no self-respecting prostitute would tolerate that. Severe evidence of self-harm hence the name Scar.'

'Self-respecting whilst self-harming? How do you square that circle?' Skeeter had a point. 'Whore, yes, professional sex worker, no.'

'So, have they closed the kebab place down?' April asked knowing the answer. They would no doubt play the race card if there was a move on that front.

'Nope. However, it didn't score well and Environmental Health have warned of further visits. I can imagine it'll not be used as an hotel any more. Thankful for small mercies. I'm also chasing about unregistered CCTV. I'll needle the bastards out with a fucking pin. Getting a warrant would answer so many questions.'

On the outskirts of Ormskirk, Quasim pedalled the electric bicycle towards the top of a passageway linking the university to the main road. It was his regular drop. Text messages gave time and location which varied. He had worked it to perfection. It was within five minutes of a remote lay-by where the van had dropped him. He would be collected at another point. The goods were round his shoulder in what looked like a laptop case. He was dressed casually and looked to all intents and purposes like another student. He wore a helmet too.

The bike was different and certainly a wolf in sheep's clothing. Normally the electric motor was governed, allowing a limited speed, but this had been modified. The bike was both fast off the mark and could achieve speeds of forty-five miles per hour. That and an ability to thread through the narrowest of gaps made it a difficult bike to chase.

The person approached on time. The relevant conversation took place and the swap was made, a simple procedure but highly effective. Three such transactions a day were extremely profitable for all concerned.

CHAPTER 19

It was 11am. Kelly waited at Gathurst Station, her hood up and cap peak lowered. She studied the ticket machine, deposited the correct change and withdrew the ticket. She leant on the fence some distance away from the only other person waiting, an elderly gentleman with a large brown dog. The bird song was vibrant but the rumble of vehicles on the M6 motorway viaduct that traverses the Douglas Valley seemed even louder. It had woken her when it was at its morning peak. She rubbed her hands. The day seemed warmer and it was good to move from her temporary burrow. Two nights in there had taught her she needed to find somewhere warm where she could get hot food. She would not return.

It took less than seven minutes to travel into Wigan. The train was quiet, the carriage empty. On arrival at Wigan, she threw her rucksack over her shoulder, found her bearings and trudged up the steps taking her from the platform. The handrails ran centrally and she took the right-hand steps before glancing at the sign written large and suspended over the exit.

Welcome to Wigan Wallgate

She paused momentarily wondering if she was doing the right thing. A flutter of nerves filled her empty stomach. Popping her ticket into the barrier she passed through the turnstile.

Like the train, the road outside was relatively quiet. Turning left she walked toward the pedestrian area. Some pubs were already open but others were boarded up. They had served their final drink. She glanced at the war memorial through a gap between two buildings and then noticed the figure huddled in a doorway. Although she did not have much money, she placed a pound coin into the outstretched gloved hand. A head looked up and Kelly was surprised to see a female face. Pausing she crouched. She studied the girl: her hair, her fingers.

'Are you alright?' Kelly's tone was concerned and sincere.

The girl wiped her nose on her sleeve and nodded. Kelly could read her like a book. She had been there herself, experienced the loneliness until being sucked into the insidious bosom of a gang. Smiling, she dug in her pocket for a second coin.

'I need help myself. A night shelter, some food and clothes.'

'Sharon,' she stuck out her gloved hand again.

Kelly was taken aback but reached out and took it. 'Kelly.' She smiled and enjoyed the human touch, the gentleness and sincerity.

After a few words, the girl pointed across the road to a narrow alleyway between a pub and a takeaway. 'At the end of there. They'll help you and ask few questions. It's secure. They're helping me. Keep safe, Kelly. And thanks.'

For the first time, Kelly saw her smile. She reached and touched the girl's hand once more. 'Thank you. Stay safe, too.'

Kelly crossed the road and headed towards the entrance to what could best be described as a ginnel. It was neither inviting nor threatening; it was a throwback to a bygone age. The narrow roadway comprised cobbles broken by two lines of flagstones, a cart width apart. They were worn from use. A boarded window held frayed and faded posters. Her attention was drawn to the largest. She could just read the greyed-out print.

Starsailor
Robin Park Arena
13th July, 2016

She had never heard of the band. She traced the date with her finger. Where was she then? The image of the band members was faded and ghostly. She stared at it, trying to bring the faces into focus, but all she could see were Abid's features appearing from within the weather bleached paper. 'I miss you, Abid.' Removing the small plastic bag containing the remnant of his clothing, she inhaled what little smell remained. 'You'd know what to do.'

Turning away she took a deep breath as if trying to purge the previous moments. There were no tears this time and she knew for her own survival that she had to turn him into the image on the poster. She had to bleach and blur him from her head, make him fade away. She had to move on.

* * *

Tony was the first to see the report from HOLMES. The addition of the link between Skeeter's intelligence and the latest information, had signalled a need to investigate. He knew that she would be fuming. He thought of sending it as a paper dart but then revised his thinking. He would just tell her.

'Shit!' The scream and the sound of Skeeter's clenched fist hitting her desk reverberated around the room. 'You have to be fucking joking! When?'

Tony held out the printed details that were at best sketchy. Grabbing the paper, she read it before raising her eyes. Tony found it difficult to return her stare.

'"A body found awaiting ID and Forensic examination,"' she continued to read out loud. '"Initial finding: severe damage to the front of the shop, the room directly above and parts of the roof. A body discovered beneath the collapsed stairs. No other persons found within the building as yet. Full survey to take place once the building has been properly secured. Victim believed to be male. Severe burn injuries." Fuck!'

'If you're going to get rid of evidence the best way is fire and water. Someone somewhere knows that we're getting warm.'

Skeeter turned her gaze on him and was not amused at his attempt at a pun. 'Fucking warm? Fuck off. Try incinerated.'

Her comment was water off a duck's back. 'My money's on the dead man being Malik. You?'

She did not answer but allowed the report to fall onto her desk. 'I'm nipping out there. I want to see for myself.'

* * *

Two people were smoking at the end of the ginnel. Kelly paused. Their similarity was striking. Both appeared grey, hooded and vaping. Huge plumes of vapour clouded above each at almost identical times as if in competition to see who could produce the larger cloud. They leaned against the brick walls, some distance apart but were somehow linked by appearance and circumstance. Neither looked her way. A blossom tree, light pink in colour, was in full flower and occasionally when the wind blew it scattered petals like warm snow. Growing on the piece of waste ground it seemed trapped, imprisoned within the urban area but the marked contrast added a certain beauty. She walked on, keeping her head down until she saw the sign. She headed for the door.

Inside was a small entrance, that too was painted grey. A man in his sixties could be seen through a glass hatchway in the wall. It was then she noticed the bell push. She took a moment before pressing it. Immediately the man turned and smiled before moving to the hatch.

'Morning. How can we help?'

Skeeter did not race to the kebab shop; she took her time to allow her anger to abate. She wanted to be able to focus on what she believed to be a case of arson. For a hundred yards to either side the road was cordoned off. A fire engine, blue strobe lights flashing, was still parked to the far side of the road. The usual collection of spectators was positioned along the tape.

Leaving the car, she mingled with the group, aware that locals at times like these might have vital information. She enquired with a degree of innocence about what had happened.

'Bloody fire love, blind or something?' The person turned and looked at Skeeter's eyes. 'Sorry, no offence. Last night about midnight. Sudden like.'

'Anyone in?'

'Strange place that, love. Sometimes see people go in but not come out. Live over there so I see what goes on. Not much else to do at my age.' She pointed to a nearby terraced house. 'Been there forty years.'

'What do you mean?'

'I've lived in it …'

'No, people not coming out.'

'Sorry, I see. Bit slow on the uptake some days. Senior moment. It's a takeaway and can be busy but them that goes in comes out a few minutes later. On occasion I've seen people go in but not come out. I've deliberately waited. Nearly wet myself one time hanging on. Don't get me wrong, it's not every day. Always wondered. Well, you do, don't you, when it's on your own doorstep?'

'Do you go in?'

'Once. Bloody place is filthy. How it stays open I don't

know. Never trust what's in them kebabs anyway. You could be eating anything. I remember what my dad told me about the war, you'd never eat rabbit again!'

Skeeter smiled and made her way to the firefighter who was rolling up one of the hoses. She held up her ID.

'There's a possibility this place is involved in distributing drugs and possibly people trafficking. I know you have a fatality. Can you do something for me?'

The officer tucked the roll away and approached, asking for her ID again.

'Can't be too careful. The press is here and would love us to tell all. Drugs and people, you say? Wouldn't surprise me. It has all the hallmarks of arson but that's my personal opinion, you understand. The team'll look at it forensically and give their verdict. I'd imagine that from what I've seen the guy was trapped on the stairs and asphyxiated either trying to get up or down. The upper floor has come through in places and covered the body with burning timbers. It'll remain there until the place is made structurally sound so he's not going anywhere. Don't forget there's an awful lot of water gone in there too.'

'Any idea where the fire started?'

'This is only a rough guess but I'd say the cooking area. Intense too.'

'Tell me,' Skeeter moved a little closer. 'Can you look and see if there's any remains of a clock on the wall to the far right behind the counter – close to the window?'

The officer frowned. 'It'll be a mass of melted plastic and metal if it's there.'

Skeeter handed him her phone. 'Please, just take a few pics and I'll know if it's the right place.'

'I shouldn't really. People trafficking you say?'

She nodded.

Taking the phone, he moved to the front of the charred remains of the shop. He spoke with another officer who turned to look in her direction and then back. She saw him nod. Within minutes he returned handing back the phone. 'There's no sign but it could have been washed anywhere by the force of the hosed water.'

She checked the photographs. There was neither sign of the clock nor the melted residue. The shelf brackets remained and the skeletal, twisted remnants of the spit but nothing of the clock. She rang Tony.

'Tony, the clock you saw at the kebab shop, like the one you have. What's it made of?'

'I think it's plastic, even the glass is some kind of plastic. It'll have some metal in the mechanism. There'll be batteries too, four I think and they'd explode in fire, wouldn't they? I'll check when I'm home. Why? Are you rooting round the wreckage?'

'Thanks,' was all she said.

* * *

The carpark was well lit and the cameras active when Mansoor Kamman approached the white BMW. Dressed in a suit and carrying a leather briefcase, he looked not only smart but professional. He had paid at the station and tucked the exit ticket into his breast pocket. The indicators flashed as he blipped the key fob. He went to the boot and it lifted with a second press. He smiled. The suitcase was waiting. Popping his briefcase to the side he allowed the boot to close before slipping into the driver's seat and relaxing. He removed his phone but there was no service. It could wait. Within fifteen minutes he would arrive outside Sadiq's apartment and that would be time enough.

* * *

The outside door released the lock with a resounding click and Mansoor went to the elevator, checking that the outside door had closed behind him. He expected Sadiq to be waiting for the elevator doors to open and he would be greeted with smiles but that was not the case. His mood changed. Approaching Sadiq's apartment door he put down the case, tapped on the door and stood back. He knew he was being observed through the small peephole. He had witnessed him do it each time someone came to the door even though he had seen them on the CCTV before allowing entry. To his surprise it was not Sadiq who opened the door but Flamur.

'Come in, you're expected. Smart, Doc, very, very smart.' He reached out and ran his fingers along the edge of his lapel. 'A beautiful case too. Heavy?'

'Expensively heavy. Where's Sadiq?'

The question was swiftly answered as Sadiq approached to stand behind Flamur. 'Just enjoying one of the pass rounds. Fancy a turn later?' Sadiq's eyes were now on the case.

Doc looked to see a young, naked girl move from the room and disappear down the corridor. She swayed, either drugged or drunk. He shook his head. 'You'll want this checking and cutting I presume?'

Sadiq moved closer and wrapped an arm around his shoulder. 'Doc by name, Doc by profession. Of course. You hear about the fire?'

He shook his head. 'Nope. Heard about Scar. Sounds like a bloody set up to me. What are you doing about it, other than shagging?'

Sadiq's expression quickly changed as he raised a finger to Doc's lips. 'Respect, Doc, respect. Remember your place.'

Doc tossed the case onto the settee. Flamur frowned. He crossed his arms and observed. Doc was no fool, he knew where the power lay.

CHAPTER 20

April had assembled them in the Incident Room. She had already marked an arrow from Malik Buruk's name and written DECEASED in red, matching that of Gittings.

'It's as if someone's clearing the deck. A spring clean of possible dead wood,' Tony announced. 'But why and who?'

'Another gang moving in?'

'Kelly?' Brad suggested with no real degree of conviction. 'Revenge for her fella?'

April turned to him. 'Have you been touching my drum sticks?'

Lucy smiled and looked directly at Brad who flushed red. April immediately sensed his discomfort.

'Please leave my desk alone, Brad.' April saw him nod.

'Sorry, just looking.'

'With these?' she waved her fingers. 'I mention this to remind you just what our job is here. We observe and react to the smallest thing. We note it and act. We share it, the good and the bad. We're supposed to be detectives, Detective

Constables. We're not detecting, sieving the wheat from the chaff. I noticed things were not as I'd left them. I predicted it might happen and I left them strategically, like bait to see whom I could trust not to touch?' She placed a hand on Brad's shoulder, shaking her head. 'Now, you all know that I have a dog?'

A number of heads nodded.

'Tico, ma'am, I believe,' announced Brad.

'Bloody hell … Bon bloody Jovi!' Tony laughed out loud. 'Just put two and two together. Tico Torres is the drummer. You like drumming and I guess Tico is your idol, the one you aspire to.'

April pointed her finger at him. 'Correct. We tend to see things in isolation, cryptic maybe, but when we look from another perspective or if we're given another clue, the opaque can suddenly become transparent and that for which we search might be right under our very nose.' She smiled at Tony. 'That's what our job is all about. It's putting disparate facts in a line or pattern and seeing if there's a connection. It's commonly referred to as good police work.'

There was an immediate lightening in the atmosphere.

'Here we're collecting facts, and it's funny that suddenly one of the facts we were given from my source is a female by the name of Gittings. She's now gone the way of all flesh. We believe that one that Skeeter's been hounding has also bitten the dust and the one she suspects has disappeared. We have no record of them.'

'His name, Flamur, is all we have.'

'We need to find the other characters.' She turned to the board. 'Asif Rehman, the Bully, Don Benson, Blusher, and Doc, let's not forget, Doc, a certain Mansoor Kamman.'

April's mobile signalled a text. Ignoring it she continued. 'I believe we've seen a slowing in the moped crime incidents?' She addressed Skeeter.

'Indeed. Another reason why Tony and I believe something else is happening. It's not been as quiet as this for over twelve months and I don't believe it's because of our man from the beach, or that Gittings and Kelly are out of the equation. It's something more than that.'

Lucy tapped the board. 'Our beach find was tortured, we know that. We have evidence Gittings self-harmed, but right now that's an assumption, and therefore we can't be fully sure. We have the fire and one seriously burned body. What state was he in before the fire, alive or dead?'

'We'll await the post mortem, Lucy, and not jump to conclusions. We've work to do.'

April moved away and found her mobile. She read the message. 'Hold up!' She turned to the group who were just leaving. 'My contact has details of a woman we might be looking for. There's no name but I'm assuming it's Kelly.'

Lucy looked back at April. 'Do I have a visit to look forward to?'

April smiled.

Kelly left the night shelter earlier than necessary. She had showered, dressed in a change of clothes she had selected from what was on offer, collected toiletries and self-referred for one more night's stay. The experience had been better than she could have imagined. The food was good as was the bed, an inflated mattress positioned next to a chair and a wall socket. She had ensured she had taken any valuables into the shower leaving only her rucksack out in the changing area. The water had been hot and she had let it flow over her for possibly longer than was advisable. The night's stay was a world away from the brick tunnel she had occupied the previous two nights. It suddenly seemed so civilised, so human. Meeting Sharon, the girl from the doorway, had made a difference. She had forgotten what it was like to chat, relax and not keep looking over her shoulder. They had managed to stay close in the dorm too and that had helped. It would be good to see her if she returned later. She glanced across at the tree a short distance from the entrance. The colour and the blossom seemed to attract her. Crossing the narrow street, she touched the smooth bark. *I'm not normally a tree hugger,* she thought. Somehow, right now, it seemed appropriate and she felt an inner warmth, hoping that one day she might be able to trust again. She belched suddenly. Her stomach seemed full for the first time in days. Giggling to herself she could not remember the last time she had eaten porridge for breakfast. The day had started well.

* * *

Sadiq had laid the contents of the case on the bed. The kilo-gram bags were neatly positioned.

'Snow White has come home and she's brought not seven dwarves with her but thirty-eight. Let's say that at today's street prices and depending on how it's cut,' He turned to look at Doc, 'We've well over the million once expenses have been taken out. We're expecting another shipment in July.

Our elderly mules are winners. Should really refer to them as Neptune's Nymphs.' He laughed but no one joined him.

Doc's face remained expressionless. 'Let me know when and where and I'll sort the rest.' He turned and went to the front door. He glanced across at the girl now dressed and standing on the balcony. 'Does the boss know you're mixing business with pleasure?'

Sadiq came out of the bedroom and closed the door behind him. He studied Flamur who had been listening to the conversation. 'I'm sure he's aware. The girl knows nothing. Thick as pig shit too although a good Muslim boy shouldn't say that. He shouldn't drink or take drugs but … besides that's for me to know. We're brothers, we trust each other and remember, Doc, there's him and then next in command, me. Don't ever forget that.'

Doc left.

* * *

Kelly went into the library. She had listened to conversations within the hostel and many had referred to the facilities. It was a shelter in poor weather and you could read or simply sleep without being disturbed. The building was modern and bright, the toilets were clean too. To her left was a bank of computers, many were in use. She, on the other hand, wanted to sit down and put her life into some kind of perspective. Collecting a newspaper, she found a quiet seat between two book shelves and settled down. She would stay an hour or so, check what money she had left and then …

* * *

'Where did you get the information from last time, Lucy?' Tony asked as he stirred a mug of coffee with a pencil. 'When you met April's informant?' He licked the end before tucking it behind his ear.

'A coffee shop on the main pedestrian area, all cloak and dagger stuff. Made a change to be honest, a break from all the normal stuff. I was apprehensive, believe me. Knew what was expected but still nervous, and to think I used to work in Wigan. You never know what you're going to meet. April's right though, when she said that things go on under our noses all of the time. To think I used to believe paying for info was illegal. Happens a good deal from all accounts. I for one should have known that.'

'Live and learn, Lucy. Live and learn. Male or female your contact?'

'Official Secrets Act, Tony. Couldn't possibly say.'

'Yes, I know, if you told me, you'd have to kill me.' He moved away shaking his head. 'We're colleagues, we're supposed to share everything.'

Skeeter was checking the report of the fire but she was more interested in Malik and Flamur. She had worked with the EvoFit team in facial recognition and they had configured images for both men. She wanted to check with Jane from Environmental Health to see if the image created matched her recollection of Malik. Jane could check against the images from her body cam. It was to be done in this order for two reasons. The first was to check her own memory and therefore the quality of the likeness produced. Secondly if she had managed to create an accurate image of him, the likelihood was she had also captured Flamur too. Facial recognition had come a long way from the days of the police artist and because of the progress the success rate had increased exponentially.

'Jane, thanks for taking part. Your thoughts?'

'Malik Buruk without question. I had him slightly more threatening but that was probably my nerves. Firstly, did you receive the images you requested looking over the counter, the still shots of the clock?'

'Received and sent to the Forensics Team investigating the fire. Thanks very much.'

'Secondly, I've just sent the still images of Malik from the body cam. I was amazed how accurate the photofit image was.'

'Technology, Jane, helps fight the bad people. Thank you for those.'

'Happy to help. Data protection prevents the sending of the whole recording but if you need it, Skeeter, you know the process.'

Skeeter waited for the file to come through. Although the body cam image was grainy, it was adequate. Tony entered the room carrying a coffee.

'Tony, a minute.'

He ambled over, dragging a chair towards her workstation before resting his mug on the mat on her desk.

'Look at this!' She handed him the printed image.

'Malik. EvoFit. That's good. Did you know the system was first used by the Lancashire force? Learned that in training.'

Skeeter raised her eyebrows. 'You're happy with that?'

He nodded and collected his mug. 'Bloody good likeness from what I recall.'

'There's this too.' She handed him the second photofit image.

'It's the one you love to hate, it's Flam or to give him his full title, Flamur. Did you know the name Flamur means flag in Albanian?'

'Tony, the walking, talking encyclopædia. No, I didn't but I do now, thanks for sharing that. Before you go, I want you to look at these. They're the shots taken in the kebab shop when I was with Environmental Health. Look at the clock, your clock, after all you discovered its secret.'

She paused and went to the computer bringing up the forensic images of the scene of the fire. She turned it so they could both see the screen before flicking through the images until she found one that nearly matched that sent from Jane's bodycam.

'There's nothing, no melted plastic, no metal parts and no sign of batteries exploding against the wall. The nail is still in the blackened wall. I forwarded images of the place when I last visited and Forensics did a specific search. Their report suggests that the clock wasn't on site during the fire hence the blackened wall. They assure me that we'd have seen a different scenario if it had been in situ. They also checked for residue but there's none. It wasn't left anywhere in the building.'

'So, what else do they say?'

'Arson is a firm favourite. Pathology are still working on the burned remnants but they've confirmed it's Malik's body. DNA shows that our plain and simple Malik was anything but. Mixed history. It's all on file and will be added for the next briefing. It'll be another twenty-four hours before they have a definite cause of death, but for me I'm convinced,

Tony, that he didn't fall down the steps carrying a candle in his cap and gown.'

'Briefing in ten. Incident Room!' April shouted from the far door.

Skeeter looked at Tony. 'Shit's hit the fan if I know that tone of voice.'

CHAPTER 21

The Incident Room was full. Officers leaned against the desks whilst some quickly checked the boards trying to see what the fuss was about. Brad was the last in and it did not go unnoticed.

'Thanks for dropping everything. This is DCI Bob Lawn, some of you may have met before. National Crime Agency. One or two of you have had your antennae ruffled with things going quiet in this area of Merseyside, apart from the one knifing and the possible arson. We believe these are linked to the same group, the ones moving drugs and possibly fuelling the motorcycle crime that's been growing over the last eighteen months.' April stepped aside.

'Afternoon. If we've not met before let me just say I've heard all the quips about my name, and no, the grass doesn't grow under my feet, size eleven too.' He held up a large and shiny brogue. 'I neither have an affinity for weeding grass out of criminals, nor do I smoke it and I know I'm not on my home turf ... But saying that, I'm always willing to hear a fresh pun.' He smiled noticing the team before him relax; it had broken the ice.

'We have firm evidence that a large shipment of cocaine is either due to arrive in Liverpool or has just arrived. We're talking a million quid plus but that's merely an estimation. We also know it's coming in by sea, but from where and to where is the million-dollar question. Things either heat up or cool down before a big shipment and looking at the statistics we see for this area it shows that pattern quite clearly. The container port is a likely area and that's being checked thoroughly by Her Majesty's Customs and Excise and Border Force is doubling its activities. This stuff could also come in on fishing boats, ferries, yachts. Everything is being tracked.'

'Liners?' Lucy asked. 'There was one in a couple of days ago and there's one due in I think Thursday.'

'Routine checks were carried out on ...' he looked at his notes. '*The Dawn Lady*. From the Caribbean. We have the next one marked for a more detailed search when she docks. To come back to your point, though, the crew list and the passenger list are being checked against the different ports at which the liner stopped. We'll be doing a full check on all passengers listed on that vessel, obviously starting with those who make regular trips to the same places. I'd be grateful if you can keep everything you find uploaded so that all intelligence is shared. If the shipment is already here, then we're probably too late. We know from experience that it will soon be distributed; they'll not keep all of their eggs in one basket. I'll be functioning from Liver Street for the next week or so. Staying at the Ibis so any tips on pubs and restaurants would be a great help. I'll give the galleries and museums a pass on this occasion, maybe next time.'

* * *

For the first time in a while, and after only ten minutes in the library, Kelly felt herself relax. She had £127.59, some toiletries, three changes of clean underwear and the clothes she stood up in. She would be able to get a change that evening and she would target a few charity shops during the day. Jeans and a few sweaters would be a start.

Collecting some paper and a pen from one of the work stations, she jotted down the numbers Abid had read to her. She smiled, it reminded her of a memory she held of her foster parent playing *little piggies*. She began to recite it, *this little piggy had roast beef ... roast beef, when was the last time I tasted that?*

She wrote down the numbers in the order she recalled before checking them against the small piece of material. On this occasion it stayed safely wrapped in the plastic: 66, 82, 69, 65, 68. She pondered the odd one out, the highest number in the group, hardly the runt. She believed that the numbers on her fingers were 66, 69 and 68. The tattoo on the index finger, a squiggle was supposed to mean *remember* and according to Abid, the last, *love*. The time seemed to pass quickly when she was focused, warm and without worry.

* * *

The evening was brighter than on Lucy's previous visit. The instructions were different too. It was a simple case of calling into a pub and asking for an envelope that had been left. Why it could not just be posted she could not fathom. On the first occasion the man knew that the information had been received and therefore payment would follow, but the collection in a pub?

She knew *The Railway*, a large, red bricked edifice opposite Wigan's main station and very close to the bus stop. Not only was the weather kinder this time, the journey was less fraught as she had travelled later. The bus had moved past too quickly for her to check to see if the head was still on the stick but as she passed the memory brought a smile.

The pub was bright and she immediately thought of April. The Victorian stained glass seemed to fill the place. Green tiles edged the bottom of the walls and the rich red of mahogany made her appreciate how much money was invested in these establishments so long ago. It had, however, kept up with the times as a large screen on the far wall displayed a football match. She ordered a gin and tonic.

'What make of gin, love?' the server behind the counter asked pointing to a vast array of bottles set before a diamond cut mirror.

'Any will be fine.'

'And the tonic ... any, too?'

They both chuckled. 'I'm a simple lass. However, I do have a special request.'

As the drink was being prepared the lady turned. 'I can't turn the football off or they'll put me in the market stocks.' More chuckles followed.

'No, I'm supposed to collect a note from a friend. They said they'd leave it here.'

'You must be Lucy, then? We do get some strange requests. Are we playing an illicit game of cupid?' She winked presumptuously as she placed the large bowl on the bar, gave it a stir and then returned to the far end. 'Here you are, love. Just sign that to say you've taken it, ta!'

Lucy felt herself blush a little. Now she knew why it had not been posted. Moving to find a quiet corner she settled, taking a drink from her glass. From the corner of her eye, she thought she saw a familiar face, a man who was just leaving. However, she was not sure if it were the man from the café. Opening the envelope, she pulled out a single sheet of paper.

The two mopeds moved along the side of the traffic, one with a pillion, the other just the driver. All three were wearing helmets and fluorescent jackets and travelling at a steady pace. A few heads turned and people instinctively moved away from the kerb. They passed by innocently. They were heading for Salthouse Quay. At this time of day, it would be busy with tourists and that meant phones, cameras and bags. They would be concentrating on their surroundings and not on them.

Approaching the Albert Dock, the rear bike slowed to add distance between each of them. The first bike turned in after allowing the traffic to pass. Everything had to look normal, it was a game of stealth, a challenge and it felt good to be back.

The tourists were there in full. The first bike pulled to the side of the road and waited. It was all about finding the right target. Sadiq's words rang in Quasim's ears.

The hunting animal chasing the herd will only see one of the many and no matter how close another of the herd comes, the hunter will stay focused on the selected one ignoring all else. That is why the big cats survive, they have an inner discipline. You will pick one target from the crowd and that is the one you will strike.

Scanning the road, he slowly moved from the kerb and followed a car along the one-way system. On turning left at the top, he spotted his target, a woman. The bag was by her feet as she steadied the camera she held. Her gaze was away from the oncoming traffic. She appeared to be alone. He tapped his pillion's knee and called out the coat colour of the target. He received a response as the pillion tapped his shoulder. They were now as one.

Twisting the throttle, the moped screamed along the road keeping as close to the kerb as possible. Quasim switched his weight to the right side expecting the pillion to lean to the left as his job was to snatch the camera. People turned on hearing the high-pitched sound, but their prey did not. In one swift, yet destabilising moment, they struck. The bag was collected from between her feet. Quasim had the camera; the strap still around her neck took her off her feet in the direction of the moving bike. The sudden force of her fall whipped the strap from her as she crashed face first onto the road. She neither had time to scream nor hold out her hands. Her face meeting the cobbles took the full force. The second bike screamed past before turning right as the lead bike went left; a strategy to confuse. Both bikes had a rendezvous planned.

Quasim steered the moped to the end of Gower Street; it meant a left turn. He instinctively bumped the kerb and drove under a stone arch – a remnant of the old docks. He was on the pavement. Here he was free to squeeze every ounce of power from the feeble machine as he dodged those walking in either direction. Those seeing the approaching bike could avoid its path and move quickly to the sides. He could see the police headquarters to his right across The Strand and he raised his right hand and then his middle finger before turning to laugh with his pillion, and so he failed to see the two officers running towards their approaching bike; neither did he see one remove his baton before he crouched. As the moped passed, the officer threw the baton at the front wheel.

Quasim felt the sudden jerk, as the baton jammed within the spokes and the forks jarred and twisted the front wheel. The sudden jolt turned the bars to the right throwing his hands clear. It took only a second for Newton's First Law to come into effect. As the bike came to a sudden halt, both bodies carried on travelling before crashing to the pavement. The bike's engine screamed as if in protest.

Both officers were prepared; they each took a youth. The pillion, who seemed to travel the further, lay motionless. The force of the immediate ejection from the bike had removed his ill-fitting helmet and the left side of his skull had made contact with the pavement. He was going nowhere. Quasim had landed on his left shoulder and he knew instantly his collar bone was broken. Seconds later, when the officer pulled both arms behind him to attach the cuffs, it was confirmed to everyone in the vicinity. His piercing cry caused the seabirds sitting along the dock railing to take to the air. The bike engine had now stopped screaming. The bag and the camera had landed further along the pavement.

A crowd quickly gathered. Those whom the bike had narrowly missed were first on the scene quickly followed by a police car. The officer let his right knee rest in the small of Quasim's back as he called for medical assistance.

CHAPTER 22

Lucy could hear the light beat of a rhythm being tapped out before she saw April. She paused and watched from a distance. April let the sticks hit the wad of paper before finishing with one last strike, the stick hit the side of a cup as if it were a cymbal. It was as that last stick struck its target that she noticed Lucy. She smiled and let one of the sticks swirl as if attached to her fingers. It was like magic.

'Very impressive. I've seen professional drummers do that. Played long?'

'Just a hobby. Gets rid of all the inner demons and by golly this job brings enough of those. Thanks for the call last night. So, we've located Kelly in Wigan and she's been identified by both name and the tattoo?'

'According to this we have. We also know where she might have stayed last night.' Lucy waved the envelope she had collected the previous evening.

'Just in case, I'm treading carefully. Don't add this to the board yet, Lucy, I have to clear a path to get to this girl without making her run. I need to find a way to communicate and get her to trust me.'

'Good luck with that challenge. It might be easier to plait smoke.'

Lucy dropped the envelope on the desk and left April as she picked up the phone. Arriving in the corridor she met Tony.

'How's my Bond girl? Good night?' He whistled the Bond tune.

Taking up a karate stance she whispered, 'Pub this time or did I already tell you that? We think we've found the girl. Sorry, that's factually incorrect being a copper. We've located Kelly's whereabouts; we just have to work out a way to get to her and then get her to chat with us.'

'Mission impossible.'

'You watch too many films.'

'A couple of homeless hostels there I'd have thought. Brad was asking earlier. Have you heard about the officer who's foiled the moped mugging? His quick thinking's got two in custody, well, one, the other has a severe head injury. Was just going to let Skeeter know. She'll be made up.'

The results of Malik Buruk's post mortem had come through. Skeeter wasted no time. Further trawling had shown his past criminal affiliations. There was also evidence that he was under surveillance by a neighbouring force for inappropriate sexual activity with minors, information which is not generally logged within the main system for obvious reasons. Aware that his name was linked with a child grooming gang, the investigation, she knew, would be kept concealed. Skeeter laughed. *It was more likely they didn't want to upset a racial applecart as we've been seeing all too clearly within other forces,* she thought, and she was not the only one to hold this opinion. Clear guidelines had dropped on most desks.

There had been too many cover-ups and she, for one, was growing tired of the manner in which certain elements of society were treated preferentially as if they were immune from public scrutiny. From directives she had received from those higher up within the force, she had on occasion, felt hobbled. It seemed she must tread on egg shells when dealing with accusations of criminal activity within certain ethnic minorities. She had been reprimanded twice for voicing her concerns. This was one reason she believed promotion was slow in coming her way.

The images of the corpse were disturbing and reminded her of victims, the white contorted figures she had seen at the museum in Pompeii, only Malik's was as black as coal. No matter how long you had been involved in this criminal world you never seemed to be able to respond without some emotional involvement. The skull, looking as if it had been in the ground for years, stared to the side. The remnants of what might be facial skin and muscle had been drawn back forcing a terrifying rictus and exposing what remained of the gold teeth. She wondered why they had not melted. Annoyingly, he still seemed to be smirking at her in death.

The torso looked as though he was curled, his arms tucked towards his chest and his legs bent at different angles as if he were about to run. It echoed a boxer's stance, but this was a horizontal pose not vertical. Previous experience had taught her that this was termed the pugilistic attitude and was often seen in severe burn victims as the body tightens and draws in. It was surprising from the report that peri-mortem injuries could not be effectively aged. Lung samples clearly showed that smoke asphyxiation was the cause of death, but it was classed as laryngospasm, a symptom which would lead to heart failure.

Skeeter referred to the detailed plan made of the building's lower floor, showing where the fire was believed to have started, the position of the rooms and crucially, the corpse. Why he was positioned where he was might never be known. Focusing on the close-up images of the arms and legs she could also detect what looked like marks around each wrist. Referring to the report there was no mention of any ligatures. She reached for the phone.

'DS Skeeter Warlock.' She began with the usual pleas-antries. 'I'm just going through the Pathology Report on Malik Buruk.' She read the reference number. 'Can you just confirm that the indentations I see on either wrist are not from ligatures?'

The answer was clear and precise. Apparently, the mark-ings she had detected were common in such cases. The pseudo ligature marks were due to the victim wearing tight sleeves or to an item of clothing that has been incinerated and contracted around the cuff area. She felt a little foolish for asking as if she were grasping at straws.

However, what did attract Skeeter's keen eye were remnants of Malik's personal items found in the vicinity of his right trouser pocket. They were clearly labelled as 'coins' and 'keys'. These objects had been trapped at the site of the body between the concrete floor and his thigh. There was also evidence of some form of plastic that had melted and adhered to the femur. Further Forensic tests would be needed to confirm but it was believed to be part of a keyring. A belt buckle was also found along with a knife and a number of small, metal containers. It was thought that these were probably stored beneath the stairs and the collapse had brought the burning timber and Malik's body into close contact.

The second part of the report had been submitted by Fire Service Forensic experts. It seemed clear where the fire had started and that an accelerant had been used. It also indicated that the same substance had been applied to the stairs and possibly linked to the initial origin. These areas were marked in red on the plan. 'Arson,' she said out loud. 'Plain and simple, but was it murder or was his death a case of being bloody careless, an accident? In either case, where was Flamur when all of this was going on? More importantly, where is he now?' She tapped the pencil against her lips, feeling as though she were no further on. Tony coming in was a light relief and his news was just the fillip she needed.

* * *

Bob Lawn sat alone on the bench on the edge of Chavasse Park, a man-made, trench-like piece of open space set within the modern development. A disposable cup of coffee rested next to him. He had come there not only to reflect on the case in hand but to pay homage to one of his heroes: Noel Godfrey Chavasse VC and Bar, MC. The very man was celebrated here and for good reason – bravery above and beyond the call of duty.

Chavasse was born in Oxford but moved to Liverpool when his father was made Bishop of the city in 1900. He was a medical doctor, an Olympic athlete and an army officer, the only man to be awarded two Victoria Crosses during the First World War. Sadly, Noel Chavasse died of wounds and was buried in Brandhoek. Although this memorial was dedicated to the family, it was Noel on whom Bob allowed his thoughts to dwell. He reread the history on his phone whilst occasionally taking a sip of coffee. Sitting back, he thought of the previous day's action that had taken place just in front of his present perch. It had been the talk of the station. It had even been captured on the cameras that were a key feature on all external walls of the police building. The action was brave, the officer stopping the speeding moped. His quick thinking and courageous action not only brought two criminals to justice but also prevented further crimes and public injury. *Bravery is still here,* he thought. *It's in us all and comes to the surface when the time is right. He deserves a Queen's Medal.* Bob doubted it would be forthcoming.

A gull screamed as it approached only metres from his head. It was refreshing to be out of the office, even for the twenty minutes it took to drink his coffee. DCI Lawn's team of three had covered twenty-five percent of the passengers from *The Dawn Lady* thought to be possibilities. The criteria for this type of investigation were pre-set and in the past had proved to be successful. There was no need to pay each person on the list a visit; that pleasure would be reserved for those who appeared towards the end of the search – the likely candidates. Bob Lawn had calculated that he could finish investigating this first liner before the next docked. The second process, however, would be more controlled as all passengers would be in situ and would not be leaving the ship until everything had been scrupulously checked and double-checked. He was a great believer in the modern criminal's rationale of sending out a dummy run, a minor prize to trick law enforcement into taking their eye off the real prize. He finished his coffee and returned to the office. He felt recharged.

It was the medical records from the cruise that captured his eye and, in particular, an accident to a passenger that had occurred a short time before the cruise's docking. He checked the date on the report and the name: *Brinkman, Lynn. Sixty-seven years of age. Tripped on the stairs causing facial bruising and injury to her ankle.* He flicked through the treatment given, cross-referencing with the passenger log. Partner was Arthur James Brinkman, seventy-one years old. He noted their address in Lytham St Annes. Within minutes he had found their booking details. The fact that they had stayed overnight and used the carpark facility for the duration of the cruise, brought a tingle, what he called his copper's nose, when the mundane suddenly becomes exciting. He would call up the ship's CCTV from the day of disembarkation and that from within the landing stage cruise terminal. He also wanted to interview the stewards who had looked after their cabin and also the porters. That request had been sent. If the itch was still there it would be to the hotel carpark he would then turn. He made a note to collate the material as soon as possible to ensure nothing was lost. He logged a Person's Enquiry but it showed no previous police record for either Brinkman.

* * *

April had wasted no time and had liaised with colleagues at Wigan Police. Their co-operation in the case was assured. They had agreed to search for Sharon in the hope that they would be in a position to offer further information. Once she had been traced it was best, they thought, to use an independent, qualified Family Liaison Officer to instigate contact. At this stage, approaching the three homeless shelters in the town would be a step too far. They treated the details of those seeking help and support with strict confidence. Many might be running from abusive relationships and this was clearly understood by all concerned. Both the police and those involved with the homeless had strict professional guidelines and each was aware that those lines, unless in the cases of serious crime or to help prevent a serious crime, should not be crossed. A briefing of the PCSOs who worked the town centre had discovered that two females were regularly moved on from doorways and parks. At this stage, it was their responsibility to find Sharon and if possible, Kelly.

What April did not want to do at this stage was to scare her into vanishing – Kelly had done that effectively in the past and she was aware that this element of police work had to be handled sensitively. She had kept the team informed in the early briefing. She checked her watch. As well as sending information down the chain of command, she also had to show progress with her superior. Detective Chief Inspector Alex Mason had invited her to his office that afternoon on the pretext of assessing how she was settling in.

Driving down to the Liverpool Police Headquarters she approached the dock road, admiring the docks' splendour. At this point they were still bustling and what she thought to be huge concrete grain stores intrigued her. She decided that when time allowed, she would find out more about her fascinating and historical new home. There were so many places to see away from the usual haunts that attracted the working police. She would make a mental list and *The Cavern Club* would be somewhere near the top.

Entering the station's security gate, the guard instructed her where to park. The large, modern, red brick building was as close to the river front as the newer builds could be, the front being a UNESCO World Heritage site. Positioned next to the bus station and *Liverpool One*, the huge shopping area, it was ideally situated. A newer Police Transport Hub had been built further out of the city centre. She stood and admired the eight or nine floors and smiled at what appeared to be copper-coloured tinted glass; an architect with a sense of humour. She chuckled to herself.

Past the initial security, she slipped on the lanyard and headed for the seventh floor. She had met Alex on a few occasions, some here in this office but generally it had been back at Copy Lane. The door to his office, if you could call a pigeonholed area of an open-plan space an office, was ajar when she arrived. Checking her watch, she was a little early. She knocked, noticing his name on the door.

'Come in April. Coffee?'

April smiled. 'Thank you, sir.'

'Alex, please, when we're within these four walls – sir we'll keep for the more formal meetings.' He raised his eyebrows as if ensuring she fully understood. He did not await a response. 'Have a seat. Milk and sugar?'

'Just black, please.'

There was only the one chair in front of his desk.

'You'll have heard we've one of the gang – the moped

boys we've been after – in custody. As my old boss used to say, "If you wait long enough they come to you!" He chuckled and brought the coffee. 'We're lucky we had a quick-thinking colleague on patrol. Anyway, the rider's downstairs. Doctor checked him yesterday and he's fine to interview. We're awaiting a Toxicology Report but we found traces of class A drugs about his person.'

'The second one, the pillion, was a little more shaken, I heard.'

'Intensive Care. Tests there proved positive for cocaine, high quality too, and there's a suggestion that it was buffed with fentanyl.' He raised his eyebrows again. It seemed a habit. 'Those supplying to these lads are not just dealing with shit stuff. Suggests these boys and girls are linked to the main supplier. The shit stuff for cutting, your caffeine and laxatives will be added lower down the chain or when they pass it on. Much of what we're seeing on the streets, as I'm sure you know, has been cut and buffed several times. Let's say the profits have been stretched as far as possible.

'We've run the CCTV of those leaving the scene of Beverley Gittings's murder and I'm assured that there's a likely match with our chap downstairs. Not too sure as to the other fellow as his face matches a bus crash at present. We'll see what he has to say for himself when we present him with a murder charge. Usually focuses the mind of even those with the lowest IQ. We might also have a name. Finger prints have revealed nothing and we're awaiting DNA. This was not a lone wolf incident, April. The bike was stolen so at least we have him on that count too! I believe Skeeter Warlock's been running that side of the investigation. Tenacious young lady whom, if I can say it in these politically correct days, you wouldn't want to meet down a dark alley. Please invite her to call in on our lad. I'd have contacted her this morning but knowing you were in today I think it's better coming from you, being her direct senior. Keeps everything in place, I think, a certain order.'

April smiled. She knew that it would make Skeeter's day.

The meeting lasted just over the hour and April came away feeling more reassured that the work she was doing was deemed both efficient and valuable. Leaving the office with a lighter step than when she had arrived, she called Skeeter, imparting the good news.

CHAPTER 23

Flamur stood by the large expanse of glass looking out across the Mersey. Sadiq paced the room. It was apparent from the raised voice that the caller on the other end of the phone was not in the best of moods.

'It's been moved, yes and Doc is doing his stuff. The cutting agents are there, I checked this morning although they're getting more difficult to come by. The prices are rising ... might have to use shit stuff if this goes on.'

The voice on the other end was raised yet again and Sadiq moved the phone some distance from his ear. Looking at Flamur, he shook his head. He put the phone on speaker.

'No, nothing on Chelle, why?' He brought the phone closer. The rant was over and he continued to listen.

'She's in Wigan. It's from a good source. Get the word out and Sadiq ... get Snow White moving and fast.'

'Yes, bro.'

'Discretion and if you're unfamiliar with the word, talk to Flamur, he's with you. He knows all about it. Trust me. And whilst you're at it, ask him to give you chapter and verse on Malik.' He ended the call.

Sadiq frowned. 'Says you know all about Malik.'

Flamur turned his gaze towards the view. 'I know more than you think about many, many things, Sadiq. Remember, it's always good to let people believe that they hold more power than they actually do. Why? I hear you think. Because, when it's taken away, they become lambs to the slaughter. You give them power and let them shout and scream, let them feel high and mighty, indispensable, until, that is, they are no longer needed or they've served their purpose. My father back home taught me. We kept goats, we reared them, protected them, fed them and bred them. We cherished them like we cherished our own family. However, when we were hungry, we killed them. Life is simple and we are life. Never forget.'

Sadiq looked at Flamur and then the phone, said nothing but understood much.

* * *

The day had felt like two as Skeeter packed away her belongings. She had to be at the main station in the city centre the following day. Adjusting the trophy that sat on the pile of papers, she took a second to study the engraved date on the dulled brass plaque. She breathed on it before rubbing it on her sleeve. It seemed like only yesterday. It was a critical Catch as Catch Can bout and a vital win. The whole wrestling competition had been difficult but the final scrap had been touch and go as to who would win. She raised her hand to her ear; the permanent swelling had been a direct result of that fight. Initially she had loathed the damage but very soon she treated it as a badge of honour.

The paper dart landing on her desk made her jump. She turned to see Tony grinning from behind his computer screen. 'When did you come back? You said you had an important call to make, that wouldn't wait.'

'Ages, you were engrossed and I didn't want to disturb you. Are we having a pint or not? Fancy a pub meal too, can't really be arsed cooking tonight.'

'I was …'

He held up a finger as he approached, took the trophy from her hand placing it back on the pile and then took her arm. 'Now or I'm going without you.'

The pub was quiet for just after six. Skeeter had a pint and Tony a large glass of red wine. They perused the menu. 'Being a Wiganer, it's got to be the pie and chips.' Skeeter picked up her beer and sank half. 'I needed that, mate. Didn't have you as a wine man.'

He lifted his glass and in doing so stuck out his little finger. 'Can't judge a book by its cover.'

He grinned, checked the table number and went to the bar to order. Tony's phone vibrated and Skeeter looked across at the screen. It rang three times and then stopped. A minute later the message tone sounded. He returned with another round of drinks. 'Save getting up when the food comes. I'll get this. Some luck on the horses. My treat.'

'Didn't know you enjoyed a flutter. Your phone rang when you were at the bar. Cheers.'

Picking up the phone he checked it, pulled a face and slipped it into his pocket. 'Loo, won't be a tick and if the meals arrive don't nick any of my chips.'

The meals came soon after he had left but she waited politely other than taking a chip and tasting it. He returned and pointed. 'That better have come from your plate, Warlock, or there'll be hell to pay.'

'Checking it wasn't poisoned. You're fine.' Her expression did not change as she plunged her knife into the pie allowing the gravy to leach onto the plate.

'This is good.' Tony looked up.

'Was the call important? You could have phoned from here, no need to go into the bog.'

Tony blushed slightly. 'Girl trouble. It'll pass.'

Skeeter was neither stupid nor foolish and she chose to store that nugget.

* * *

Bob Lawn checked his watch, he seemed to be doing it a lot lately. He had sent the other members of the team off an hour ago. Sitting back in the chair he put his hands behind his head and stretched. He wanted to check the video of the disembarkation of the The Dawn Lady. He had viewed footage of the couple, the Brinkmans, and he was beginning to doubt his initial premise. He had allowed himself one more hour and he would be meeting the group at an Italian restaurant by the Wheel of Liverpool.

Bob allowed the video footage to speed through, his finger on the mouse ready to pause at any moment. It was seeing the wheelchair that made his finger click on the mouse. He enlarged the image, and although grainy, it was clear enough to make out the crutches held to the side as well as the porter and Arthur. Bob focused on the bag Arthur Brinkman was carrying; for hand luggage it appeared larger than those carried by other passengers. Returning the video to its normal speed, he watched as Lynn took herself unaided from the wheelchair before moving to a seat. The crutches seemed ineffective as if she had not used them before. His curiosity was spiked. He saw Arthur tip the porter after he had returned with three other cases. They would have been checked as they were taken through customs. He paused the video again taking a screen shot of the luggage. On restarting the video, he witnessed Arthur lean and kiss his wife before he left wheeling the case that had never left his hand. Within fifteen minutes he reappeared in the car, helped her into the passenger seat and loaded up.

'Now why did you take that case all the way to the garage when you were bringing the car back here? Why not leave it with your wife and your other luggage?' Bob pondered out loud. The same strong nag now returned, a copper's curiosity as his wife called it. He knew it was usually accurate and suddenly he felt rejuvenated. Pausing the tape again, he saw the porter return waving something which he quickly realised was a book. What really caught his attention, however, was the car stalling as it pulled away. Just a stall, moving a foot too quickly off the clutch. That, to an experienced driver at least, occurred when flustered or anxious.

Something did not gel. Having watched others depart there was not all of this fuss. He wanted to look at the footage from the hotel carpark but his stomach protested in a different way and angrily at that. It had been neglected since breakfast, and besides, he had to meet his colleagues. One thing was sure, he had much to discuss.

CHAPTER 24

Bob Lawn had not been the only one working late. Lucy had delegated a search through the statements to ensure everything had been logged. DC Michael Peet was on lates. He enjoyed the station when it was not operating at full blast, he could concentrate. He had always wanted to be a lawyer but his partner's pregnancy in the second year of university had stopped that idea in its tracks. Quickly married, he joined the force and with the arrival of a second and then a third child, he saw his police career being the one he should focus on. Working lates also gave him respite from the kids.

It was whilst reading the report taken during the interview with Eileen Toland that Michael's sharp eyes spotted something that might not have been fully considered. He checked all the details for the man found on Ainsdale beach before progressing. His hunch proved to be correct. The report stated that the male staying at the flat, the man believed to have been found on the beach, was a bit of a geek and that he owned computers. It was the term 'geek' and the sentence 'a couple of those laptops on the go' that arrested his attention. Michael jotted down the notes, sent a copy to April and attached the other to the Incident Room boards. It was highlighted in blue. According to the reports neither of these computers had been found during the forensic search of the flat.

He went for a coffee and mulled over certain questions: had anyone searched or considered searching the lower apartment? Excepting personal items, the contents of the upper flat belonged to the Tolands. They had a key. When both occupants went missing how easy would it have been to take valuable items into safekeeping? These notions were accompanied by what seemed to be a small alarm in his head. A second gatekeeper's job was to look beyond the obvious, and not just what might have been missed, to try to knit the evidence together. That was his job tonight and it might have paid dividends. He decided to call his boss. It was nine thirty.

April was soldering the last of the joints on the second side of the stained-glass windows when the call came. He explained his findings and his thinking.

'That's another lead we need, Michael, good work. I'll sort out a warrant to search tomorrow. I'll ring DCI Mason in a moment. As it's a murder inquiry he should have no problems. Toland, on the other hand, will be a different kettle of fish. Something else, you're good with computers and such. Our man was murdered for some reason. From the evidence he was tortured before he was killed, you've read all of that. The question is, why? He was found with two things, the fake police medal and the Perspex disc. We know from where they originated. Please, give it some thought, see what clear thinking brings to that particular anomaly, and

Michael, thanks, and well done. If anything comes to mind, please leave your notes on my desk and any links you think relevant.'

April stood back. Such a simple thought but it could be a vital clue missed. She propped up the window with a light source behind it. As the glass was yet to be cemented in place, it rattled within the lead. Immediately the whole concept, the pattern and colour took on a new dimension, it became real and vibrant. It made her think of Michael. Looking with fresh eyes certainly helped you see things differently.

It was 7.45am when Sharon placed her two bags in the doorway of the old bank building, a place she had occupied for three days. As it was shallow and on the main road, the smell, unlike some empty shop door ways, was not reminiscent of a urinal. Tucking her knees to her chest, her hood up, she waited, staring at the immediate area before her like a patient kingfisher on a branch, only less colourful and certainly less successful.

Within thirty minutes she felt the presence of company. A woman dressed in a waterproof cotton jacket held a large takeout cup of coffee before her. Crouching on her haunches she leaned against the stone wall.

'Sharon?'

The girl did not move and her hands remained under the small blanket.

'A friend asked me to call, it's very important. This conversation and your help could save the life of someone you met recently … Kelly. She's in trouble with a gang which has already killed. We believe they will kill again.'

Sharon took the coffee.

'You can see my name on the cup and there's a phone number too. At the moment I work with the police although I am not a police officer. I work with people like you, Sharon, who might have accidentally found themselves vulnerable. I'm someone you can trust. If I found you, so can the gang. Where I want to just chat, they, on the other hand, will want immediate answers … I needn't say more. You're not naïve.'

Sharon looked at the cup before turning. 'Paula, when?'

'I think there's never a better time than the present.'

Paula stood and helped Sharon collect her things. Taking the cup from her she dropped it into a litter bin. Walking down Wallgate they reached the main railway station where a car was parked. The driver walked up to them.

'He's with me it's fine,' Paula reassured her.

He smiled and took Sharon's bags before putting them in the boot whilst Paula held open the rear door. Once closed she went around to the other side. Within minutes they were gone.

* * *

Skeeter arrived early at the Liverpool Police Headquarters, if only to look at the young man who had plagued her for quite some time. She had seen his photograph sent the previous day and had also watched the CCTV footage of the bike appearing from the Albert Dock and recklessly running down the pavement. Even knowing the final outcome, she still cringed as the pillion took the full force of the impact. Still, she could not prevent herself from smiling.

Once in the building, the formalities attended to, she met with DCI Mason in an office normally reserved for visiting solicitors.

'We'll use this and save going upstairs, Skeeter. Great to see you looking so fit and well. Still throwing your weight around in the wrestling world?'

'You know me, Alex. Keeps me physically and mentally fit. I get rid of all the crap this job throws at me and believe me you'd go mad if you didn't.'

'I could do with that myself. How are you taking to your new boss?' He looked away as if it were a casual, throwaway remark but she knew him too well.

'She's crap, Alex, if you want the truth. Couldn't find her arse with her hand in her back pocket.'

Alex Mason turned immediately but only found her grinning from ear to ear. 'She's my boss, new at this stage in the game and so she deserves and receives my trust, loyalty and respect just as you do. I neither tell tales out of school nor throw witches on the fire. You should know that but I'll be happy to castrate the little shit you have downstairs should you require. I've brought these.' She held out her hands in a cupping position. 'It'd just take a gentle squeeze.'

'I'm sure of that, I've felt your handshake.'

They both planned the strategy for the interview understanding that initially they would get, as Skeeter so aptly put it, 'diddly squat'. They were in no hurry. The other character involved was still in Intensive Care and so he would be going nowhere for some time unless he was called by a higher being. Considering his history, there was only one direction in which he would be travelling.

Quasim sat with only two legs of his chair pirouetting on the grey, polished floor. His knees rested against the edge of the table allowing him to swing gently back and forward. His hands were cuffed in front. The ceiling mounted cameras were trained directly at him and the microphones were positioned to catch every word. A large, intimidating officer stood by the door. Quasim hummed some indeterminable tune. Skeeter and Alex watched from the Control Room as if privately becoming acquainted with their subject.

'Ready?' Alex asked as he picked up the electronic tablet.

'Yes, indeed I am.'

The officer moved towards Quasim and lifted him to his feet as the door opened. Alex and Skeeter sat before him and strong hands forced him to sit.

'This is DS Warlock. You know my name and title but just in case it's slipped your mind I'll remind you, DCI Mason.' He watched as the suspect stared at his colleague.

'Warlock?' His tone was questioning as if asking him to clarify.

'DS Warlock. Correct.'

Quasim leaned forward. 'I've seen you before. I've seen those fucking googly eyes but you've never seen me. Knew you were a copper, a fucking ugly one. You look like a fucking witch too – googly-eyed fucking witch at that.' He grinned and started to swing again on the back two legs of his chair.

'Please don't swing as you might tip backwards, otherwise we'll remove the chair and you'll stand for this interview,' Alex instructed emphasising the word *tip* as he looked at the officer by the door who remained motionless. He had witnessed this before and knew the outcome.

Quasim continued to perform the action and he grinned directly at Alex. Skeeter slid her foot beneath the table and caught the front leg of his chair before applying a little upward force, tipping him just out of balance. His cuffed hands flew as if trying to catch the edge of the table to stabilise his backward rotation. They missed and he crashed to the floor. Skeeter looked at Alex and shrugged her shoulders.

'If the lad refuses to listen to reason.'

'You did that you poxy fucking witch, you kicked the fucking chair.'

She stood. 'Look at my legs. Are they long enough to go all the way under this table? I'm like you, vertically challenged.' She emphasised every syllable.

'Fuck right off.' He brought both hands up in front of him and extended the middle finger of each.

Skeeter smiled. She was getting beneath his skin just as they had planned. Even in today's sophisticated society there was still room for the good cop, bad cop routine. It was amazing how often it succeeded.

The officer lifted Quasim to his feet before moving the chair to one side. He returned to stand directly behind him.

'Quasim,' Alex started, bringing a frown to the lad's face. 'Yes, we know your name. We put the word out. Amazing what a few bob will buy in this fair city. Do you have a nickname? Let's guess … Grumpy? You know who he is, Quasim? No? He's one of Snow White's boys. All we want from you is Snow White's real name.'

Alex allowed the pause to linger as they both stared at the

lad. 'We have your DNA, lad, and we have DNA from a number of crimes and incidents. The bike attacks, the knife attacks, even a murder or two. Stays in place a long time DNA and can be found on skin, material, stone. A stone was next to where Beverley Gittings was cruelly knifed to death. Did you kill her?'

Quasim's eyes grew wider and they watched as his head involuntarily shook. He remained silent but the defiance was beginning to slip away.

'Evidence could point that way. Your DNA is left anywhere you've been so once the samples have been processed and checked against every crime in the city for the last few years, we'll be able to charge you for more than simply falling off a moped. We'll be able to charge you with murder. You'll be away a long time and if you come out, we'll be retired and a good deal of water will have flowed to the sea.'

It was Skeeter's turn. 'However, you've not heard the best. When we find the others who are responsible, we'll let them know just how co-operative you've been, how quickly you squealed. We'll even ensure you're allowed out early to see the grass grow. You know the term *grass*, Quasim, and you know what happens to those who are known to grass?'

She stood and went to the door. 'Now where did I leave my broomstick?' Turning she winked at Alex and left.

CHAPTER 25

April checked the boards in the Incident Room noting those highlighted in blue. She felt an eager anticipation to discover what Michael might have left on her desk. She was not disappointed. Next to her drum sticks was a blue folder, her name neatly written in block capitals. She removed the contents.

Not much, but it's a start! You might be familiar with some of the facts.

The discs were used as three-dimensional props on large cardboard advertising boards. These were usually placed in indoor shopping areas such as Liverpool One. Here's an image of that one in situ. The Perspex discs were stuck with a type of glue you find attached to your credit cards when you receive them by post or the front of a magazine cover when it's promoting something. It's easily removed. There are a number of makes and I've added a list on a separate attached sheet. I believe Forensics identified a trace on a disc found on the beach.

These boards were advertising bitcoins. You might remember a while back the value of this virtual currency started to climb at a phenomenal rate making some people bitcoin millionaires overnight. Although you invested real cash, you received virtual money that was stored on your computer. You could cash this in at any time or buy more. If, however, you lost the computer, you lost your investment whatever that might have been. Initially, some people invested and within months realised they were sitting on a fortune, then they realised they had disposed of the computer!

Bitcoins are made by 'mining' (I'd have to talk about that as it's not with a pick and shovel) and believe me, to mine one needs a great deal of computer power. It takes time, making some more valuable than others. As I say, that is a fascinating area of study but unnecessary to understand fully at this stage.

I've added links should you not be able to sleep and you need something soporific to help ... read these!
Theory One: Our man invested his own money in these coins. Two laptops, one he kept safe and possibly hidden unless seen by a nosy landlady. Whether he's worth a fortune we might never know unless we find them.

Theory Two: People heard about his investments and tortured him to get to them. If he made a fortune initially, withdrew it as cash and then invested again when the coins went rock bottom, he'd still have a tidy sum. To get to it they'd need his passwords, his bank account and knowledge of the worth of his investment.

Theory Three: He's been shifting their money into his accounts short term, making a fast buck and quickly withdrawing the funds.

That way he retains their cash but makes more. At first when the stock was rising rapidly, he might have thought he was onto a winner but with a sudden crash ... What do gamblers do? They push more in and keep their fingers crossed. It's an addiction and when you're playing with criminal proceeds you could get your fingers burned or possibly in his case ... removed!

Anyway, hypothetical rambling from a copper working the late shift but one based on facts from this case. It's now yours. By the time you're reading this I shall be in bed.

Michael

April read it through again, twice. In some ways she could see the logic, particularly in the third theory. She had seen avarice destroy coppers let alone criminals. An initial run of good luck can turn anyone; people who do not seem to have two pennies to rub together buying lottery tickets when there is more chance of being hit by a meteor than winning the jackpot. She was not foolish enough to believe people needed a light at the end of the tunnel. If it were the person's money they could do with it as they pleased but if it were not ... She would also run it past those in the dedicated Cyber Crime department to see if the theories were credible.

Within minutes she had sent the file to her team and her boss in the hope that it would speed the warrant to get into the Tolands' apartment.

Bob Lawn watched the CCTV images taken on the date of the *The Dawn Lady's* docking. Security at the hotel had been cleared to allow him access to the garage parking CCTV for the area used by the cruise company and long-stay customers. Should it prove useful to the enquiry, he would seek to get it copied for evidence, like he had done with the ship and the dock. He was fortunate to know the exact time Arthur Brinkman left the terminal area and could find that point on the recording with ease. He had also tracked the car and its registration; a white Skoda Superb. Within two minutes of the recording starting, he saw Brinkman, case in hand, approaching the lift. He appeared on the fourth level. Bob could clearly identify the Skoda even though it had been parked in a corner as far from the camera as possible. The next move both surprised and excited him. The indicators on the car positioned next to Brinkman's illuminated and flashed twice. The case was put into the boot. He appeared to remove a small bag before the lights flashed again, this time more quickly. He locked the car. The Skoda's lights then performed a similar ritual. Within five minutes Brinkman was heading for the ramp that would take him to the exit.

Bob made notes of the times from the markings to the bottom of the video. They were to the second. What he needed now was to find when that car in which he deposited the case left. Somehow, he felt it was going to be a long day.

* * *

April and Brad sat further down the road from the familiar address, that of the Tolands. They both knew the hostility they were about to face but it was a job that had to be done.

They had organised members of a specialist search team who, through experience, knew where to look. It was experience backed by scientific, social and psychological training. People, they had told April, tend to follow similar patterns, and by knowing and analysing those you could become extremely efficient in performing the job.

Looking in the rear-view mirror, Brad saw the van pull in behind. He eased the car forward affording them more room. April climbed out and walked to the van.

'Give us fifteen minutes or so. We'll give you a shout. This will go one of two ways but from meeting her before, I've a strong hunch which way that will be.' She pulled a face and ran a finger across her throat.

Brad left the car and they approached the front door. The Aspidistra was still in the window.

'Bet that's frightened of bloody wilting,' Brad remarked, 'no matter how close to death it gets.'

April pushed the bell. Within seconds, a face appeared by the moving curtain next to the plant. It was Francis, the husband. Moments later the door opened.

'Mrs Toland, DI Decent and DC Bradshaw. May we come in?'

Moving aside, Eileen Toland did not let her face slip. She wiped her hands on her apron and pointed to the mat. Brad immediately complied and wiped his feet.

'Go through to your left and take a seat.' The tone of her voice was sharp and direct leaving them in no doubt of her annoyance. 'And to what do we owe the pleasure of this visit?' Her tone swiftly changed as she raised her voice. 'Francis, we have visitors.'

For April, it was the perfect opening gambit. She did not

take up the offer of a seat but stood. Knowing from her attitude there was not going to be an easy way of approaching the reason for their visit, she decided to be direct. Francis appeared from the kitchen. Brad was disappointed, he was expecting him to be wearing Marigolds.

'You can sit, we'll not charge.' Francis's voice was light and he seemed a little nervous. April detected genuine concern. 'Have you found Chelle?'

It took the wind from her sails. She realised that they thought they had come to bring news, possibly bad. Taking a moment, she looked at them both. It was true, they were waiting for her response. She had badly misjudged the situation.

'Sorry, no, unfortunately. However, we do know she's safe. I don't think she'll be coming back here. Mrs Toland, you mentioned on our last visit that you thought her partner was,' she glanced at her notes, 'a geek. He had two laptop computers. Is that correct?'

'He did and in my eyes he was. Whenever I went up to see Chelle, check the place, like, and collect rent, or if something needed attending to. Did that regularly, saves trouble as everyone knows where they stand. It keeps the standards high. Where was I?'

'Her partner, computers.'

'Yes, sorry. He would be on the thing, sometimes two at the same time. On occasion he'd pick them up and go into their bedroom leaving Chelle and me to chat.'

'Did they have a big computer or did you only see laptops?'

During the interaction, Brad was observing Francis. He noticed that he looked anxious. He was wringing his hands.

'When was the last time you saw the computers?' April stared at Eileen and then at Francis.

'The last time I was in there with Chelle. They were on a table. If I remember correctly, one was on top of the other.'

'Was her partner still there or had he left?'

Eileen thought for a moment. 'If I'm honest, it was after he'd gone. Just before she went too. Yes, I'm sure, Inspector Decent.'

'I want you to think carefully before either of you answer this question and I also want you to come to the window.'

They moved over and April slipped back one of the curtains. 'You see the two people in that van?'

Francis and Eileen took it in turns to look and nodded, curiosity written all over their faces.

'Well, they're specialists.' April removed an envelope as they returned to the centre of the room. 'In here is a warrant to search the whole of these premises, not just the flat upstairs and the yard as we have already done, but also this flat.' She paused allowing the information to sink in. 'Those two people in the van, the specialists, are expert at finding missing objects – hidden objects, particularly things that people are apt to conceal.' Turning to look at Francis, she deliberately targeted him when speaking. 'Criminals have ways of making things, let's say, disappear but those two know every trick in the book. We believe those laptops are key pieces of evidence in solving a crime, your missing tenant and the death of the man we found on the beach, also the reason Chelle disappeared. They, and possibly other items, hold vital clues and we're desperate to find anything that will help us understand the reason for his death. Believe me, it was not a pleasant death either. Maybe, those responsible are also looking for the items too. As they weren't upstairs during our initial search and we don't believe Chelle took them, they must either be here or have been smuggled from the flat by somebody else. Mr Toland's mystery call from Chelle mentioned the person who came for her things when she was visiting her mother ... accident, she'd had an accident you said? When we were last here, you also mentioned that Chelle had given her key to someone.'

Francis flushed again. He nodded. 'That's what the person said when they rang. I assumed it to be Chelle. Didn't see them, like I told you last time.'

'Do you have a computer, Mr Toland?' She immediately saw him stiffen.

'No, never had one. Use one at the library occasionally, but, no.'

April smiled at Brad. 'Bring them in.'

Turning to the door, Brad left. 'We need to sit down. We never know how long these things take. The search could be all over in fifteen minutes or could take all day. They'll be as careful as possible, Mrs Toland, don't worry yourself.'

'Is this allowed? It's our home?' Eileen blustered; aggression again evident in her voice.

April handed her the warrant. 'Totally legal, Mrs Toland. If you'll kindly show them the rooms in the flat and then come back here. Once they are orientated, they'll do their stuff.'

'There'll be no dogs? Francis is allergic to dogs,' she pleaded.

'We're looking for computers, not drugs. There's no dog.'

* * *

Sharon had been co-operative and once over the initial anxiety and uncertainty of knowing she was in the company of the police, she quickly realised the gravity of Kelly's position and opened up to Paula. She described her time sleeping rough and how her experience of such people had educated her, not only about the kindness fellow human beings can demonstrate but also the sheer evil and cruelty of which they are capable. They had talked of her first meeting with Kelly and the short time they had been together in the night shelter. She had spoken to Kelly longer than she had talked to any person for as long as she could remember. Paula listened to the recorded informal interview.

'Kelly seemed relaxed throughout. Even when we met, she was kind, gave me a couple of quid. I could see that she'd not been on the streets long and I don't mean ... you know. I told her about *The Corner Stone*, the charity set up to help the homeless and support families in need – food banks and the like. They run night shelters around here. It was there we met again.'

'Was there anything you noticed about her?' Paula hated the sound of her own voice and cringed a little. 'Did she talk much about her past?'

'She went through everything. I thought I'd had a bad life but she ... and her being in a gang. She used to call herself Chelle Pearson ... think it was Pearson, and then with the loss of her fella.' There was a long pause. 'She told me his name too. I try to remember by putting the things or names next to a picture. She had a piece of his clothing; said she could still smell him and that helped.'

'What was his name, Sharon? This is so important.'

CHAPTER 26

B ob Lawn paused the fast-forwarding video each time someone appeared in shot. He had decided to concentrate on the one camera showing the car until the owner arrived. From tracking times, he could look at the others from around the building. On this occasion he slowed the moving image as the smartly dressed man, briefcase in hand, approached the car.

'Bingo!' He continued to observe. The pattern was familiar. The boot was opened and he saw him drop in the briefcase. He watched as the other case, the one Brinkman had left was checked: it was not opened, only weighed in his hands before being replaced. It had been over forty-eight hours since the case had been deposited. *This group was good. Professional and not hurried,* Bob thought, *but maybe just not good enough.*

He viewed the other cameras in the building and still images of the man were taken to be run in conjunction with facial recognition software. Bob already knew that the car plates were cloned. However, the information came back suggesting the car had recently been resprayed a different colour and was stolen a month prior to the car being detected. Finding it now would be useful but not essential and if he were honest, unlikely. He organised a watch on Arthur and Lynn Brinkman's home. He also requested details of their banking history.

* * *

April watched as Eileen Toland grew more anxious as the noise of the search became louder. The occasional crash brought both frustration and anger to her features. 'Damage will have to be paid for, you do know that?'

April did not reply. Within twenty minutes of searching the area under the stairs, an officer dressed in a full protective paper suit, gloves and shoes appeared in the room. Approaching April, he raised his eyebrows. April stood and followed him out of the room. He pointed to the door. A free-standing lamp had been erected.

'Far end.'

Two laptops were visible along with a small velvet box. She removed her phone and took a photograph as did the second officer. Returning to the lounge she immediately returned to her seat, remaining silent for a moment. She allowed her gaze to pass from one Toland to the other, becoming aware of Francis's increased anxiety. Brad glanced at April and frowned.

'Do you want to tell us anything, Mr Toland? I seem to recall you suddenly had a memory flash on the previous occasion we met.'

He lowered his head and nodded. 'I took them,' he mumbled, his words being swallowed by his cardigan.

'Sorry, we didn't catch that,' April responded, raising her voice so everyone could hear.

'I took them!' he yelled, startling Brad and making him jump. It was the first time they had heard his voice raised. He turned to his wife. 'Say not a bloody word to me, you!'

The mouse roared, thought Brad as he quickly positioned himself between husband and wife, unsure as to what might happen next on seeing her face contort in pure anger.

'You?' Eileen asked. 'You?'

It was clear that it had been as much a surprise to her as it was to April and Brad.

'She, Chelle, gave them to me. She said they were Abid's, her bloke's, and she was frightened someone might take them when she was out. That was a while after he went missing. Gave me the box too to keep safely. I put them under the stairs, well out of the way behind years of crap.'

'Francis! Language. Watch your language in this house!'

He just turned and glared at her, angered by her pettiness.

'Did you look at them, open them, the box?' April pressed.

'No, I just wanted to help the girl. She was always civil to me, as was her bloke, like. One good turn and all that. What harm could it do? I could tell from her face she was worried. Maybe her mother's accident.'

'Did she actually mention her mother at that time?'

'No. That was said in the call. It makes sense though, doesn't it?'

April left the question hanging but his wife had something to say.

'And you didn't tell me about your little liaison with the

girl from upstairs and her giving you things ... *to look after?'*
She emphasised the words making it seem sordid and illicit.

'For that very reason. You'd have said, no.'

'We'll be checking them, the last time they were used will
be stored. You've not used them, Mr Toland?'

He shook his head. 'No, and there's nothing else unless
madam here took anything when she went rooting round
her flat.' He looked directly at Eileen, a look of defiance now
clearly written on his face.

'How dare you! How bloody dare you!'

'Language, dear, language.' A smile cracked Francis's lips.
Clearly, his day had come.

Once the officers had photographed, bagged and labelled
the items, they put them to one side. They opened the small
blue box. Inside was some jewellery and a computer memory
stick along with three small pieces of card. On each was a
word: RADIO, COURIER and TRUCK. These items were
probably the most precious objects they had ... but the
cards?

'Possibly passwords,' Brad offered.

'You'll be hearing from us again. I'll ask just once more.
Did she give you anything else for safe keeping or have you
taken anything that you've failed to tell us about today?'
April regarded each in turn.

Francis immediately answered in the negative but Eileen
went into the kitchen and brought back her purse. She took
out forty pounds and handed it to April. 'This was found on
the table when I went in on the last occasion. I was going to
put it towards their rent, only ... it wasn't those exact notes
you understand.' There was embarrassment in her tone as
she handed them over.

April took the money before handing it to Brad. 'You'll be hearing from us again have no fear of that. We'll send you a receipt for the items we removed today.'

The officers in the hallway were clearing their equipment. They all left together.

'Bloody hell, I wasn't expecting that!' Brad chuckled. 'There's going to be a few strong words spoken in there today and strangely, ma'am, my money's on Frankie boy, like.' He grinned, mimicking their penchant for finishing sentences with the word *like*.

'What do we have, DC Bradshaw?' April asked as she climbed into the car.

'Two laptop computers, a box, and some cash, ma'am.'

'Is that all?'

Brad turned to her and looked her in the eye. His puzzled expression clearly demonstrated a thought process. 'A possible future domestic?'

'You disappoint me, DC Bradshaw. Your mind was obviously somewhere else. We have a name … Do you recall now?'

Brad turned the key and started the car. 'Nope.'

April looked at him again. He had been taking notes. 'You'll need to keep a close eye on the Incident Room boards.'

* * *

Sadiq's phone rang. The tone told him who was calling. He knew to listen.

'Are we nearly done? Where's Doc?'

'Hi, bro. Yes, should be. Doc? He's at "Effing Street",

where we always work. Flam's there too with the others so all will be well. Being bagged and readied for distribution as instructed.'

'Rumour has it the police have been around the terminal and the carpark. If that shit, Quasim, has been squealing, I'll have him.'

'He'll not squeal, he was there when we did Abid. It shook him. He's only too aware of the action taken against traitors to the group. He also realises that it doesn't matter if he goes down, his lights will still be put out wherever if he squeals.' Sadiq did not intend for his words to come out so flippantly.

'You'd get to him like you can get to the girl? So, what about Chelle? Kelly, you know she's really called Kelly, right? They've found a girl who knew her, in Wigan. If they get to our girl this could start to bubble and bubble. Get the stuff shipped and clear up. No more attacks for the time being.'

The phone went dead. Sadiq grabbed a coat. Within fifteen minutes he was approaching Effingham Street.

* * *

Skeeter had ten minutes with Bob and mentioned the discovery of the laptops and the name, Abid. She voiced her desire to confront the suspect and it was agreed.

Quasim was sitting next to his legal representative and it must be said, his demeanour appeared far more respectful on this occasion. Skeeter and Bob Lawn entered the room. The attending officer helped Quasim to his feet.

'Sit when the officers do, lad, otherwise you'll be standing for the interview.' The officer tapped his shoulders like an old friend.

Quasim obeyed.

'Quasim, let me introduce you to DCI Lawn. He's a police officer who specialises in bringing drug dealers to justice and he's very successful at it.'

Bob shuffled the papers in front of him but did not look up.

Skeeter continued. 'You might be wondering one of two things. Number one, why have you been held a long time, longer than normal? Your legal representative here may well have explained or will give you the reason for that. Secondly, why are you being questioned by this man, knowing his area of expertise, when you were arrested for robbery and ABH? You were also in possession of a Class A drug, traces were found on your clothing and in your system. It is our belief that you, young man, are involved in dealing and running drugs. We have the results back from the tests.' She pointed to the file on the table. 'You're a mule. We also believe you've been involved in many crimes involving motorcycles and the like, and in some cases including threats and violence. We know that you were involved. DNA proves it.'

Quasim looked at his lawyer and then back but did not respond. He had listened well to his instructions.

It was Bob's turn. 'Remember that you're still under caution and this interview is being recorded for your legal benefit as much as for ours.' He smiled fleetingly as he turned a photograph over and pushed it in Quasim's direction. 'Have you seen this man before?' Bob sat back and steepled his fingers.

Quasim did not pick up the photograph. He looked carefully before turning to his lawyer and then back at Bob. He shook his head.

'You're shaking your head. I take it that means, no?'

'No,' came back, the word like a shallow echo.

'Let me give you this photograph.' This too was pushed across. 'I take it you recognise one person on that photograph; the one facing the camera?'

'Me.'

'And the other person?'

The lawyer picked up the photograph. 'It shows the back of someone's head, Detective Inspector.'

Quasim nodded and smiled.

'Try this then,' Bob slid across a third photograph. 'Here you can see the person to whom you were speaking has kindly turned and is now facing the camera. What do you notice between the first photograph and this?'

'It's me and the man in the first pic. You asked me if I knew him!' Quasim's voice was raised. The officer near the door moved closer.

'I asked if you'd seen him before. We can replay the tapes.'

The lawyer whispered into her client's ear.

Skeeter took up the line of questioning. 'We know who he is, we know his full name. We even know him by the name with which you might be familiar. Let me tell you some of those familiar names, Quasim, just to jog your memory. Bully, Blusher and Scar. Scar, yes and you may well be aware that she's no longer with us.' After a moment she leaned closer towards the table before putting her finger on the third photograph. 'He has a criminal record. Drugs and violence. Getting warm?'

'Doc,' admitted Quasim.

Skeeter looked at Bob and then at the lawyer. 'Mansoor Kamman, better known as Doc because allegedly he was a doctor, and that's possibly true. We haven't traced his educational history but we know what he does.' She removed a strip of paper on which was written a name. 'I take it you can read, Quasim?'

He nodded. She pushed the paper forward tight-lipped. There was an immediate negative response on seeing the name. He stiffened and looked to one side as if rejecting the idea. She did not pursue it, what she had witnessed was enough to confirm her suspicions.

Bob took over. 'If we said the name, *The Dawn Lady*, what comes to mind?'

It took a further thirty minutes and they had a vague confirmation of what they believed to be the import of a significant quantity of drugs. All the pieces of the jigsaw were now facing the right way, picture side up. All that was needed was to slot each one into the correct place. There was something that Quasim had uttered that stuck in Skeeter's mind: *We were told that we'd always be one step ahead. Make no silly mistakes!*

CHAPTER 27

April Decent stood in the Incident Room staring at the photographs taken of the items found at the Tolands' flat. The laptops had been opened and started up but were password protected, as was the information on the memory stick. Once cleared by Forensics they would be handed to the IT team. The techy people, as she liked to call them. The photograph of the three words found in the box had also been added. Brad stood and considered the evidence.

'Abid.' He turned and smiled at April. 'Sorry, now I recall. It may well all open up when we get inside those computers. The reason he was killed, his life, photographs. A veritable Aladdin's cave, ma'am.'

'Or a huge Pandora's Box.'

Skeeter appeared at the door and thrust an arm into the air, a victory punch. 'We have another of Snow White's men. We have Doc and we also have a canary. I was going to say *grass* but in respect to the leading officer, DCI Lawn, I thought better of it. The DNA match at Gittings' murder turned the tables. He was with her, attacked by three, one he believes he knows. Speaking to his brief she's optimistic we might be able to negotiate. Bob Lawn is keen to move on this as soon as. Quasim has confirmed the name, Abid. Says that he was once with them. He has more to say on that matter, I feel sure. DCI Lawn's gone to pay a visit to the couple he believes brought the shipment into the country, a Mr and Mrs Brinkman – Arthur and Lynn. Both pensioners. To think a few years ago people of their age played bowls and knitted hats and mittens. Now they serve as drug mules. Funny old world.'

April breathed deeply. For the first time since the start, she felt as though they were coming to terms with the case. What seemed like a rash of moped crime had morphed into a major murder and drugs investigation. What was reassuring was that she was surrounded by a quality team of investigating officers. She had made the right decision to transfer to this force.

Tony came over with Paula, they were chatting. Paula was very animated. She looked at the board and tapped it next to the name, Abid. 'Kelly's partner. Kelly showed Sharon a piece of his clothing she keeps, said his smell was still there, a type of comfort blanket she thought. There was also a series of letters or numbers marked on it, she couldn't be sure. She told me Kelly said that it was Abid's recipe if things got bad. They were the markings on their fingers.'

April frowned. Tony made notes as she spoke.

'Kelly then showed Sharon. She did this, I'll show you.'

She stretched her fingers out. Taking Skeeter's hand, she straightened hers. She then asked her to do the same and she gently slid and they docked fingers until each was linked.

'This might sound garbled but I'm telling it as I heard it. Kelly told Sharon the marks were significant as they spelled out a word or words about a person. She didn't really know who, only that it was some kind of warning. I presume she meant Abid, as it's him that she was obviously most concerned about. Sharon has agreed to call when she sees her. They're ready to take Kelly into safekeeping.'

Tony looked at his colleagues and left.

Skeeter watched him leave before turning back to look at Brad. They both pulled a quizzical face.

Bob Lawn glanced at the white windmill that stood on Lytham St Annes' seafront. The skeletal sails seemed to be frozen in a gentler time zone. Within minutes the cars turned away from the coast and were soon on an estate of fairly modern, similar-looking bungalows. Lawn's car pulled up behind the lead vehicle containing two officers from the Lancashire Constabulary who were now liaising. There was another plain police car further up the road, a watchman. On seeing his colleagues arrive he left the car and came down to meet them.

'DCI Lawn?'

Bob moved across. 'Morning.'

'Nobody in or out since six this morning.' He stretched. 'Could kill a brew. The house to the right, sir. Number Fourteen.'

Bob and two of his team talked with the uniformed officers and then again to the watchman. 'Thank you. Come with me, it'll take your mind off tea.' He quickly pointed to the other officers. 'You stay here until you're called. Considering the couple's age, I'm not expecting anything but initial politeness and co-operation, but then I've been wrong before.' He smiled briefly and raised an eyebrow. Ringing the bell, they stood back from the door. It opened on a security chain.

'Mrs Brinkman? DCI Lawn.' He held out his ID. 'May we have a chat?'

'It's not Arthur, is it?' Anxiety was immediately etched on her face.

Bob shook his head. 'May we come in?'

The door was closed and Bob heard the chain slide before being welcomed in. 'Goodness, my heart was all a flutter. I do worry about him.'

'Is your husband at home?'

'No, he went out about, let me see,' she looked at her watch, 'must be over an hour ago. A walk and a coffee on the seafront. His morning constitutional he always calls it. He was then going to visit a friend of his. He told me he'd not be back till later this afternoon. May I offer you some tea?'

Bob smiled. 'No thank you. What time would that be?'

'About ten I suppose.'

'Ten, right. Don't think me rude but does your husband always begin his morning constitutional by climbing over the back fence?'

'I'm sorry, I don't understand ... Back fence? Whatever do you mean Inspector? He left by the same door you entered. Back fence? You know he's over seventy?'

'Indeed, I do. You see, Mrs Brinkman, this officer here has been positioned outside your home since six this morning, possibly earlier, and he can assure you that no one apart from us has used that door today.'

'Mr Brinkman opened the door to take in the milk at,' he checked his note book, '7.48, sir.'

Bob smiled. 'Thank you. The bruising to your eye looks calmer. What about the ankle, and then there's the crutches? You seem to be managing better without them than when I last saw you. You were in the process of leaving the ship.'

The look in her eyes reflected everything she was feeling, but mainly defeat. 'You saw me?' She brought a hand up to her mouth, flopped onto the settee before taking a deep breath. 'I told him, the silly man, but he wouldn't listen.'

'Where is he or do I have to send this officer to look for him? We know he's somewhere on the property.'

There was a long pause. 'He's in the garden shed. Sorry.'

'While we go and get him, you put the kettle on, we'll have some tea and you can both help yourselves by telling me all you know.'

Sadiq had left the car on Effingham Street. He was greeted by the lad watching the door. The building, once a busy, large brick warehouse was now empty. Most of the external windows were sealed with steel plates. Having six floors, it was spacious. The upper floor level was illuminated by natural light. Rows of north facing windows, set at angles, ran from one end to the other. The opaque wire glass was cracked and damaged in places but secure within the iron frames. Regularly placed cast iron columns supported the roof.

'We need to be out of here as soon as.' Sadiq's voice echoed within the void as heads turned but no one spoke. Working on a stainless-steel table, dressed in a white coat, gloves, mask and goggles was Doc. He was the only one who remained focused. Digital scales sat to his right alongside a neatly stacked assortment of clear plastic bags. A large roll of what appeared to be clingfilm was held on a stand. Bikes and mopeds were leaning against one of the walls. Five card-board boxes no more than twelve inches in depth, width and height were taped shut and stacked on a separate table. Each had a Greek letter written on the side. Sadiq went over and ran his hand along them.

'Still using Abid's system. Gone but not forgotten. That man was truly bloody weird. Fucking geek. A, B and fucking C would do just as well.' Looking down he counted the boxes. 'Tidy sum there, my friends.'

He approached Doc but stopped short. Buffing was, to the man in the white coat, an exact science. There was a maximum he could go to in ensuring a balance between the best profit margin and good quality. He prided himself in doing just that every time.

'I'll be done by tomorrow. I'll finish this batch and they can go. Last one tomorrow. Once this natural light begins to fade, I can do no more. Has payment been received for yesterday's delivery?'

Sadiq just nodded. 'Payday for you boys will only be when the last lot is shipped. Hopefully a bonus too.'

'There'd better be and it better be an improvement on what they gave Chelle.' Doc's tone was flat with little feeling. 'If not, this'll be the last time.' His words were cold and direct.

Sadiq frowned. 'Let's all do what we're paid to do.' He quickly left.

* * *

Kelly was sitting on a bench by the Leeds–Liverpool Canal, her bags to one side. The large coffee cup was still warm and she wrapped both hands around it. She had found this place, this oasis of calm, after hearing someone mention it in the night shelter. It comprised a small, grassy park-like space with a few benches. It seemed quiet. She had been disappointed not to see Sharon, particularly as she had informed her she had booked for another night. She unwrapped the sandwich she had bought and nibbled it. Some ducks swam enthusiastically to the side and fluttered from the water and onto the bank, all noise, splashes and optimism. She admired the drakes' coloured plumage and their selfish pecking as an attempt to achieve some kind of order. It reminded her of the gang. Throwing some morsels into the canal, the majority turned and raced in pursuit. The noise level rose. One fowl remained and looked at her. Breaking off another piece she tossed it on the ground by her feet.

'Just how brave are you, little one?' she whispered.

The duck waddled up quickly and took the bread.

'When a duck is not a sheep it is rewarded.' She finished her coffee.

A couple approached. Both looked to be admiring the ducks before turning to Kelly. 'They're always hungry.'

'Greedy, the majority, but there's always one in every crowd who is patient and unafraid.' She pointed to the duck near the bench. 'My new friend until my food runs out.'

'It's Kelly I believe?'

Kelly immediately put down the remains of the sandwich, ready to flee.

'Don't be alarmed. We're friends too. Sharon spoke to me about you. May I sit and explain? If you don't like what I'm about to reveal you can just collect your things and go.'

Pulling her belongings closer, Kelly nodded her approval and pointed to part of the bench. 'My name's Paula and that's Chris. Like I said to Sharon, I'm working alongside the police, I'm a Family Liaison Officer. We know your circumstances and we know about Abid. I'm sorry, love, truly.'

The stranger's mention of Abid's name brought a degree of fear. Kelly wrapped her arms around her lifted knees and rocked slowly. Paula cautiously moved her hand to cover Kelly's and then drew closer. Immediately the flood gates opened and Kelly broke down. Her deep sobs were heartbreaking. She had kept everything contained for so long. The sorrow and the fear had been a toxic cocktail that had festered within. Suddenly it erupted in an emotional tsunami of tears, snot and spittle. Chris tapped her other shoulder before handing her a clean handkerchief.

'Can we talk, Kelly? Sharon is at a safe address and I know she'd love to see you make the right decision. You cannot run for ever.'

Paula just held her until she calmed and then moved back, giving her space. Kelly looked at Paula then Chris and nodded. 'You'll not hurt me?'

Paula placed her hands to either side of Kelly's face and lifted it. She looked directly at her. 'I promise to protect you. We'll not hurt you or Sharon. You have to trust me. Read my eyes, Kelly. They give the same message as my mouth.'

Right now, whoever these people were, Kelly had come to the end of the line. She had no more inner strength left. Studying her hand, she rubbed the gecko on the side of her palm as if secretly wishing the fairy story she had once been told would somehow be real and a genie would magically end all of this and bring Abid back. *If only you were here*, she thought. *If only you were still with me.*

CHAPTER 28

A part from Bob's formal caution and the dictaphone placed on the coffee table, the meeting had all the appearance of an afternoon tea party and not that of a police interview. The domestic ornaments, the soft furnishings, the best cups and saucers and plates of biscuits, all suggested a relaxed informality, but it neither had the corresponding atmosphere nor ambience. There was an air of anxious nervousness that stifled a readiness to speak, or to commit. In Bob's experience, informality and friendliness reaped dividends. He believed there was a reduced threat when those accused were interviewed in the security of their own home. On home turf, he liked to say.

Bob spoke first. He had judged the mood perfectly. Arthur's hand locked with his wife's as they sat as close as possible on the settee as if seeking mutual physical support.

'Just tell me why?' The question was so simple but it was like a recently recovered lost key slipping into the lock and opening a door of guilt. A psychologist would see it as a way of offering an opportunity to finally admit and reduce the burden of guilt that weighs heavily on those not used to wrong doing.

'It was all my idea, Chief Inspector Lawn. Lynn just had to go along with it once I'd told her but that was not until we were on our way back. I didn't want to spoil the first part of the cruise. She'd looked forward to it so much and I couldn't deny her that pleasure. Once I'd told her ... I've never seen her so angry but I fully understood her ire, I was prepared. Besides, what was she going to do, report me to the captain? No, we've been together too long, through the good and the bad, sickness and health. I'd betrayed her trust but she stood by me.'

Bob checked the Dictaphone and placed it back on the coffee table. Two other officers were taking notes.

'My morning walks, my constitutionals? They're not what she believes them to be. They satisfy an addiction. I'm lost to gambling.' He lowered his head before turning to her and mouthing the word, *sorry*.

Lynn moved to the side and regarded her husband with a look of sadness and surprise.

'I look after the household accounts, always have. Let's say at first I was able to manage, as the outgoings were not too bad. You wouldn't believe how much you can feed the slot machines. I'd go up to Blackpool. It's just around the corner, meet mates, but I always went too far. Look, to cut a long story very short, I borrowed money. The house is paid for so the loan was just for the bills and repayments on the car. Anyway, as an anniversary was coming up Lynn wanted to go on a cruise, and the only way we'd be able to afford that was through my getting another loan. There should've been cash in the bank. Lynn believed we had enough and by rights we should've had plenty. God, we'd been prudent throughout our lives. We've no kids and both worked but then she didn't know the truth.'

He pulled her hand closer and whispered again. 'I'm so, so sorry, love.'

Bob spoke. 'Go on, in your own time.'

'I was telling all this to a guy in one of the casinos in Blackpool, and he brought one of his mates to see me. We had a meal and a drink and then he stated he could sort me out with cash and a cruise but … It sounded so plausible, so easy. Three weeks in the Caribbean, collect a couple of rucksacks in Trinidad and bring them home. It was just like he said. We went off with the cruise logo bags and just swapped them. Well, what happened was so efficient. We left them by our sun loungers and went for a swim. When we returned, what looked like the same bags had in fact been swapped for identical ones apart from the contents. I neither saw who did it nor did I want to.'

'You placed a case in a car and that was it?'

'Yes, more or less what was in the bags was transferred to a large case, the one I carried off. I never met the initial contact again. I met a foreign gentleman, young. He went through all of the details, even what to do if the ship went down with salmonella. Everything was so precise. I was given the car key and told it would be parked next to mine on our return and it was. Lynn, as I say, through love and misguided loyalty played along. When she knew I'd blown our life savings what could she do?'

Seeing tears appear in her husband's eyes Lynn moved back closer and wrapped an arm around his shoulder.

'For better for worse and you don't get much worse than this but … he's my husband.'

Bob looked around the room and saw a few grown men and one female PC emotionally challenged by what they were witnessing. There was now a sadness in the room that weighed heavily on everyone's shoulders.

'How much did they pay you?'

Arthur stood and went to the kitchen before returning with a supermarket carrier bag. He put it on the table. Bob did not move but looked.

'It's all in there. Twenty thousand pounds. What I'd asked for. Enough to clear my debts and get the loan sharks off my back and then deposit some back in the bank. I was going to deposit it bit by bit.'

'Have you taken the money out of here? Counted it?'

'We looked in the bag on the way back, expecting to find fake or plain blank bundles of paper but it's real. I took one note out and spent it locally. There was no problem.'

One of Bob's team slipped on a pair of gloves and collected the money from the table. It would again be bagged for forensic testing.

'Collect some things and secure the house. You'll face the consequences of your actions. Once at the station, I'd like to see if you can recognise some faces.'

'I'll need to wash these dishes before we go, Chief Inspector, I can't leave the place like this.'

Bob nodded his consent.

Skeeter Warlock sat in the Incident Room and stared at the boards. Something had been bothering her for a few days and she had failed to win the previous evening's bout at the wrestling club. For once she had conceded and it rankled. The words she recalled from a film came to mind, *Failure is not an option*. It referenced both her hobby and her professional conduct.

She scribbled down the three words found on the cards at the Tolands' apartment. They made no sense. She then looked at Brad's report from the tattoo parlour. Collecting her jacket, she left.

Within twenty minutes she was walking down County Road. The traffic was light considering the time of day. She could see *Jesters Ink* on the opposite side of the road. Checking both ways, she crossed. Skeeter was pleasantly surprised by the professional appearance of the shop front. She entered. A heavily tattooed young man was sitting behind a computer screen. He greeted her.

'Just a minute and I'll be with you.' He leaned round and smiled. Once he had finished tapping on the keyboard he spoke again. 'And ... save,' he said with a flourish, hitting the key with an exaggerated flamboyance, like a concert pianist hitting a critical note.

Skeeter held out her ID.

'Foolishly, I thought your popping in here indicated you might want a tattoo. How wrong of me. Never mind, how may I help?' He grinned.

'I believe you tattooed a young man with a gecko here, depicted in simple red-and-black lines and lettering or numbers, some kind of lines here.' She demonstrated on her own hand.

'That was me,' a voice from the back called and a young woman appeared.

Skeeter was impressed by the tattoos that spread up both her arms. She pointed and whistled. 'Now that's class!'

'Why thank you. All his work. Do you have any ink?'

'One.' Skeeter opened her jacket and lifted her shirt from the waist band. To the left they read the fine script tattooed in black. 'It's in Latin.'

They looked at each other and back at Skeeter. 'And it says?'

'It says, or should say, *By any available means or method.* I follow that code in all things, always have since I was a kid.' She tucked in her shirt and closed her jacket. 'According to the report you gave my colleague, you were trying to trace the tattoos you applied to the fingers. I take it you haven't found them? Too busy, I guess.'

'I sent them, an image of each. They were Arabic numbers and some symbol or sign.' She moved through to the back and returned with them. 'Here, the punter wanted them small and just above the nail. I sent the images to your colleague the day he came here, late in the afternoon. He thanked me so I know he received them.'

'May I take a photograph of these?'

'Please, anything to help, and if you consider adding to that one of yours you know the quality of work we do.'

Skeeter thanked them and left.

* * *

Kelly's reunion with Sharon brought tears to both girls. They moved across the room and hugged.

'I'm sorry but I thought it was for the best, Kelly. Are you alright, Babe?'

Kelly nodded. 'I think I'm fine. I'm tired and hungry and lonely and I've been bad but otherwise I'm good.' Both girls laughed.

Paula came in with coffee and cake. 'It's important we talk now, Kelly. Sharon do you mind?'

'She can stay, I'd like that,' Kelly announced before reaching for Sharon's hand.

Paula nodded. 'Tell us about your man and then we'll work backwards from there.'

Kelly looked at Sharon who smiled. 'Go on. It'll be fine.'

'He was part of the gang when I was recruited. I've always been around lads and gangs and he encouraged me and gave me confidence. I could ride, see. Good on a moped or motor bike. Proper fast. Daring too. They liked that. We were busy. Abid made me laugh. He didn't ride, he did more important stuff, computers, meetings, business. Travelled abroad at times. Soon we were together in my flat.'

'Computers and meetings?'

She nodded. 'He was really clever. Before he left Albania, he told me he'd been studying computer sciences. It felt as though he spent more time on the computer than he did with me. We'd row about it sometimes but always made up.'

She took out a plastic disc. 'I believe this is why he was killed.' She handed it to Paula.

Turning it in her hand she recalled the reports she had read on the man's death. 'Why do you say that?'

'He'd been following this virtual currency, bitcoins, and as he was handling the money for Sadiq he decided to invest, gamble a bit and in his words, *take a few risks*. It was really successful. A couple of us tipped over some of our cash for him to invest on our behalf and we each received one of these.' She pointed to the disc. 'He traded, that's the term he used, and made quite a bit. He sent money home, he was good like that, kind and that's why he was different. I really loved him. Then it all went wrong. Overnight everything crashed. He said the bubble had burst and that he'd lost thousands. He was shit scared, really frightened. At first, he didn't do anything. He waited, thinking it might be a blip, but it wasn't. Loads of people lost huge amounts of money.'

'Why didn't he just go home, back to Albania?'

'Because they were linked. A man called Flamur was the key, money went both ways. I saw them, all apart from one person, the one they called boss. Sadiq seemed always to call him bro: hi, bro, yes, bro, two bags full bro. Abid approached Sadiq as he thought he could trust him. How wrong he was. Sadiq went nuts. It was then he said he'd contacted the true boss and he told Abid that he'd give him a month for the market to change, and if it did, all would be forgotten, but if not ...'

'And if not?'

'He never said but I can guess. I remember the evening he came home. They had slapped him about but he didn't complain. He then did something strange. A day or two later he had the tattoos on his hand. He hadn't any money but he did that. It was so out of character. He then persuaded me to do the same. He took me to a friend. Here, see.'

'Are the tattoos identical, Kelly?' Paula took her hand and studied them.

'This one is but these, they were different. If we put our fingers together like this, just to the first knuckles he said they created a recipe, a secret recipe that he wouldn't explain. He also told me to believe nothing and trust no one. I don't know why I'm trusting you.' Pausing she turned to Sharon. 'Sometimes I just wish I was dead.'

Sharon leaned forward and hugged her. 'You're doing great.'

Kelly pulled away, blew her nose on the handkerchief she had been given and smiled. 'There was something else too.'

CHAPTER 29

A rthur Brinkman looked at the first photograph. He shook his head. 'Sorry, no.'

The second photograph, although poor, brought an immediate response. He tapped his finger on it. 'This is the young chap I met a couple of times, the one I mentioned to you. Met at different places. They called me and we'd meet. My constitutional. Dreadful photograph, looks like a corpse.' Looking up he smiled and then saw Bob's expression. He quickly removed his finger.

'Did he have a name?'

'No, nothing like that. I received money to purchase the tickets and that was it. We met again when he gave me the instructions to follow when in Jamaica and also when the ship docked at Liverpool. Nothing was written down. I made notes but he told me to just keep one-or-two-word reminders. That seemed sensible. They were very cautious and that gave me confidence.'

'Your wife's fall. Was that all part of it?'

'Yes, we thought it might help. She was getting rather

jumpy once we'd collected the stuff. The closer we came to the UK she started to have a few too many from the courtesy bar. I can hardly blame her. I was frightened too. That was our excuse!'

'You'll be charged today and you can either appoint your own lawyer or we can do that for you. The same for your wife.'

Arthur stood and held out his hand. 'DCI Lawn. On behalf of my wife and I, may I thank you for your sensitive handling of this situation and will you please accept my sincere apologies. I've been a bloody fool.'

Bob reached out and took his hand. 'Good luck, Mr Brinkman. Your co-operation has been noted.'

Skeeter sat in the carpark for more than an hour. Something stabbed at her, a disquiet that was uncomfortable. She could not fully understand elements of the investigation. Quasim's words accompanied by the sarcastic grin niggled, *one step ahead*. She needed a walk.

Paula wanted to photograph Kelly's tattoos but was conscious of her fragility. There would be time for that later once her confidence grew and she believed that she was in safe hands.

'You collected a parcel, something purchased from the internet?'

Kelly was surprised by the question. 'You know a lot. Yes,

I collected it for Abid. He sent for that after he'd had the tattoos. He wanted me to collect it. It was a kind of medal. He showed me, held it to my chest and told me I deserved one for putting up with a loser.'

'What happened to it?'

'A day or two after, Abid didn't come home. He went missing but then it seemed as though he wasn't missing if that makes sense?'

Paula nodded. 'Perfect sense. Go on.'

'I was riding with Quasim and he informed me that Abid had asked for the medal. He was away for a couple of days. We went to my flat and I got it and gave it to him. He said it was urgent, that's why we went home on the bike, something we'd normally never do unless I was on my own.'

'You didn't see Abid again after that?'

'No. The items never really crossed my mind until I saw the report with the disc, the medal and the body. At first, I thought it was Quasim, but I saw him again when he was riding. I knew deep down that the body was Abid's. The image I saw in the paper was awful and I had to look away. I was really scared. I asked Francis – he's the nice man married to that fucking cow, my landlady – if he'd look after Abid's laptops and a box of our stuff. I really was frightened that something was going to happen to me.'

'What was in the box? Do you remember?'

Kelly picked up her cup but it was empty. 'Do you have more?'

'Certainly, but first tell us about the box you left with Francis.'

'It had one of his computer things, a memory stick, some jewellery I had, not much but one of the rings was special, and I think there were three pieces of card that Abid told me referred to a place, an important place. What with his recipe and the medal and the cards, I never knew what to think. He talked in riddles at times, things I didn't understand. He was acting so strangely, probably the worry over the money. He said they'd called him a traitor. I understood that.'

'I'll get the coffee.' Paula left the room, requested coffee and took her mobile from her bag. She rang the Liverpool extension. It was Brad who answered and he revealed that April was in a meeting. He did not go into details.

'Sorry to bother you. I'll try her mobile.'

'You could do but I can see her mobile's sitting here on her desk. I can give her a message for you.'

'Tell her we have Sadiq's address.' She read it out and Brad scribbled it down. 'We also believe the three cards found in the box refer to a location. That's it. She'll understand. I'll send a full report later but the girl's being very co-operative.' On putting down the phone she realised she had not asked for the officer's name.

Brad returned the phone and left a note regarding the information he had received on April's desk before collecting a mobile from his drawer and making a call. He glanced at the poster of the silhouetted figure set amongst the Post-it notes. How he would love to be walking on that beach right now. There was only one place he could be – the Incident Room.

The three officers working in there turned and smiled. He reciprocated as he turned to stare at the words pinned there: COURIER, TRUCK, RADIO. 'An important place,' Kelly had told Paula. Walking to the nearest computer he tapped in his ID and password before Googling, *find places with three words.* He was surprised to see a number of sites in the search but the main one was What3Words.com. He went to the site and read.

The company had assigned every part of the world's surface to three metre squares; each square had been given a unique three-word address that would never change. The example showed a location in London. He typed in the three words in the order in which they appeared on the board adding a full stop between each. It immediately showed *No Result.* Looking carefully at the website, he realised he had added a space after each word, the example did not. Retyping he quickly had three addresses, two in California and one in Dumfries and Galloway. He rearranged the words: TRUCK.-COURIER.RADIO. This time he had Alaska, Essex and California. *How many bloody combinations could there be?* he thought as he tapped the table with his fingers. RADIO.TRUCK.COURIER. An address in Bootle appeared. 'Bingo!' he called out involuntarily causing those in the room to turn.

'Lottery win?' one said and the others laughed. Brad joined them.

'If I had, people, I'd keep it quiet and just bugger off,' he sniggered.

Clicking on the box it brought up the exact three metre square. It was a warehouse positioned between Millers Bridge and Effingham Street. He sat back and stared at the map. 'Well, well, well. Who would have thought it? The wonders of modern science.' Removing his phone, he made a call before moving back to the office to find Lucy.

'Come with me. A tip off.'

Lucy looked up. 'Where, and what?'

'Tell you on the way. Just need to call DCI Mason.' He lifted the phone receiver on Lucy's desk and it rang twice.

Mason answered. He listened as Brad described the conversation with Paula before asking for clearance to check out the location. He thought bigger guns would be needed at the designated address knowing an inappropriate action could jeopardise the chance of surprise.

'Just look and make discreet enquiries. If you think you're on to something get it secured. No heroics. Understand?'

It would take DCI Mason forty-five minutes to receive the necessary clearance, check the address and plan the tactical assault. Nothing was taken for granted. If this address was indeed that of the gang, then firearms might be present. Procedures had to be adhered to. Once instructions had been delegated, they could move. It was a matter of safety, timing and efficiency – teamwork as Mason was always banging on about. CSI would be waiting in the wings.

It took twenty minutes before Brad and Lucy approached the end of Derby Road. Owing to the dual carriageway they had to cross at the junction and approach Effingham Road from the river side. Brad pulled up and took out a print of the screen capture he had made, highlighting the square.

'It's up near the top.'

Once out of the car, Lucy scanned the brick buildings that dominated either side of the road. Steel, blue *taking-in* doors were recessed, one for each of the six floors and all looking as though they had not been used for years. There was a chill in the air as the sun failed to reach the narrow road. Cars were parked on either side and further down some units were open. Brad walked down and entered. Two men stopped working on a flatbed truck.

'Can we help you?' The question was neither welcoming nor cordial.

He showed his ID. 'Information, sorry to distract you.'

Both men wiped their hands on pieces of rag as they approached. He showed them the paper.

'Is this building occupied?'

'The one next door is used for storage and after that they're all empty. Been like that well on two years. Occasionally see people if we're here late, probably security. Never see any damage to the place. Bit out of the way. Another few years and they'll be posh flats. Funny though about half an hour ago I saw some people leaving. They had a few boxes. How strange is that?'

Lucy put her head back out of the door. She saw someone outside the building in which they were interested before they climbed into a van. She started to run in the hope of seeing the number plate before it turned left at the junction but it moved off too quickly. Brad appeared at her side. She explained. They both went to the door by which she had seen the man leave. He called Control requesting two officers to attend to stand by until access could be organised. He also gave the address and requested a search on the owners.

'Check the places at the top for CCTV possibilities and I'll check along the bottom road. Back here in ten.'

Regent Road boasted only a closed café and a hotel some distance away, but neither had cameras outside, nor did a chemical works opposite. He jogged back up to the car, his breathing heavy. Lucy was just returning. She watched him lean against the car gulping air.

'Are you alright? You're very red.'

'Unfit and getting fat but otherwise I feel bloody brand new. Anything?'

'There's a camera top right at what appears to be some sort of garage but they told me it's trained on the doors and their forecourt. There's a monitored camera on the junction of Balliol Road. Looks directly down Millers Bridge. The lady in the garage says there's been activity here for a few weeks. She wondered if some firm was preparing to move in. I've called for the junction camera to be reviewed. Time and van colour. It should give us an idea of its direction at least.'

'Good, the woman in the garage, did you get her name?'

Lucy just looked skyward as her expression conveyed the contempt he deserved. Fortunately, the police car approached and Brad waved the driver down. It saved his receiving an earful.

Mason, alongside three officers and a Firearms Unit, approached the modern tower block. Plain police vehicles were positioned to close the road and were ready to block all entry and exit points. One was positioned across the underground automatic garage doors. As Mason's car pulled to a halt the firearms units moved in as a semi-lockdown started.

Flamur was driving the battered Sprinter van. He was the only one in the cab. He was also very much aware of the cameras in the warehouse's vicinity. They had always ensured they approached the area from Regent Road. The van had become a familiar sight with those working in the road. After padlocking the steel shutter on the warehouse door, Asif Rehman had been the last to climb in through the vehicle's side opening. The van was already accelerating when he slid the door closed. The action was helped by the sudden braking as it stopped suddenly at the junction. Asif was tossed forward as the door slammed closed. Don Benson was sitting on two clingfilm wrapped cardboard boxes, holding the sides. He farted.

'Better out than in.' His grin spread across his naturally red face.

Asif recovered his composure and thrust a fist in Don's chest as the pungent aroma filled the enclosed space. Doc sat quietly propped against the rear door, mulling over the recent call he had received. He was neither happy nor comfortable with the latest setbacks and he could see the writing on the wall. He would be leaving the van before the rest. For the moment, his job was done. Arrangements for his payment were in hand.

Once through Great Crosby, the van increased speed before pulling up as it came into the neighbouring Little Crosby. Doc pulled open the side door and slid out. Flamur glanced in the side mirror and caught sight of Doc's raised hand. He pulled away. Doc would now have a fifteen-minute walk to his car. It had been left the day before on a quiet side road. After that he would become smoke and hopefully vanish for a while.

The van continued before turning onto Southport Old Road and then Broad Lane, a contradiction in terms as it was only wide enough for one vehicle. It was also a dumping ground. Strewn in places, a variety of items from televisions and asbestos sheeting to broken household furnishings could be seen. In some areas, huge swathes of the ditch running next to the golf course were overflowing.

The lane gradually lost the tarmac skin and potholes of various depths appeared causing the van to sway and rattle. The two remaining occupants in the back could only hang on.

The air was cool; the place private. In the distance a tractor could be heard but not seen. It was now a matter of waiting. Don and Asif sat in the open doorway and each lit a cigarette. Neither knew the other man's thoughts but they were both pondering the same thing. Why the sudden rush, the swift clearing and packing? The phone call had brought a controlled panic to both Doc and Flam and it had unnerved them. Now, sitting here they felt more in control.

Mason looked around the apartment and the *Marie Celeste* sailed into his mind. Moving to the window, he stared down the Mersey. It was evident from the way in which things had been scattered that whoever lived there had left in a hurry. The only advantage to that was it would be awash with DNA and evidence. He was also aware that criminals of this calibre had escape plans. Key documents, cash and credentials were always stored to be accessed at a moment's notice. Looking around, it appeared as though they had done just that. 'Fuck!' was the only word he uttered as he stepped into the elevator.

CHAPTER 30

A pril finished her meeting with the techy boys and dropped the report on her desk. She was neither pleased nor disappointed. The information retrieved would be collated and matched with what they had already gathered. It was another step in the right direction. What excited her more was the pending briefing planned for four o'clock. Bob Lawn was due, along with her boss. She had heard that Paula had concluded her chat with Kelly who had been taken to a women's shelter alongside Sharon. April had requested Paula's personal attendance. It was always better to discuss evidence received face-to-face with the team present. Memories and ideas could often be jogged from dark corners where they lay temporarily forgotten. She was also aware that Bob had a positive ID on Abid from the interviews with Quasim. Another session with the suspect was planned for later in the day. It was only then did she see the note from Brad. She dialled his mobile.

'Brad, I take it you're at the location?'

'Effingham Street, just off Derby Road, Bootle. Just on my

way back. Lucy's with me. We've secured the place and started a search for the owner. Need to get a team in there as soon as, ma'am. According to witnesses here, there's recently been a good deal of fresh activity. Looks like our dead man has tipped us the wink. What did you tell me on the day we were at the burial site? *Dead men can tell tales*. You were spot on.'

'That was from my first boss. A wise fellow. Four o'clock, conference room and don't be late. Thanks for the note.'

April greeted Paula and escorted her to the conference room. They chatted briefly. Paula enquired about the information she had sent. 'Thought that it was critical, urgent. You saw she identified Quasim and gave a description of Sadiq. She'll be brought here to work with the EvoFit technician in the hope you can get an accurate image of Sadiq although the CCTV from the address you gave has turned up a veritable treasure trove. The coverage is being checked as we speak.'

'Kelly's coming here this evening,' April informed Paula.

'And Sharon too? They've become inseparable and that, for me, is useful. They've made a request too, a rather unorthodox one. I've told them I'd see but couldn't promise. Hope you didn't mind my leaving the information with the officer when I rang your extension. I was so determined to get it to you quickly, I didn't get to ask his name. I usually work after the case has run its course and not when it's at this stage.'

'It was Brad. He acted immediately on both fronts, checked the site and secured it but the other …' She did not elaborate, but kept her suspicions to herself. The least said the better. 'That was quick thinking and you've achieved a miracle with the girl. Acting immediately can be crucial, so no problem and the more faces we collect, the better. Thanks.' She tapped Paula's shoulder. 'Good to have you working with us.'

'Kelly's been very co-operative, frightened but you can understand why. It's all in the report. I've brought twelve copies.' She handed April the documents.

Skeeter was the next to enter as the room quickly filled. She sat to one side. Lucy and Brad were last in. April wasted no time and started the briefing but it was to be led by DCI Alex Mason.

'Thanks, a welcome back to Bob and a new welcome to Paula, the Independent Liaison Officer who's been working with Kelly. If you can listen and read at the same time then Paula's findings are in the file in front of you. She'll brief you shortly. The latest progress is a mixed bag. As you know we've checked out Sadiq's alleged address, turns out it was on a short-term lease. We're checking the holder's details but as you know ...' He looked at the audience and many knew there would be little to track to a suspect. 'On a more positive note, we've also been directed to a location derived from the three words found on the cards at Kelly's place. It's been secured and will be checked as soon as the teams arrive. When we get the call, I want Tony and April out there immediately.' He checked his watch. 'April, please begin as you might disappear at any minute.'

April was prepared and moved to the front. 'The laptops have revealed a good deal about the man, Abid. Kelly tells us that he was a computer expert, working on computer sciences at an Albanian university before coming here. I looked up the term as I was unsure what computer science involves. I discovered that it was the study of the processes that interact with data. It's about the use of algorithms to manipulate, store and communicate digital information.'

Moving to the nearest whiteboard she wrote down the words, *manipulate, store* and *communicate*.

'I feel these words may be a key, a possible code for us to decipher. He also worked with something called ASCII. This too may be a link. It's an abbreviation for American Standard Code for Information Interchange. To me that suggests passing something from one to another, part of his code? As we sit here, better brains than mine are correlating this data with the information we have. Whilst with this criminal group we know that Abid specialised in their planning and dealt with certain accounts. We also know he worked with the mules, our cruisers, the Brinkman, who are now in custody. His role, according to their dealings with him, was setting up their cover and the feeding of information. Now, according to Kelly, she was aware of a change in Abid's personality after he took a risk. He purchased crypto currency. This would've been fine had the money been his. It wasn't. It was purchased through a website called Clickfolio. He'd purchased a considerable amount of a specific currency called Zil and he'd initially done well.'

Brad tapped his pen on the desk as he looked at his mobile. April stopped. Brad looked up, realised his error and mouthed an apology. She raised an eyebrow and continued.

'If you recall, a few years back this form of investment crashed after meteoric increases. Millions were made and lost overnight. Since then, things have stabilised, but there are still peaks and serious troughs. We identified his pass-word. Can you believe the word *6eck0*? You see the connection was key. It was their matching tattoos. We could track his transactions. Initially, he did well, however, a month ago, his whole investment dropped off the cliff reducing it to a pittance. We know from Kelly that he was given time to recoup as the majority of the investment was not his. It was then he had the tattoos done and bought the medal. I strongly believe these may well be part of his escape plan.'

Skeeter looked at the words April had written and then back to the report. She scribbled some notes. It was like the penny had finally dropped.

'You'll read why the Perspex disc is relevant. I have a hunch as to how it came to be found at his burial site. You may, too, when you've digested Paula's report. We couldn't get into certain parts of the hard drives as the tech people believe they are mined. If they get it wrong a set number of times, the disc will either be wiped clean or it will destroy itself. We'll have to be patient before we discover anything else. It's the same with the memory stick we recovered. It seems he wanted us to find only certain things and not others. It's as if we're being drawn along. Now, whether that's safe is for us to decide but time is ticking and it's my hunch we don't have too long.'

The phone in front of Alex pinged. April and Tony stood as they looked across at him. 'Go! Firearms are on their way. Road and area's secured. You're expected.'

CHAPTER 31

Don finished a second cigarette and lay back in the van, his eyes closed. His feet dangled over the edge, just touching the ground, as he clasped his hands across his stomach. He inhaled and a smile came to his lips.

'This is the life. Heigh bloody ho, it's off to work we don't bloody go.' He opened an eye momentarily and chuckled.

Flamur looked at Asif and smiled before running a finger across his throat. Asif moved sideways and studied the prostrate and slightly rotund figure. He focused on the exposed throat. Feeling the bone on his wrist, he turned his palm and made a rigid, karate-type hand pose before lifting it. The first blow had to be accurate. He brought it crashing with full force onto Don's Adam's apple and the dull crunch of the hyroid bone disintegrating echoed within the thin, metal van walls. Immediately, a sharp and desperate gurgling and gasping noise erupted from Don's mouth. Snot exploded from his nose as the air was forced outward. His bulging eyes neither focused nor blinked as his hands moved towards the damage.

With another swift action, Asif slipped his arms behind Don's bent knees and lifted, pushing sideways until his body was shoved into the van. He followed. Dropping onto the victim he forced his hands across both his mouth and nose. Don struggled but not like a man fighting for his life. He was too busy trying to get air into his lungs. Only seconds later the backs of his shoes kicked feebly at the van's floor like diminishing cymbal strikes. On hearing the last one register, Asif rolled off his victim and began to breathe deeply.

Flamur turned and looked inside. 'Well done, Bully.' He always used his nickname. 'Neat, very, very neat. Now we need the boxes out.' Picking up his phone he sent a message before scanning the road. Sadiq should be joining them shortly. They would burn the van. Down here it would be ash before it was discovered.

CHAPTER 32

The meeting continued. Skeeter looked across at Brad as he watched them leave. His phone was now on his knee. Occasionally the screen lit, illuminating the area beneath as he checked it. He did not seem to learn. She returned to Kelly's file, scrutinising the images of the tattoos on her fingers and then the drawings she had recovered from the girl who had tattooed Abid. Arabic numbers. The similarity between the two was apparent but one was of a higher quality than the other. Kelly's looked the more amateur. She needed to know what numbers they represented. The squiggles, too, had a relevance, but they seemed impossible to identify. Knowing the group was still unaware of the significance of Abid's tattoos, she struggled as to whether to divulge what she suspected. In the end she felt as though she should keep it under wraps until Brad released the evidence. She believed that he knew. It had been confirmed to her in the shop.

Paula highlighted her report consolidating what April had reported and answered questions. Brad had returned his phone to the desk and gave his full attention to Paula's statement. He enquired where Kelly was housed but simply received a stare suggesting he should know better. That information could not be disclosed.

DCI Mason rounded up the briefing. 'I'll be interviewing Quasim this evening and formally charging him. Skeeter, I'd like you to assist seeing it was you who started this whole investigation. He also seemed to like you in the room!'

She nodded and smiled, not knowing if he was being polite or cynical.

Checking his watch, he stipulated, 'Twenty minutes.'

Skeeter collected her things before heading into the ladies' toilets. She locked herself in a cubicle, requiring the maximum, uninterrupted time. Within minutes she had Googled 'Arabic numbers' and cross-referenced. She had five numbers. Considering how the fingers interlocked, she realised that they would be in a certain sequence starting and ending with a squiggle. She had 66, 83, 96, 65 and 68. Immediately she thought of bus numbers and chuckled to herself. *You wait all this bloody time and five come along all at once!* she thought. She sent a text relaying the images of the three unidentified tattoos to an Arabic speaking translator she had used in a previous investigation, requesting a favour. Within minutes she received a reply.

Two are the same, the ones marked 'B', although not of the same quality of script. This can be interpreted as 'betray' or 'betrayed'. The one marked 'A' I feel is the idea – 'remember'. Hope that helps. You owe me! :)

Skeeter looked again at the marks. *Who's betrayed whom?*

* * *

Quasim sat, his arms resting on the table as he lightly drummed his fingers on the surface. He was still nervous. His lawyer sat next to him; the files set before her. As the door opened, Quasim stood immediately and looked round. Skeeter could not help but notice a nervous smile cross his lips, it was neither in defiance nor arrogance. For the first time she saw a youth and not a thug.

'Thank you. This will be the final interview and the last time you can help yourself. Drug dealing, theft, ABH and GBH will be on the charge but murder may be hovering in the wings? We still await evidence. It would be a positive step if we could say that you led us to the gang leaders. It would certainly go some way in your favour in the jury's eyes.'

Bob turned to his lawyer. 'Do you agree?'

'We always encourage our clients to be fully co-operative and honest during interviews remembering they have taken an oath.'

'Why did Abid want you to have the plastic disc and the medal?'

Quasim was taken aback by the question but quickly recovered. 'He was scared that he would be killed and should that happen, he'd asked me to hold them and make sure that I put them with his body. In his hands if I could. He said it was important to him. He was a friend, a brother. He also told me not to say a word.'

'And you did? You did as he asked?'

His lawyer leaned towards him and spoke. He nodded.

'I have to say this as it's the truth.' His eyes were intense and his knuckles white as he spoke. 'I know they killed him

266

in the warehouse but I wasn't there. I was only there when we took the body to the sands. I was chosen as I was fairly new. They told me the same would happen to all traitors who betrayed Snow White.'

'Did you put them in his hands?'

'Only the plastic one as I was on that side. Had I gone to the other they'd have seen. I was very scared just doing that. It wasn't easy as the hands were stiff and partly wrapped.'

'And the medal?' Skeeter asked.

'I dropped it in the sand as we covered him, tried to bury it with the toe of my boot. I couldn't let them know it was there.'

Skeeter could see a tear begin to form in his eye. He brought a hand up to wipe it away.

'Quasim, why the chain? It was with the body.'

'It was believed if it was found like that it would suggest the body probably had come from the sea. I know that I've been a fucking shit but I've never killed anyone. I've stabbed at them when I've been on the bikes but I could control that. I wasn't there when they did him.' He looked at his lawyer. 'I'm telling the truth. I was with Beverley when she was done but that was a guy called Hoover. He's with a rival bike gang trying to trespass on our territory. I can tell you it was him, I saw him.'

'Does Hoover have a real name?'

Quasim nodded. 'Mark Dyson.'

Skeeter turned to Alex.

'This warehouse you mentioned. Where is it?'

* * *

On arrival, Derby Road had been closed to traffic and a diversion was being set up. April and Tony took the dock road before forcing their way through, sirens and lights forging a path as cars moved onto the kerb. An officer directed them to the right and onto Effingham Road. It was evident from the commotion at the top that it was to be their destination.

Armed police were just standing down and loading their van. The building was clear. CSI vans were positioned near the door as the technicians carried in a variety of boxes. April and Tony slipped on overshoes and gloves before entering, adding their names to the Crime Scene Manager's list.

'Very top floor. Sorry no lights!' He handed them a torch.

The steps of those climbing ahead of them reverberated against the cold, brick walls. Places such as these seemed to be made for this type of crime. Even when the sun shone, the space was cold. As they passed the doors on the different levels, they could see how dark each floor was. Occasionally, a laser of light penetrated, illuminating small areas. The top floor was very different. Daylight flooded through the rooflights even that late in the afternoon. They stood just to the side of the door and surveyed the large space. In the centre was a stainless-steel table. Some chairs sat to the far side and leaning along another wall were some electric cycles and mopeds. To one side was a primitive large dumbwaiter.

'That's how they brought up the bikes as they sure didn't cart them up those stairs,' Tony grumbled.

Looking beyond the gated opening something on the far wall caught April's attention. A large mural filled it, a naïve drawing of Snow White and some dwarves. It was incomplete. Beneath the finished images were the names, Doc, Blusher and Scar. Simple outlines had been started for three others. It was drawn in what appeared to be chalk.

'The information was accurate. Amazing!'

They kept their intrusion of the crime scene to a minimum. Step plates had been placed to an area to one side where the CSI equipment was stored.

A senior CSI was shining a UV light around the table. 'Blood stains. A lot of them too. Here also. There's a line as if plastic sheeting were used from this point.' She traced the contrasting line clearly displayed in the light.

'It's going to be a long day, ma'am. Shall I call it in?'

April nodded.

CHAPTER 33

'The Effing Road we called it. Top floor. It's where we did the drugs, got them ready, boxed and shipped as Sadiq would say. Kept the bikes there too. We had to tune them somewhere else otherwise those things screamed when revved. In there they would have woken the dead. We arrived and left in the van with the bikes and took them in.'

'How did you deal with the heavier machines?' Skeeter quizzed.

'There was an old hand-pulled lift-type thing. It creaked and groaned. The bikes we could take up the stairs but the mopeds went in that one at a time. Doc called it a dumb-waiter to match the dumb arseholes he worked with.' There was a pause as Quasim's facial expression changed and a smile appeared. 'I drew a murial on the wall.'

'A what?' Skeeter asked.

'You know? A murial. A big picture. Snow White and the dwarves. Sadiq liked it but Doc said it was foolish and that I shouldn't sign it considering what went on there. I was just trying to brighten the place up and kill time between jobs.'

There was a knock on the door and an officer entered dropping a note in front of Alex. 'Thought you'd like to know straight away, sir.'

'This might interest you.' He looked across at Quasim. 'A white Sprinter van has just been found. Body inside. The same van that left that very warehouse in, what you call, Effing Road, today. Burned out. It looks like Snow White is slowly getting shot of her dwarves. Looks like you, young man, are in the safest place you could be, surrounded by coppers who need to keep you secure.'

Quasim turned the colour of the van.

'Broad Lane mean anything to you?'

Within ten minutes he was charged. Skeeter and Alex left as a second officer entered the room. Looking at the lad, they would have little trouble.

'We'll not request bail,' were the last words Alex and Skeeter heard from the lawyer. Alex just raised his hand in response.

Skeeter left the room. She needed to get back to Copy Lane. Knowing there would be congestion on the lower road, she travelled the longer route.

* * *

There was always someone working. DC Michael Peet was in the far corner, his face illuminated by the light from the computer. He looked up as she entered.

'Bloody hell, Wicca, you're grabbing some overtime. Thought you'd be tearing someone limb from limb on those wrestling mats of yours.'

'Home soon, believe me. Just need to check if anything's come in.'

She passed Brad's desk. The Post-it notes were still over his board but no longer fluttered; the computer was off. She was about to move away when she realised something was missing.

'Mick, I'm supposed to be a detective. What was here on Brad's wall?' She pointed.

'It's Another Place, you know the Gormley statue, the sunset and silhouette. Crosby.'

'When did that disappear?'

Michael just shrugged his shoulders.

Moving to her desk Skeeter switched on the computer, typed her password into the space and the page appeared. She checked her internal mail. There was one titled 'ASCII'. She read it and printed the attached item before removing her phone. The numbers were written in her notes. Scribbling them down she cross-referenced. It made no sense. Searching the top right corner of the screen she checked the time, 19.21. Time she was home. She would give the gym a miss. The drive to Orrell would be enough. Passing the desk, she signed out and handed in her lanyard to the duty officer.

'You'll be glad you're back here. Flap on in town,' the Duty Officer remarked. Skeeter paused allowing her eyes to focus directly on his. 'Some witnesses have gone AWOL. Bit of a cock up from all accounts but I haven't heard the full story.'

Skeeter took the lanyard back and pushed her pass against the electronic key pad. She shouldered the door before going to the nearest phone.

April answered her mobile. 'The girls, Sharon and Kelly,

are missing. You need to get down here if you're still at Copy Lane. We daren't post on SM as it might just attract the wrong attention.'

Skeeter rang another number. Michael answered. 'Get your arse down here now, your presence is required.' As Michael arrived, she removed his lanyard and tossed both over the desk as she grabbed the startled officer by his arm and encouraged him to run to her car.

'I'll explain in the car!'

* * *

April was pacing the Incident Room and Paula was sitting by the wall, a mug of tea in her hands. Looking at her face it was obvious she had been crying. She turned and looked down at the floor as Skeeter and Michael arrived, embarrassed by her inadequate and unprofessional actions.

'We'll discuss the start of this later. They were going to look at the Wheel of Liverpool. Apparently, Kelly had told Sharon about it and she'd promised to show her when things got better. Paula decided there would be no harm in showing them. The WPC who was with them for the trip back to Wigan had apparently gone along with the idea. Once there the girls just vanished into the ether.' She turned and looked at Paula. 'The officer is out looking along with as many others as possible. Lucy and Tony have seen her picture so they're helping co-ordinate the search. We're starting at the Wheel and moving out.'

Skeeter went and crouched in front of Paula wrapping her hands around her wrists. 'What was said in the car on your way there?'

'I'd never seen Sharon so excited. She kept thanking Kelly.'

'And Kelly?'

'She was Kelly. It was nothing to her. She'd seen it so often and had probably travelled on it.'

'Was she reluctant?'

Paula considered the question before answering. 'In a funny way, yes.'

'So, you think this was Sharon's and not Kelly's idea?'

'Do you know, Skeeter, I really couldn't say. I've been taken for a fool. I'm so sorry.'

Skeeter reassuringly squeezed her wrists. 'We'll find her.'

'Is Brad looking?'

'He's gone home and is not answering his mobile,' grumbled April. 'Closes the hangar door when he can. Always has. That's what my dad always recommended I do.'

'Permission to follow a hunch, ma'am?' Skeeter looked at April.

'Michael, remain here and contact me on my number if you need to. Look after Paula. Control will keep you fully informed. DCI Mason is co-ordinating along with DCI Lawn. We've issued photographs of both girls to all officers working this evening.'

Skeeter handed Michael some papers then spoke quietly. 'See if you can work it out. If you do text me. I need confirmation – it's critical do you hear?'

April and Skeeter left the room. Michael looked at the phone and the information relayed on the white wall-mounted screen. Paula was still feeling guilty and was at this moment ineffective. He looked at the papers Skeeter had handed him.

CHAPTER 34

The warm ambience of the evening did not benefit the police as a large number of people were out enjoying the sunset and the sights. A concert at the dockside arena had also exacerbated the situation bringing a youthful crowd to see Stormzy. It was easy to see how the girls could simply disappear within this melee. It was also a concern that a large police presence was in place as security against possible terrorism. Since the Manchester Arena bomb, the potential threat was being taken extremely seriously.

Sharon held onto Kelly's arm and laughed as they mingled amongst the crowd. 'Thanks, Babe, just needed to taste freedom again. We'll go back in an hour. You know where the police station is?'

'Always tried to avoid it until now. Suddenly it feels the safest place in the world. An hour and no more.'

Sharon checked her phone was on then returned it to her

pocket. 'Down here!' She broke into a run moving between the people heading towards the arena.

'Sharon, wait!' Kelly followed, occasionally looking back towards the area where the police HQ was housed. She wanted, needed, to stay close. Two PCSOs were in the crowd and Kelly saw Sharon turn away. Within minutes they were reunited.

'Don't leave me again, Sharon. I just can't take this.'

The crowd was thinning as they crossed a carpark. Sharon found a bench and flopped onto it. 'Let's just watch.' She slipped her hand onto Kelly's. 'I'm so glad we met. Who'd have thought you'd find me when all along I was looking for someone just like you.'

The noise of traffic and people seemed so far distant. Neither noticed the car pull into the side nor DC Bradshaw approach. Sharon caught a glimpse of him in her peripheral vision and raised a protective arm as his fist slammed into Kelly's right temple causing her head to collide with Sharon's elbow. Kelly made no sound just slumped onto Sharon. Brad smiled. 'You OK?'

Sharon did not respond as they each locked an arm under Kelly's armpits and lifted her to her feet. As they approached their car a couple stopped.

'She alright?'

'My daughter. Got a call to say she'd over done it. Her birthday. Could you get the back door please?'

The man laughed. 'Been there and done that.' He opened the door and watched as Kelly flopped onto the rear seat.

'You were supposed to be looking after your cousin.' Brad's voice was stern and the couple moved away. 'Thanks. Daughters!'

Once in the car Brad relaxed. 'Tracked your phone. Well done.' He handed her an envelope. 'You need to disappear and get rid of that phone. There's one in there. The river's the best place.' She climbed out and lost herself in the crowd.

* * *

Michael had sent Skeeter a text. He wondered what all the fuss was about. It was hardly challenging. He turned his attention to his hunch. Working on the computer, he occasionally checked the large wall screen. He cast a solicitous eye over Paula. She had recovered a degree of composure and had protested her innocence a couple of times but her remarks had largely gone unheeded and she returned to the chair.

It was Sharon's face that had sparked his curiosity. He had seen her before when he had been checking the CCTV in the entrance of Sadiq's apartment. Letting the film run at speed, his finger hovered over the mouse. It was only on one occasion if he recalled and she had been accompanied. The person with her was aware of the camera and never looked in its direction. He clicked the mouse, enlarging the image. On cross checking, he realised his hunch had borne fruit.

He called Paula over and showed her both images. She leaned closer. 'The same girl. Involved? But Kelly didn't know her. I might seem a fool but I know my job and they hadn't met before. I can assure you of that.'

'In gangs like this there are people who will never meet. It's done that way for security. Trust few and if possible, trust no one. That's their motto.' He rang April.

CHAPTER 35

Night had overtaken the evening and the eastern sky's black cloak had settled along the west coast. There was nothing facing but darkness as they approached the carpark by Crosby Marine Lake. Skeeter checked Michael's text one more time before driving to the far end and manoeuvring round some bollards. The footpath along the lake edge was made from tarmac and was a car's width.

April looked around her. 'Where the hell are we going? We're supposed to be looking for the girls. Kelly may well be in harm's way and we're joyriding here!'

Skeeter turned briefly; her one blue eye bright in the dashboard lights. 'You'll have to trust me.'

As they approached the sea, the track ran parallel, becoming a wider promenade. The beach wall and fence sat to their left. It was then Skeeter saw the car. She turned off her lights and stopped. 'Out!' She ran towards the car. It was empty. Approaching the sea wall, she peered into the dark. Eyes focused, she scanned a one-hundred-and-eighty-degree panorama. The sea's surface reflected light and showed the water to be relatively close; the tide was on the way in. Following the steps down to the beach, she paused. Two indented lines, almost parallel in the sand, were clearly marked and brought an immediate end to her doubts. The start of an adrenaline rush heightened her senses.

April had also seen the tracks but they only brought further confusion. She just followed. It was then things changed rapidly. Crouching, Skeeter stopped and sent a hand signal to April to pause and remain silent. She had first seen the faint silhouette of an iron statue and then that of a figure appear from behind it. The person walked towards them, head down. There were no identifying features, the darkness had disguised those but she knew the gait, the height and the drop of the shoulders. The sound of his feet slopping through water grew louder. She waited, looked back at April before darting directly at her target. The sand, now wet underfoot, splashed as she pounded through the thin upper tide.

Once close she launched herself at the figure taking him completely by surprise. Her arm wrapped around his neck. An animalistic grunt surged from her taut lips as it always did when competing. She took hold before pulling the figure towards her, sending it upward and backward as she fell and twisted. The screams came spontaneously as he was hurled brutally over her right shoulder. Every move she made was controlled and precise. The man's now stiff and unforgiving body mass arched through the air before making contact with the hard, wet sand. A slapping, splashing sound erupted that brought a smile to her lips. It was a perfect suplex under difficult conditions. She dropped his face into the water each time he struggled. He soon got the message.

April approached and switched on her phone torch. 'It's Bradshaw! Skeeter, listen, he's one of ours! It's Brad!' As she spoke, she frantically tapped Skeeter's shoulder in an attempt to get her to hear and respond.

'Ekmek … fucking bread or as I call him, fucking barm cake.' Her breathing was heavy but controlled. 'Get help. He's going nowhere and then check down there towards the statue. Bradshaw is going absolutely fucking nowhere.'

April called in for assistance and cautiously walked a short distance in the direction Skeeter had indicated. Water lapped even further over her shoes. To the front of the statue facing the sea was a prostrate figure. It seemed to levitate face down in the rising tide. The water's incoming move-ment caused it to sway gently back and forth. April spotted the rope attached to the base of the statue and to the neck of the figure. An anchor. She turned the head out of the water. It was Kelly. Swiftly she checked for a pulse but there was none. Even so, she untied the rope and slipped her arms beneath her shoulders, dragged her up the beach and began CPR.

* * *

The foil blanket wrapped around Skeeter's shoulders reflected blue as the number of strobe lights from the response vehicles illuminated the surroundings. A ship out in the estuary was a bank of lights. It attracted their gaze as they sat on the steps in quiet contemplation. The red beacons on the wind farm even further out in the Irish Sea, blinked their warnings to both those at sea and in the air.

'How did you know?' April moved the foil around Skeeter's shoulders.

'I discovered Brad hid part of the evidence from the tattoo parlour. At first, I thought it was his bloody absentminded-ness, you know what he's like. When we had both tattoos, they gave us a series of numbers and some Arabic squiggles. Abid was Albanian but I guessed he knew some Arabic. I asked one of the translators we use, a doctor from Whiston Hospital. He told me they roughly mean *remember* and *betrayed.* Didn't make sense to me then but I knew it was significant. Michael helped solve the other elements. The numbers were linked with the ASCII code. What it really is I don't fully understand but I knew numbers referred to letters and the numbers spelled BREAD. It took a while but it eventually dawned on me – Brad's tattoo, his holiday embarrassment. EKMEK, Turkish for bread, remember? Abid needed to send a message whether that was to Kelly or to us, the police, I don't know. The tattoos were permanent. I believe that was deliberate. Then there was the cloth he'd given her, the piece of his clothing.'

'Bless her, it was in her clenched fist when they put her in the ambulance.'

'It was as if it were Abid's final act of defiance against the leader, a leader whom he believed to be Brad. Remember what Quasim said about them always being one step ahead. Tip offs and a bent bobby.'

'The apartment and the warehouse. Brad received that information before everyone else,' April remembered as the fog was being lifted from before her eyes. 'Bob Lawn said it was like the *Marie Celeste*. Just emptied.'

'I'd been worried about Brad for some time. He was

always on his phone during and after briefings. Asked a lot of questions. Never thought in a million years he was bent. Then there was the police medal. He seemed overly fascinated by it at first and then cast it aside as if it wasn't linked to the body. It was a vital clue, Abid was giving us a pointer, hence his insistence that Quasim bury it with him. That brought another piece of the jigsaw into place. He was brave to do that.'

'You didn't mention these things.'

'If I had then the person leaching the information would know we were getting close. Some things you keep to yourself. The penny dropped earlier this evening as I interpreted more information. Finally, what made me fully convinced that Brad was bent, was when Michael contacted me as we arrived at the carpark here, tonight. He'd recognised Sharon from the CCTV of Sadiq's apartment, realising she'd obviously been part of the gang. Strange that Kelly didn't know her. Maybe she was just one of the tarts, I don't know.'

'You know Sharon's disappeared?' April asked, her frustration apparent in her tone. 'So, tell me, Skeeter, why in all of Liverpool did you come here and not another place?'

Skeeter turned. 'Another Place, precisely. A hunch, woman's intuition. Brad always had a poster of this place next to his desk. He told me he came here to think and clear his head after a bad day. I noticed the poster had gone. At first, I couldn't remember what was missing and it was again Michael who remembered. I just had to make an informed guess but we weren't in time. I failed.'

'We got a pulse and the paramedics believe she'll pull through. Kids like Kelly feel responsible for the way adults have always treated them, as if the early physical and emotional abuse was somehow their fault. She needs a break. She needs help and we let her down.'

Skeeter turned to April; her light blue eye now contrasted markedly with the other. 'I could have killed the bastard. You know that?'

'No, you wouldn't. Your training wouldn't allow that. I had total confidence in your ability to apply just the correct amount of restraint. You're one fine team player and I'm proud to work with you. It's certainly been a baptism of fire.'

'Well, boss, teams are what you make them. You're doing just fine.'

A blast from the departing ship's horn made them both turn to observe, the breeze blowing their hair.

DCI Alex Mason and Bob Lawn walked up towards them. The blue strobes had begun to disappear down the promenade.

'Just come to congratulate you both on some lateral thinking. It might just have made a massive difference to a young woman's future.'

April stood. Skeeter remained seated. 'Anything on the van?'

'We believe the body found is Blusher's.'

'I need a drink.' Skeeter stood.

'It's on me.' Both men replied in unison.

'Then you can make it a double.'

CHAPTER 36

The final solder and the rest of the hour was spent sealing and polishing the stained glass. April held it to the light. The depth of the low evening sun breathed life into the assorted colours.

'Well, Tico, what do you think?'

Tico turned, yawned and replaced his head on the cushion.

'Thank goodness it's not for you!'

Skeeter arrived at Copy Lane and collected a coffee before going to her desk. Looking across, she was pleased to see DC Bradshaw's desk had been cleared. It was strangely quiet. She checked her watch. Michael popped his head round the door. 'Briefing, Wicca, you're late.'

Leaving her brew, she followed him. He opened the door allowing her to enter first.

'You're on lates, Micha ...' She did not finish as the cheer drowned the last of the sentence.

It seemed as if half the force had crammed into the room. DCI Mason and April stood near a table on which a few gifts had been placed, one of which was April's window.

Looking at the crowd and the gifts Skeeter realised they were for her. She immediately felt more anxious than she had done during the whole incident. For the first time April saw her blush and in Skeeter she immediately realised that she had found the perfect professional partner.

ANOTHER PLACE

Crosby Beach made a perfect setting for the denouement to 'Catch as Catch Can'. The one hundred cast-iron Anthony Gormley sculptures are both stunning and mysterious. They change with the seasons and the elements. Those constantly being submerged are strangely deformed adding a warped beauty to their overall appearance.

The life-sized figures are spread over three kilometres of foreshore and stretch a kilometre out into the sea. Each weighing 650 kilogrammes, they are made from a cast of Gormley's own body. The sculptures all face the same way, staring out over the Mersey Estuary towards the horizon.

Crosby was not their first home. They were exhibited in Cuxhaven in Germany, Stavanger in Norway and De Panne in Belgium before being transported to *Another Place* to become a permanent feature at Crosby Beach.

According to Anthony Gormley, Another Place harnesses the ebb and flow of the tide linking man's relationship with nature.

The seaside is a good place to do this. Here time is tested by tide, architecture by the elements and the prevalence of sky seems to question the earth's substance. It is no hero, no ideal, just the industrially reproduced body of a middle-aged man trying to remain standing and trying to breathe, facing the horizon busy with ships moving materials and manufactured things around the planet.

For me, *Another Place* is certainly a jewel in Merseyside's crown and I feel privileged to be able to experience this ever-changing art installation.

MALCOLM

ABOUT THE AUTHOR

You could say that the writing was clearly on the wall for anyone born in a library that they might aspire to be an author but to get to that point, Malcolm Hollingdrake has travelled a circuitous route.

Malcolm worked in education for many years, even teaching for a period in Cairo before he started writing, a challenge he longed to tackle for more years than he cares to remember.

Malcolm has written a number of successful short stories and has more than ten books available (and more to come).

Born in Bradford and spending three years in Ripon, Malcolm has never lost his love for his home county, a passion that is reflected in the settings of several Harrogate Crime Series novels.

Malcolm has enjoyed many hobbies including works by Northern artists; the art auctions offer a degree of excitement when both buying and certainly when selling. It's a hobby he has bestowed on DCI Cyril Bennett, of his characters in the Harrogate Crime Series.

ACKNOWLEDGMENTS

Writing is a selfish pastime that allows only me to travel to a fictitious world. I have a wonderful time creating the characters, researching the crimes and the elements that make up all aspects of the writing but there comes a time when the ink is dry that I need others to help. Without the interaction from the readers, I do not believe I would achieve the same degree of satisfaction. It is clear to them, from our chats, that for me the characters created within the pages of my books are real. They trudge the streets, drink in the same pubs as them, they admire the same scenery yet cringe when the shadows grow long whilst delivering justice. I try to make them live and breathe. Creating not only Decent and Warlock but the lesser characters brings the same degree of satisfaction. It will be interesting to see who will grow into the light in future books.

For this creativity to happen, however, I'm grateful to many people and I would like to tell you about some individuals and some groups. Obviously, I cannot name them all and if any should slip through the net, my apologies.

My wife, Debbie, must take centre stage. Her dedication, understanding and patience are limitless and I could not do this without her. Thank you. x

To Helen Gray, my sincere thanks for casting your professional eye over each and every word.

Caroline Vincent has been a true friend and guardian angel from the very beginning to whom I shall forever be grateful.

What would authors be without the advanced readers and the blogging community? Those prolific, enthusiastic readers who turn a pleasure into a profession. My thanks to each and every one. It is here I must also mention the reading and book groups who spread the word; please remember how vital you are.

Sincere thanks to Carry Heap, Ian and Gill Cleverdon, David and Jan Johnson (whose lovely cottage now belongs to Skeeter during the course of this series!), Georgie, Lucy and the staff at Cordings, who have always been a strength, Lucy Sampson and Samantha Brownley from UKCBC, Donna Morfett, Dee Groocock and Craig Gillan for your unfailing support.

A special thanks goes to Royce Banks of Royce's Gym, for his guidance with all things wrestling.

Receiving an acceptance to join the Hobeck family has given me a tremendous boost and I look forward to working alongside the many fine authors now signed. Thank you, Rebecca and Adrian, for seeing something in my writing that attracted you to the series.

Finally, to close, as always, last but certainly not least, I mention you, yes you, holding the Kindle or paperback, the reader, for without you I would not be here. Thank you for buying and reading this the first book in the series. If you have enjoyed it then please mention my work to friends and family, as word of mouth is the best way to see more people discover Hobeck Books.

Until Book Two

Thank you

MALCOLM

HOBECK BOOKS – THE HOME OF
GREAT STORIES

This book is the first in the Merseyside Crime Series, the second book, *Syn*, is also to be a Hobeck Books publication. There will be many more to follow after that (we hope).

If you've enjoyed this book, please visit Malcolm's website: **www.malcolmhollingdrakeauthor.co.uk** to read about his other writing, inspirations, writing life and for news about his forthcoming writing projects.

Malcolm is also the author of the acclaimed Harrogate Crime Series of which there are ten books.

Hobeck Books also presents a weekly podcast, the Hobcast, where founders Adrian Hobart and Rebecca Collins discuss all things book related, key issues from each week, including the ups and downs of running a creative business. Each episode includes an interview with one of the people who make Hobeck possible: the editors, the authors, the cover designers. These are the people who help Hobeck bring great stories to life. Without them, Hobeck wouldn't exist. The Hobcast can be listened to from all the usual platforms but it can also be found on the Hobeck website: **www. hobeck.net/hobcast**.

Finally, if you enjoyed this book, please also leave a review on the site you bought it from and spread the word. Reviews are hugely important to writers and they help other readers also.

Printed in Great Britain
by Amazon